Piece of Cake

Kingston High Book One
SUNDAE LEIGHTON

Sullen Press

Piece of Cake (Kingston High Series, Book One)
Available in these formats:
978-1-7350077-6-2 (Paperback)
978-1-7350077-7-9 (eBook AZW)
978-1-7350077-8-6 (eBook EPUB)
Copyright: © 2021 Sullen Press, LLC

This book is a work of fiction. Name, characters, places, incidents or otherwise are written from imagination only. Any resemblance to actual persons, things living or dead, or events is coincidental.

This book is intended for mature readers 18 years and older. It contains sexually explicit and graphic scenes and language that might be offensive to some readers.

All characters in this work and all my works are 18 years of age or older.

All sexual acts are consensual.

Beta Reader: Stephanie Cooper
Cover: Books and Moods
Editor: My Brother's Editor

For my father.

I hope you're proud of the woman I've become.

PLAYLIST

Bad Guy – Billie Eilish
Ghost – Halsey
Criminal – Britney Spears
Break Apart Her Heart – Good Charlotte
Good Girl – Carrie Underwood
One of My Turns – Pink Floyd
Need You Now – Lady A
Jar of Hearts – Christina Perri
Mine Would Be You – Blake Shelton
Shallow – Lady Gaga
Everything Has Changed – Taylor Swift
Atlanta – Stone Temple Pilots
I Hope You're Happy Now – Carly Pierce and Lee Brice
Tin Man – Miranda Lambert

Chapter One

Brett

I clutched the steering wheel in front of me in a death grip as I stared at the sprawling building before me and instantly regretted not hitching a ride when it was offered to me last night. This wasn't the first time I had to start a new school in the middle of the year, but it was the first time I had to do it as a senior, and that's why it felt different.

I was furious with my mother for doing this yet again after she promised the last time would be it. Senior year was supposed to be the best one because you were going to graduate, move on to the real world, and most likely, if you were lucky, never have to see the rest of your classmates again. I had been at my last school for nearly two years, and felt a little more comfortable than I should have, which is why I should have fucking known Ruby, that's my mother, would pull the rug right out from underneath me.

Of course it had to do with the fact that her boyfriend broke up with her. *Everything* Ruby Cake did was always man motivated. We moved to the last place because of him, and now we moved here because of him, too. He wanted us out because he was sick of her shit, and so? We moved to Kingston, Connecticut, which was the town my mother grew up in.

I swallowed nervously as I watched a couple of girls climb out of the car parked directly in front of me. They looked happy and excited to be going to school this morning like it wasn't actually boring as hell, full of assholes, and something I probably would have dropped if I hadn't promised good old Ruby I would get my diploma because she never did. My phone buzzed next to me and I grabbed it to see who it was.

Palmer: Are you here yet? I'm waiting inside by the office for you.

I sighed. Palmer Wilson was the daughter of my mother's best friend and she now insisted that it was fate that we were going to be best friends, too. I had met her a few times in the past when the two of them had come to visit us and she seemed nice enough, but I never let myself get close enough to anyone. Girls my age were catty gossips and I didn't have time for that bullshit. Plus, we moved around so much that I didn't want to make friends with someone that I might not ever see again.

Brett: I'm here. Just give me a minute.

I opened the door and dragged myself from the seat, making sure to slip my phone into my back pocket. Being the new kid was always rough, but when school had already started, it only seemed to make it even fucking worse. All the damn questions, the stares, the rumors that everyone was going to spread about me without even actually knowing who I was because they judged the way I looked. They never wanted to get to know me because spreading rumors was so much more fun and I never bothered to correct them. I wasn't a slut, I wasn't a partier, and I most certainly didn't go to any football games or hang with the popular kids because that wasn't who I was.

I tugged my bag up over my shoulder and headed toward the door, making sure to keep my eyes down so that I didn't catch anyone's attention. I had almost made it into the building without anyone talking to me or trying to get my attention, but it was my own fault. If I had been watching where I was going, I would have been fine. Instead, I slammed right into someone and then landed right on my ass.

"Shit, cupcake, watch where you're going." His voice was deep, throaty, and when I glanced up, I swear my heart stopped beating for a minute. He was tall, with dirty blonde hair, a five o'clock shadow that did not belong on some high school boy, and the bluest eyes I had ever seen in my life. I glanced at his broad shoulders before my eyes flickered over the blue Red Sox shirt he was wearing. His jeans were blue, tight, and clung to his thighs like a second skin. Wait a second, did he just—?

I narrowed my eyes. "Did you actually fucking call me cupcake?" I started to climb to my feet, but instead, he leaned down to hook an arm around my waist so he could hoist me into a standing position like I weighed next to nothing.

Okay, this was not happening. This man-boy was beyond attractive, and I wasn't even prepared to have this conversation right now. Did he actually think that line was going to work on me?

He chuckled softly. "I sure did. It's the hair, boo, it reminds me of icing on a cake." He smiled and exposed a set of even white teeth as he casually tugged on my ponytail like it was something he did every day. "Cash Donovan." He bowed slightly at the waist.

"Sure, well bye now." I started to walk around him, but Cash grabbed me by the elbow and turned me back around.

"Not going to introduce yourself, newbie?"

"Nope, so please release me from your claws before I kick you so hard in the nuts that they shoot up your throat and out of your mouth."

Cash threw his head back and laughed. "I like you, boo." His smile was so bright it was almost blinding as he released my arm and then tossed his own around my shoulders like he did it all the time. "I won't ask you the lame questions that everyone else will about you starting school a month in." Cash started walking, so I had no choice but to move with him since he was at least a foot taller and a hundred pounds heavier than I was. "What's your favorite fruit?" he asked.

"My what?" I stared up at him in disbelief.

Again that smile, and I'd be lying if I didn't say my knees went weak.

"Fruit, newbie, what kind of fruit is your favorite? Don't be lame and say strawberry because I can already tell that isn't who you are." Cash tilted his head as he looked at me.

I shook my head. "I don't have a favorite fruit." That was the truth. I liked my food fattening, sugary, and as unhealthy as possible like most kids my age did.

"Liar." Cash high-fived another guy as we walked inside the building and maneuvered us around a crowd of kids. Another high five with someone else, and then we were standing in front of the office. "You need to go in here first." It wasn't a question.

I shrugged off his arm and caught Palmer staring at us with her mouth hanging open. "Yes, thanks," I told him. I glanced slightly to his right to find a group of girls in pleated red and white skirts staring at me with fire in their eyes. Great, I've already pissed off the cheerleaders, which had to be a new record for me.

"Not a thing, boo, not a thing." He nodded. "So, I'll just wait here and you can get your schedule so I can show you to your first class." Cash lifted his hand so he could run it through his tousled hair.

"Not necessary, I have someone—"

Cash leaned closer. "I'm starting to think you don't like me, cupcake, and frankly, that hurts me right here." He brought both of his hands up to the left side of his chest and formed a heart. That might have sealed the deal for me if I was interested in dating high schoolers. Or anyone at all, for that matter.

"I don't," I assured him, and pushed the door open. It was mass chaos inside the office with one girl standing there with her schedule in hand and crying that this wouldn't work for her. The secretary behind the desk looked like she desperately wanted to be anywhere else but here, and it sounded like there were dozens of phones ringing off the hook.

"Be right with you, hon, just take a seat." Another secretary caught my eye as she answered the phone and I might have backed out of the room if I didn't suddenly have a heavy hand on my shoulder.

Cash's lips were right against my ear when he spoke this time. "Trust me when I say you'll thank me again when this is over." His breath was hot against my skin, and when I glared up at him, all he did was wink at me.

"Mr. Donovan!" the secretary called him over. "What can we do for you this morning?" I noticed the way her cat earrings swung back and forth when she moved closer and the blush that crept up her neck.

"Not for me, Mrs. Blake, my new friend here." Two large hands landed on my shoulders as he pushed me forward.

Mrs. Blake's eyes took me in and I'm sure she had a few choice words that she would at least keep to herself, but tell her husband tonight over dinner. My bright purple hair always seemed to catch people off guard, and that was only the beginning. I had chosen an oversized AC/DC shirt this morning which I paired with blue skinny jeans and my combat boots. Her smile slipped only a second before she spoke. "You must be Brett Cake."

"Yes ma'am, I just need my schedule so I can get out of your way," I assured her.

"Cash, can you do something about my gym class?" The girl who had been hysterical when we walked in now had her brown eyes turned on my new friend. I would be forever grateful if he would help her, so I could shake him and get on with my morning.

"Marley, we've talked about this," Cash calmly reminded her.

"But, your mom—"

"Just because my mother is the principal of the school doesn't mean I can move your schedule around. I know you hate having gym right in the middle of the day, who wouldn't, but it's not forever. Maybe instead of freaking out about it, you could try and make the best of it?" Cash suggested. "You enjoy running, right?"

I attempted to tune out the rest of the conversation as I waited for Mrs. Blake to give me my schedule. I didn't give a shit about Marley, her unhappiness about her gym class schedule, or anything else that was going on in the office. What I needed was my class schedule so I could get out of here and out to where Palmer was standing. I'm sure she had a few questions for me which I wouldn't even bother answering.

"Here you go, Miss Cake." The secretary held out a sheet of paper. "I hope you enjoy going to Kingston High School." She flashed a smile that didn't quite meet her eyes.

I nodded. "Thanks." I grabbed it from her before I tried to make a break for the door, but I wasn't fast enough. Cash was right behind me.

"Brett, Brett, Brett, when will you learn you can't escape my amazing charm?" he teased before he tossed his arm around my shoulders again.

"When will you learn that I don't them?"

Palmer was still waiting outside the office and she planted herself directly in front of us. "Hi." She beamed happily at me with eyes wide. "I thought we were going to meet up before your first class, B?" She had decided I needed a nickname and that was the best she could come up with.

Cash squeezed me closer and I couldn't help but lean into him. It was almost like a magnet drawing us together. "Where is your first class?" He snagged my schedule from my fingers before I had a chance to answer him and nodded at Palmer. "You two know one another?" he asked.

Palmer blushed as her brows dipped. "Uh, yes. Brett and her mother are staying at my house until they find their own place," she blurted out. Wow, new best friend, wasn't there some sort of girl code you weren't supposed to break here?

I glared at her just as Cash started walking and dragging me with him. He was like a damn freight train. "You know, I can move on my own since I have my own pair of legs," I insisted, but that only made Cash dig his fingers into my shoulders.

"Hey Cash, who's your new friend?"

"Great timing, cupcake, I want you to meet Jameson Hamden. One-half of the Hamden twins." Cash grinned happily.

I sighed. "Please stop calling me—" I stopped mid-sentence when I glanced up into the face of God. Did this place just breed beautiful boys or was I just used to the ones from where I had just come from? Because they didn't look anything like these two Greek gods that stood before me.

Jameson was shorter than Cash, but they both towered over my five-foot-two inches. He had dark brown hair that was in desperate need of a haircut, and chestnut brown eyes that lit up like a lightbulb when he smiled, which he was doing at this exact moment. He was dressed almost identically to Cash with a baseball shirt and the blue jeans, but his pants hung loosely around his slim hips. The look on Palmer's face had turned to sheer horror when I cast a glance in her direction.

"Do you use cupcake on everyone?" Jameson snorted as he rolled his eyes. "So original, bro." He shook his head. "It's nice to meet you." He stuck out his hand. "Wait, do you not shake hands because I know some people are weird about touching, but I assumed it was cool since Cash's all possessively holding on to you." He jutted his chin at the arm around my shoulders.

I shrugged out from under Cash before I awkwardly took the hand held out to me. "Uh, nice to meet you too and I'm Brett, not cupcake." I glanced up at both boys before I started to move into the room.

"Wait a second, cupcake." Cash swung me back around like a doll. "You just can't walk into the room without saying goodbye. We're besties now. When am I going to see you again?"

Jameson laughed softly. "Subtle, dude," he muttered.

"How about never?"

"You're killing me, Smalls."

I sighed before I turned back around to shove my schedule at him and folded my arms across my non-existent chest. "Fine, you tell me, bestie, you have my schedule in your grubby claws," I teased.

"You hear that, Jam? She called me bestie." Cash giggled happily before he coughed and tried to keep his face serious. He smoothed out my schedule and nodded. "No, no, yes, yes, oh lunch with us, yes, no." He grinned at me before he handed the paper back over. "We have three classes and lunch together, newb." He broke into a little dance.

"You're nuts." But I couldn't help the smile that tugged at my lips as Cash continued to wiggle around.

Jameson nodded at me. "He's been declared clinically insane, but he's heavily medicated now." He winked. "Hey, boss, come meet Cash's new best friend." He waved his hand out.

Palmer suddenly grabbed my arm. "Brett, you really shouldn't do this," she hissed into my ear.

"I thought we were your best friends, asshat," a deep yet cranky voice answered.

Cash shook his head. "A guy can have more than one bestie. Besides, have you seen her?" He grinned like a little kid before he attempted to wrap his arm around me again. He really was a touchy-feely kind of guy.

I glanced up, and up again, into the angriest green eyes I had ever seen in my life. He had his baseball cap on backward, but I could still see the inky colored hair that curled slightly underneath, and I watched as his fiery eyes searched my face before they dropped down my body without hiding the fact that he was checking me out. His jawline was perfect with his five o'clock shadow even more prominent than Cash's and his shoulders seemed broader if that was possible. I noticed his brawny, thick arms covered in bright colorful tattoos, and the fact that the Pearl Jam shirt he wore looked ready to burst from his chest. What exactly did they feed these boys at Kingston High because they were ridiculously good-looking?

The bell chose that exact moment to ring, and I swore I nearly jumped out of my skin. "Oh, hey, I don't want to be late on my first day." I darted into the classroom as fast as I could, but I swore I could still feel him staring at me with those eyes. I felt myself break out into a slick sweat when I noticed him walk into the room with Jameson and continue to glare at me while I stood there with the teacher.

"Brett Cake, right, the new girl. I'm Mrs. Rhett." She nodded at me. "There are a couple of empty seats in the back if you want to pick one. I'll get you a textbook," she added.

"Yo, cupcake, you're with us," Jameson called me over, and I saw a couple of female heads turn to stare at me again. I was so good at making friends today—*not*. I flashed a brief smile as I sunk into the seat next to him and he beamed happily at me. "That sourpuss is Easton Kennedy, who you didn't get to meet before, but he's part of our little group, too. More like the guy in charge, actually. Cash was too busy planning your matching best friend bracelets to actually introduce the two of you," he whispered as Mrs. Rhett placed a book on my desk before she walked back to the front of the room.

I glanced over at Easton, who was now staring straight ahead, but I couldn't help but notice the perfect cheekbones, and the ridiculously long lashes that framed his eyes. He turned slightly so that he could glare at me again for a second before he turned his attention back to the front of the room just as Mrs. Rhett started talking.

Well, it was obvious that he didn't want me to join his little group of friends. Not that I had any plans on it.

Chapter Two

Easton

Purple hair? Who in the fuck had purple fucking hair and looked like that? Brett fucking Cake, that's who. She was drop-dead gorgeous with those big blue eyes, that ridiculous hair, and even though she tried to cover herself up with that giant shirt, I could see the curves. The perky round ass and tits Brett hid underneath. I didn't like her one fucking bit, but Cash, mister fucking friendly, wanted to bring her into our little circle of friends. He was always trying to save strays, but this time I was putting my damn foot down.

"No." I shook my head as I glared at him.

Cash rolled his eyes. "Dude, why not? She's cool," he insisted before he twisted his large frame to see if Brett had walked into the cafeteria yet.

I grunted. "Because she's not one of us. She's an outsider. We don't fucking befriend outsiders, or did you forget that part already?" I reminded him. "We don't need another person in a fucking circle, never mind a girl, Cash." I pointed out just as Brett walked in with Palmer Wilson. I found it interesting that they were so chummy since Palmer was her complete opposite. Tall, blonde, and brown-eyed, she was one of the most popular chicks in school. Not to mention one of the head cheerleaders which I somehow doubted Brett was going to be prancing around in short skirts for the football team. My dick twitched at the image that popped into my head, and I silently cursed myself.

Cash stood up and waved them over. "Don't be such a douche canoe," he sneered at me. "She's new, needs some friends, and I—"

"You sly fox. You fucking like her." Oswald Maxwell pointed his fork at me before he shoved his salad into his mouth. Dude ate nothing but organic shit these days because Coach Best told us to, and right now he was in the middle of devouring the biggest chef's salad I had ever seen. He wasn't nearly as tall as I was, but what he lacked in height he made up in brawn. Guy was built like a tank.

My brows dipped. "You can just fuck right off." I shot out of my chair just as Brett approached the table, holding her lunch in her hands. She stared up at me with those big eyes and I was surprised when I saw curiosity flash through them. I was used to being able to stare people down, or have girls throw themselves at me, but I already knew that Brett wasn't like anyone else I had met. I marched past her and Palmer without saying a word and headed outside to the courtyard. I took a few deep breaths as I tried to calm myself down and leaned back against the cool brick wall as I closed my eyes.

"Easton? Can I talk to you for just a second?"

Just the sound of her voice caused my cock to stand at attention and I found her standing there watching me with those fuck-me eyes. I gritted my teeth and narrowed my eyes. "What do you want?" I demanded.

Her pink tongue came out to lick her kissable lips before she answered. "I don't want to be part of your fucking little group, okay?" Brett continued to stare up at me, but I saw her chest move faster as her nerves began to take over. "You know Cash better than I do, but I guess he's just trying to make me feel welcome." Her sweet raspy voice was music to my ears.

I didn't say anything as I pushed off the wall and pulled off my hat. I brushed the hair back from my forehead before placing the hat back on my head with the bill facing forward. As I waited for Brett to leave, I folded my arms across my chest and continued to glare at her. She apparently didn't get the hint because she was still just standing there.

"I can't help but like him, you know, he's probably the friendliest person I've ever met," she went on. "No one has ever welcomed me like Cash has. Not once, even though Palmer is trying her best, but Cash is different." Her lips turned up slightly. "Anyway, he's the one—"

I waved my hand. "Whatever. It's fine, Brett." I needed her to leave before I did something I couldn't take back. Like stick my tongue down her throat while I finger fucked her against the wall so that everyone could watch.

Her nostrils flared. *Gotcha.* "Did you just fucking dismiss me? You know what? I can see there's no getting through your thick fucking skull." She swung around on her heel like she was done with me, but I grabbed her and pinned her back against the brick wall. "Let go, dickhead." She pushed at my chest with the palms of her hands but I didn't budge. Probably because I was pushing two hundred plus and Brett couldn't be more than a hundred ten pounds soaking wet.

"You're going to be nothing but trouble, aren't you?" I made sure my eyes stayed on her face because if they moved anywhere else, that would only make things worse. My dick liked this girl, not me. "I'm not sure where you came from, but I got some news for you. You're not in Kansas anymore, Dorothy," I hissed through clenched teeth.

"Whoa, whoa!" Cash's voice was suddenly in my ear. "Release her, boss." He gripped my arm tightly. The only one that could match my height, and probably my weight, I listened to what he said. "Cupcake, you alright?" He stepped in when I moved back, and I watched as he cupped Brett's face with his hands.

Brett nodded. "I'm fine." This time I saw the fear I wanted flash in her baby blues and triumph soared through my veins.

Cash wrapped his arms around her which caused a jolt of jealousy to rip through me. "What the fuck, dude?" He kept Brett tight against his chest as he turned to glare at me.

I opened my mouth, but then slammed it shut and stormed back into the school without another word. I could hear my friends calling out to me, but I didn't bother to turn around. They could eat my balls for all I cared at this point. After school, I would be able to talk to them alone and convince Cash that bringing a girl into our mix was a bad idea. He would have no choice but to see it my way, break it off with her, and I wouldn't have to see her ass again. But what an ass it was.

I HAD JUST FINISHED changing into my uniform when Oz and Cash walked into the locker room followed by J2. I acknowledged them with a quick nod as I slipped my Kingston Knights hat on. "We need to talk." I sat down and brought my right foot up to my knee.

"If this is about Brett, you can forget it." Cash stripped off his shirt as he turned his back to me. The ugly scars he carried were on display for a minute before he pulled on his Knights shirt. "She's in." Oz looked between the two of us as he stripped down to his boxers, but didn't say anything. He just continued to change into his uniform while I stared down my other best friend.

I stood up. "She's not."

"She is."

"She's not."

Oz threw up his hands. "Jesus fuck!" He whirled around. "I'm not going to stand here while the two of you fight over this like a couple of toddlers. If Cash wants a new friend, what's the big deal? Because you want to stick your dick inside of her or because he got to her first?" He narrowed his eyes.

I rolled my eyes. "Neither of those things," I scoffed, but I knew that they knew I was lying. We had been friends since we were in diapers.

"I don't want to fuck Brett," Cash spoke up. "Sure, she's cute, but not really my type, East. You're sort of spoken for anyway, so maybe just don't get involved and don't ruin our budding friendship?"

I slammed my fist against the locker and ignored the pain that shot up my arm. "I don't want to fuck Brett!" I exclaimed. "Get that through your fucking thick ass skulls. I can have my pick of any damn girl in this whole town and she is the last one on my list," I lied. "I'm done with this conversation." I waved my arms around. "You can hang out with Brett all you want, but count me out." I strode through the locker room, ignoring my other teammates. When I hit the ball field, I was fired up, and I hoped Coach Best worked us hard today.

AFTER PRACTICE, I SHOWERED and changed back into my street clothes. I hadn't said more than two words to my friends, and it was starting to bother me. I found the three of them standing around waiting for me when I stepped outside.

"You good, boss?" Cash's brows rose slightly.

I shrugged. "Whatever." I started to walk toward my bike and they followed. "Tate still having his fucking party tonight?" I swung my leg over the seat and sat down.

Jonathan nodded. "So we heard. We going or are we going to do our own thing instead?" He glanced at his brother before they both turned their identical eyes on me.

"Guy's a tool," Cash answered as he slipped his phone from his pocket.

Oz snorted. "Understatement of the century," he grunted. "Who the fuck are you texting?"

"Piss off," Cash answered without looking up.

"Is it your new girlfriend?" Oz lunged for the phone in his hands, but Cash blocked him. "It is, isn't it?"

Cash shook his head. "She wouldn't give me her number, so I'm asking Palmer." A sly smile slipped up his face. "She wants to play hard to get, but she totally wants me."

Even though I knew he was joking, green jealousy ripped through my body at a lightning speed.

I sneered at all of them. "I'll meet you all at Oz's place before we head over." His parents were never home these days so we could pre-party beforehand. I kicked the starter, so that my bike roared to life and slipped my helmet on over my head before I took off from the parking lot.

I didn't go straight to Oz's place even though I could have let myself in. I needed to get in some fresh air and the open road before this party tonight, considering there might be a chance that Brett would be there, and I couldn't react the way I had before. She didn't seem like the party type, but that didn't mean Palmer wouldn't convince her to go. Maybe suggest it would be a way to meet more kids at school or something along those lines. If I took a spin over to her place—

I shook my head. No fucking way was I going there. One, I would most likely end up confronting both Palmer and Brett, which wasn't the best idea. I slowed down for the four-way stop sign in front of me before I sped right through when I didn't see any cars. No, the best thing I could do tonight was ignore Brett if she was there. Cash could be laughing it up with her all he fucking wanted, but I wanted nothing to do with her.

I took a right to drive up Oz's street and I parked my bike in the driveway so that I could wait for my boys. Cash was my best friend. I trusted him more than anyone, and that was saying a lot because there were only a few people I let into my inner circle. I gave him a hard time only because if anyone could take my shit, it would be him. We grew up next door to one another and had bailed one another out on more than one occasion. When my dad died, he was there for me. When his dad beat the shit out of him, it was me that was there for him. We weren't brothers by blood, but it didn't matter. We were brothers when it mattered.

Oz was my third in command. Crazy, mean, and ruthless, he was the one I called when I needed help with the dirty work. The guy was born with a silver spoon in his mouth, but he didn't act like it. He drove his fancy fucking cars, but still dressed in jeans and T-shirts like the rest of us did. He enjoyed a good time, but only if *he* was the one throwing the party. His parents moved Cash, the twins, and myself in when things got too rough for us at home without a second thought and didn't blink an eye when we needed anything, although we hardly asked.

Jameson and Jonathan were our backup. The twins were never without the other long enough for most to be able to tell them apart except for the three of us. I'll admit there were times we couldn't even tell them apart. We were all only children except for J2, but they acted more like one unit than two different entities. They were the ones who suggested we join the baseball team freshman year of high school, and it turned out to be one of the best decisions of our lives. The Kingston Knights hadn't won a game in twenty years until the five of us joined the team. They had never won a championship until four years ago. We made that team what it is today and Coach knew it.

I stood up as Oz's silver Tesla slid up the driveway and watched as one by one they all climbed out. I hooked my helmet back on to the bike so that I could follow them inside.

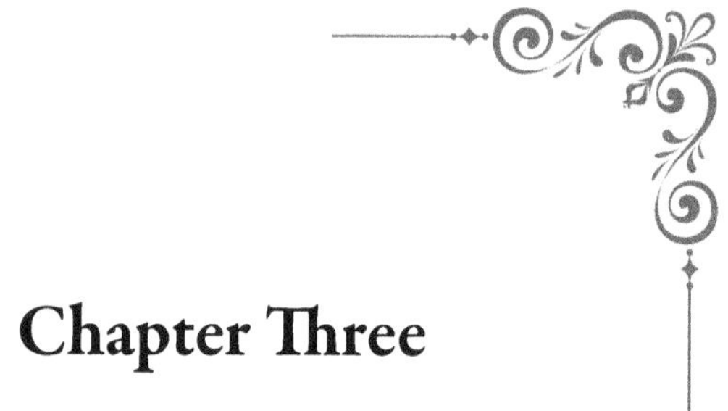

Chapter Three

Brett

I was absolutely freezing right now. I should have listened to Palmer when she told me to dress warmer, and change out of my T-shirt, but I didn't. It was the kind of weather that made you wish you had that special someone to snuggle up close to or just huddle around the bonfire. It was crisp and cool, but not yet that blistering freezing feeling that comes with the turning of the leaves. It was too bad that I was currently standing in the middle of some godforsaken town party I didn't want to be at while nursing the same beer someone shoved into my hand the moment I arrived two hours ago. I looked around the fire and realized that I was either going to have to go find Palmer or just leave her here.

It was Palmer's fault I was here in the first place. She wanted to spend time with a boy named Bentley Baker, and for some reason thought it would be a great idea for me to tag along. Except, it really wasn't because the moment she spotted him she disappeared and I hadn't seen her since. Palmer was the busty head cheerleader with the perfect blonde curls that fell in springs around her shoulders, the kind of hips that boys loved, and brown eyes that made your heart melt. She wore her makeup so that it didn't look like she had any on while her lips were the perfect shade of red. Palmer was loud, but friendly and her laugh sounded like some sort of love song. I was surprised that she didn't have guys lined up outside her door.

It was actually kind of funny that she wanted to be my friend. We were complete opposites in every possible way. I was short and would never be caught dead prancing around in some skirt that barely covered my ass. Or any skirt, for that matter now that I thought about it. Back where I lived before I never attended one single baseball or football game. I could see the way everyone was watching me, the new girl with the lavender hair. My actual hair color was dark brown, but I bleached it years ago to start dying it fun colors. My eyes were blue, and if I wore makeup, it was dark eyeliner with matching mascara. I was blessed with hips made for babies, or at least that's what I was told once, a small, almost nonexistent chest, and a sarcastic, no filter personality. I wasn't here to make friends or impress anyone in this cow town because once I graduated, I was out. If I even stayed here long enough with the way my mother was.

I took a sip of my now incredibly warm beer before I spit it right back into my red Solo cup. *Nasty.* I should have stayed back at the house like the loser that I was so that I could work on some paintings or drawings instead of being forced to hang out with these kids who wanted nothing to do with me. Or that I wanted nothing to do with.

No one had even tried to interact with me. Not the redheaded guy standing by the keg with the mean piercing green eyes who kept shooting me looks from time to time when he thought that I wasn't looking. His hair was so bright it was almost electric, and I assumed that was why he kept it in such a tight buzz cut. He was about average height, thick shouldered with a stocky build, and I wondered if maybe he was on the football team, too, or just hanging out for free beer.

I knew for certain the guy standing next to him was not a football player or on any high school team. He had a head of greasy blonde hair along with a face full of acne and beady brown eyes. He was dressed in a ratty Twenty-One Pilots shirt that looked like it had never been washed and the same could have been said of the jeans he had on. He was thin, rail-thin, and I got the feeling he was talking about me more than once when he would lean into the two girls that were standing there only to have them giggle and look over at me.

High school really was the fucking worst.

"You're new." The girl next to Twenty-One Pilots' left spoke first. She ran her hand through her short blonde hair while her blue eyes looked me over. She leaned closer to him as she waited for my response.

"How did you guess?" I raised my eyebrows. "What else have you and your friends been saying about me? You seem like a couple of regular fucking Einsteins."

Buzz cut snickered, but stopped quickly when Twenty-One Pilots shot him a look. "Your hair is purple." He pointed his cup at me.

Fucking high school boys. I couldn't help the words that tumbled from my mouth next, nor did I want to. "Do the two of you share a brain?"

This time Twenty-One Pilots stepped forward. "You know who I am?" He narrowed his beady eyes at me. "Tate

Bernard." He said his name like it was something special; like I was supposed to curtsey for him or something.

I stared at him, waiting for him to go on, but when he didn't, I realized he wanted me to speak next. I blinked a few times. "I have no fucking clue who you are, Taint, and honestly I don't care."

"It's Tate."

"Isn't that what I said?"

Tate rolled his eyes over to the blonde girl. "You believe this shit, Ash?" He shook his head. "Look, new girl—"

"Brett Cake," I stopped him.

"What?" Tate looked confused.

I smirked as I glanced around. "My name, Taint. It's Brett Cake." I needed to get out of here before this got out of hand.

He threw his head back and laughed. Laughed loud, hard, and so forced, I knew what was coming next. Tate had an ugly smile on his face when he made eye contact with me again. "Your last name is Cake?" he grunted. "Oh, this is going to be a fun fucking year of high school."

"Tate," Buzz cut started to talk, but was cut off.

"No, man, she doesn't get a pass. She could have played nicer, but not now." Tate put his hand up in front of his friend. "Isn't that right, fudge cake?" A wicked grin spread across his ugly face.

Yep, time for me to fucking jet.

I took one step back, but instead felt myself make contact with something or should I say *someone* else. A very hard someone else. I slowly turned around and looked up into the green eyes of Easton fucking Kennedy.

I had been at Kingston High for nearly three weeks now, and he had done everything he possibly could to ignore me. It didn't matter that his best friend wanted me around, Easton made sure to act like I didn't even exist. I had lunch with the Knights every day because Cash wanted me there, but Easton never looked at me, spoke to me or even reacted when his friends mentioned my name. It was like he had erased me from his mind without a second thought.

Was he taller than the last time he pinned me against the wall and made me silently beg him to kiss me? Fuck me right there up against the wall of the high school so everyone could hear and see us. Easton wasn't wearing a hat this time, which gave me the chance to see that his dark hair was shaved slightly around his ears and I instantly wanted to run my fingers over it. His lips were a perfect pink and cupid shaped. I hadn't noticed the lip ring earlier, but it only made him sexier with his thick shoulders covered in a worn leather jacket. His eyes were nearly burning a hole through my face and that old familiar ache began to slowly build again.

"Everything alright here?" His eyes moved over me. "Tate, are you being your usual charming self to my new friend?" His voice was deep and thick.

"Sure, we were just talking. Isn't that right fudge cake?" Tate slurred, and I heard the sound of laughter behind me.

Heat flashed in my cheeks and I felt tears prick my eyes as I started to walk around Easton, but he put his arm out to stop me. *You fucking assholes,* I wanted to scream at the top of my lungs, but that wasn't who I was. "I was just leaving." I tried to go around him, but he didn't budge.

"Do you need a ride?"

Did I... was this guy fucking serious? "What?" I blinked up into Easton's eyes as I tried to make sure he was speaking to me.

"I'll give you a ride home." Cash suddenly popped out of the trees with that huge smile on his face. He ran his hand through his hair and looked around. "Jesus, Tate, didn't you assholes get the memo?" He quickly moved to where I was and threw his arm around my shoulders. "Brett's with me. She's one of us now." For a split second, I saw something flicker in Easton's face before he looked away.

Panic and fear ripped through Tate's face. "Shit, I didn't know." He swallowed, and I watched his Adam's apple bob slightly. "Sorry, man." He didn't look at me when he spoke but instead kept his eyes on Cash.

Cash chuckled. "No need to be sorry, Tate, just don't make the same mistake twice." I felt every muscle in his body tighten against me. "Remember yourself," he added before he started to drag me away with him. "How did you get here, cupcake?" he asked casually once we were out of earshot.

"Palmer."

"Of fucking course."

I shoved away from him. "I don't need your protection, Cash." I jutted my chin slightly as I looked up at him. "I am perfectly capable—"

"Are you fucking serious right now?" Easton roared. "You weren't handling anything, Brett, and what would have happened if we hadn't shown up? Do you have any idea what type of guy Tate Bernard is?" He folded his arms over his massive chest. "Christ, you must be freezing." He suddenly shrugged off his coat. "Put it on," he ordered. Cash's eyes were nearly bulging from their sockets when I looked between the two of them. "Damn it," Easton muttered before he hung the coat around my shoulders.

I was totally confused about this entire situation unfolding right now as my mouth dropped open. This guy hadn't acknowledged me in weeks, but now he was going out of his way to help me? As I slid my hands inside the armholes I noticed that the jacket was huge, while my hands were suddenly warm and hidden causing electricity to course through my body like it was on fire. The coat was nice, soft, and... holy shit, it smelled amazing. Whatever cologne or aftershave Easton wore was sweet, spicy, and made my knees grow weak.

"Thanks." I dragged my teeth across my bottom lip.

Jameson appeared seemingly out of nowhere along with Jonathan or maybe it was the other way around. They were dressed in the same pair of blue jeans, but had on different shirts. How could anyone tell them apart? "We heading out already?" One of them nodded at me. "Good to see you, Brett," he added.

"You, too." I left off the name because I wasn't sure who was who.

"Jonathan." The one in the blue shirt pointed to himself. "Jameson." He hooked his thumb at his brother. "Don't worry, these three can't tell us apart most days." He grinned at me. "Tomorrow you'll have no fucking clue if I'm myself or my brother, but I thought I would at least help you out tonight."

Cash nudged my shoulder with his. "We can give you a ride, cupcake." His eyes were full of happiness. I had never met someone as easy-going as him before. Kind of sickening if you asked me, but at least I had someone looking out for me tonight.

I shook my head. "It's not necessary."

"That's where you're wrong."

I looked up at Easton.

"Clearly you can't be trusted not to run your pretty little mouth." His eyes had grown dark. "You need to watch your step at all times, Brett." He sucked his piercing into his mouth as he met the eyes of his friends. "You need to be with one of us," he added.

"I don't—"

Easton narrowed his eyes. "You do, babe, trust me." Then he started walking, and I had no choice but to follow since Cash grabbed my arm to pull me along. We walked a little in the dark, listening to the sounds of the party behind us, and the crunching of leaves beneath our feet.

My jaw fell open slightly when I saw Easton move to the sleek polished motorcycle parked in between a shiny Tesla and a black SUV. He was not only drop-dead gorgeous, but he drove a fucking bike? It nearly made me want to drop to my knees and suck him off right there. "That's yours?" I blurted out.

"What? Don't I look like the motorcycle type?" A smile tugged at his lips. "You're with me," he added.

I shook my head. "I'm not getting on that thing." I shrunk closer to Cash. "Can't you give me a ride instead?" I gave him my best puppy dog eyes.

"No can do, cupcake. Boss man has spoken, so you're with him." He grinned down at me. "Don't worry he's a safe driver, only had one or two accidents this month." Cash threw his head back and laughed when he saw the look on my face. "Relax; Easton has never had one single accident."

I had never actually ridden on a bike before. My mother dated a guy once who had one, but she said they were death-traps, and wouldn't let me do anything other than sit on the seat. I took a couple of timid steps toward as Easton patted the back. Jesus, I would have to touch him, too?

"Wait." Easton stopped me before I could hoist myself behind him. "Wear this." He grabbed the helmet from his head and held it out. "I only have the one, babe, and I don't want you to feel anything other than safe with me." His eyes moved over my face.

"Th-thanks," I stumbled over my words and pulled the helmet over my head. I struggled a bit to get the clip fastened until Easton reached out to help me. Our fingers brushed slightly and I sucked in my breath at the contact.

Easton nodded at me. "You don't have to look so worried. Like Cash said, I am a very safe driver," he tried to assure me. "Not one accident to my name and I've never dumped her if that's what you're really worried about."

I wasn't worried about any of that now. I was worried about what would happen the second I sat down. The moment I wrapped my arms around this way out-of-my league man. I eased my right leg over the seat and then the left. It wasn't too uncomfortable. Almost like sitting on a bicycle.

Easton glanced at me over his shoulder. "Brett, you need to hold on to me or you're going to fall off which would be bad for both of us." I wrapped my arms around his waist so he could start the bike, and when I pressed closer, I resisted the urge to moan. Easton smelled like fucking heaven on a stick. The feeling of the bike between my legs was odd and as Easton started to back up into the street, my stomach did a funny flip and I found myself hugging him a little tighter.

It was actually kind of nice, the feeling of being on the motorcycle, and I would be a liar if I didn't say I enjoyed hugging Easton, too. The way his muscles tightened and flexed with the movements of the motorcycle, not to mention how easily he managed the machine. As my nerves relaxed and I was able to enjoy the ride as the wind whipped by, I noticed just how carefully Easton took the corners and how careful of a driver he really was. Before I knew it, we had pulled up in front of the house, I couldn't think of it as mine, and I realized I would have a million questions to answer when I went inside.

Easton ran his hand through his hair. "Pretty cool, right?" I noticed the way his lip ring moved when he spoke and wondered why he didn't have it on at school. I might be becoming a little obsessed with it.

I nodded and handed him the helmet he had lent me before carefully climbing off the back of the bike. "Thanks." I looked up at Easton shyly. "Why are you being so nice to me now?" I blurted out without thinking. As usual. "Earlier today I got the impression you hated me." I chewed on my bottom lip as his eyes grew hard and bottomless. "Wait, I didn't mean—"

"I know what you meant, Brett." He shoved the helmet I just had on over his own head. He didn't say anything else as he started the bike and the sound of the engine roared to life.

Then he drove off, leaving me standing there in the dark. I didn't understand him. One second he was nice and then the next he was acting like he couldn't stand the sight of me. I glared down the street where he had just driven off before I rolled my eyes and went into the house.

Chapter Four

Easton

I ignored all the catcalls and obnoxious noise the moment I walked into Oz's place. When Cash, J2, and I moved into the house, his parents turned some of the guest rooms into rooms for us. I tried not to think of the place as my home, but it was nice to have a place to feel safe in since the one I came from had never been without my father there. I stormed through the living room, past the kitchen, and straight up the stairs so that I could hide and think without them bothering me, but not before they tried to give me shit.

"How'd it go, lover boy?" Cash called out, but I only tossed my middle finger up as I continued to my room. That got them all laughing again, and I hated Brett for that.

Brett fucking Cake. God, the way it felt to have her arms wrapped around me for even a short trip had made me rock fucking hard, and I had to scratch the itch. I had already texted my girl to come over and help me out, but until she got there, I would have to try to think of someone or something else. I swear I could smell Brett on my shirt, which only made me yank it off and toss it onto the top of the hamper.

Those blue eyes, those perfect fucking lips... I wanted nothing more than to kiss her so hard until she couldn't see straight before I buried myself so far inside her cunt she couldn't walk for a week. I told the boys I wasn't interested, but I was a fucking liar.

"Knock, knock." The sound of Josie Silver's voice caused me to turn toward the door where she stood.

Josie was no fucking Brett. With her long auburn hair, green emerald eyes, and the caked-on makeup? She would never even be close. We'd been on again off again since we were just kids, but she was good at getting me off and tonight I fucking needed her more than ever. Josie was dressed in a tight brown dress that clung to her like a second skin and despite how hard I was, the sight of her did nothing for me. It was Brett I wanted, but could never have.

"About time," I growled as Josie sashayed over to me.

She batted her lashes at me while she slid her hands up my chest. "Rough day, baby?" Josie purred as she licked her lips.

I shook my head. I hadn't asked her here to talk. I pointed to my cock. "Suck it," I instructed before I sat down.

Josie smirked at me as she unbuttoned my jeans and slowly pulled down the zipper. "Baby, you know I'll do much more than suck you off." She didn't need to remind me. Her hand dipped into my pants and I groaned as she wrapped it around my shaft to pull it out. "You're so hard, Easton," she murmured as she ducked her head so that she could press her tongue against me.

Hard for someone I shouldn't be, I thought, and closed my eyes as Josie swallowed my dick all the way down to my balls. Fuck, all I could see was Brett, and I reached down to grab a handful of Josie's hair in my hand to try to get her out of my mind. She whimpered as I curled it around my fist and yanked.

"Baby, let me fuck you," she cooed. "Sit right there and I'll do all the work." Her tongue danced around the tip before she glanced up at me with lust-filled eyes.

I didn't want her to fuck me, but it would ease the ache of my balls if I did. When I nodded, Josie yanked her dress up around her waist before she climbed up to straddle me. I felt her stretch and clamp around me as she eased down my aching shaft, her mouth landing on mine. I nibbled and pulled on Josie's lips with my teeth as she moved with me, her soft moans only growing louder.

"Faster, baby," I urged as she rocked her hips. "Fuck, that's it." I gripped her legs in my hands as she began to ride me.

Josie let out a low groan as she began to slip up and down my cock. Her mouth opened slightly, her eyes closed, and with her hair hanging down her back, I forgot what I called her here for, only for a second. The minute I closed my eyes as Josie muttered obscenities to me and an image of Brett appeared behind them. I pictured the way her tits would jiggle as she took my cock, and when the pussy that was currently wrapped around me began to clench tightly, I wondered what Brett would feel like. What her mouth would feel like on mine, on my body, and wrapped around my dick. Would she like it dirty? I bet she would. I bet Brett would let me make her scream, slap her ass, and maybe even—

"Fuck, I'm going to come." I gritted my teeth together as I let go and let out a low moan. I wished it was Brett I was coming inside of, thought of spraying my semen all over her tits, and I bit down on Josie's neck as I shuddered beneath her.

Josie licked her lips as she continued to bounce on my lap. "That was hot." She pinched and pulled her nipples as she threw her head back. "I don't think I've ever felt you come like that before."

I practically shoved her onto the floor. "Leave." I shoved my dick back into my pants before I zip them back up. "Now," I growled.

"I wasn't done yet."

"Yes, you were."

Josie smoothed her dress down around her legs. "It's that new girl, isn't it? The one with the absurd purple hair." She pouted as she looked up at me.

My blood began to boil. "I won't tell you again, Josie. Get the fuck out of my room." I marched past her into my bathroom. "Or else I'll have Oswald remove you himself, which you don't want," I called back over my shoulder. I slammed and locked the door as I heard Josie mutter under her breath about what an asshole I was.

I turned on the shower and stripped off my pants before I stepped inside the tub. The water felt perfect as I stood beneath it to wash over my skin, but when I closed my eyes, I only saw Brett's face. "Fuck," I muttered. What was with this girl? Why couldn't I get her out of my head even after I fucked someone else?

Once I was done with my shower, I wrapped a towel around my waist and marched back into my room. I dug around for a clean pair of sweats which I slipped into and without thinking I grabbed the shirt I had on earlier. The one that smelled sweet like... shit! Brett still had my damn coat. I had given it to her because she was cold at the party, and I never got it back. I took the stairs two at a time. "She has my coat." I pointed at Cash.

Cash grinned at me as he brought his beer to his lips and took a long swig before he answered. "I didn't see Josie walk out of here with your coat." He snickered.

I pinched my lips together. "You know who I'm talking about. Your new girlfriend. Text her. I want it back," I demanded.

Oz pulled his face away from the girl he was currently lip-locked with to glare at me. "Go get it yourself, asshole, you're a big boy now." He climbed to his feet and the girl did the same.

"Sorry, bro, but I don't have her number." Cash's brows dipped. "Yet." He finished off his beer.

"Then go get it."

Cash tilted his head. "Something wrong with your bike? Did your legs stop working or something?" He sat back and stretched his own up to rest them on the coffee table.

"Go fuck yourself, Donovan," I snarled at him and as I turned to go back upstairs, a thought occurred to me. "If I have to go back to her house—" I stopped myself. "Never mind," I hissed under my breath.

Back upstairs in my room, I couldn't seem to stop pacing. That jacket, my father's actually, meant nearly as much to me as the bike I drove. I wore it after he died even when it was too big, and now that it actually fit? Well, I couldn't just leave it with some random chick that had no business having it. I chewed on my thumb as I tried to decide what

I should do. I could wait until Monday at school and hope that Brett brought it with her to give it back. Or, I could go over there first thing in the morning to demand she hand it over. Or... or what? I didn't have her number or Palmer's either. My phone buzzed in my pocket.

Cash: Since you're being a giant turd, I texted Palmer who said she would have Brett bring your coat to school on Monday.

Easton: I need it before then. We have a thing tomorrow night.

Cash: Shit, right. Okay, well, tomorrow I'll go get it for you.

Jealousy reared its ugly head at the thought of Cash going to Brett's house. To where she slept, ate, and changed her clothes.

Easton: I'll fucking do it myself.

I tossed my phone onto the bed and ran my hands through my hair. Looks like I was going to have to make a trip to Brett's after all.

OVER BREAKFAST THE next morning, Cash was still complaining about how he still didn't have Brett's number and he was going to go over to Palmer's house to get it today if she didn't give it up to him.

"Why?" Jameson poured himself a second bowl of cereal and added the milk.

Cash wrinkled his nose. "Why, what?" He spooned a mouthful of frosted flakes into his mouth.

Jameson held up his hand as he finished chewing. "Why is she living with Palmer?" he asked before digging into his food again. I was curious about that, too, but I kept my face void of expression as I listened to them all gossip like a bunch of girls.

Oz stumbled into the kitchen in his pajama pants and looked over at us. "Ugh, how can you eat that junk? Please tell me someone made coffee." He looked hungover as hell.

"You didn't seem to have a problem sucking down bottles of booze last night." I grabbed the box of cereal before Jameson finished it off.

Oz smacked his fists together, Ross Geller style. "You fucking purple-haired freaks now?" he shot back.

"Watch yourself," I warned.

Oz rolled his eyes. "I'm scared, boss."

Cash shot to his feet, but I put my hand on his arm. "Relax, man, no one is talking smack about your girl," I assured him.

"I am," Oz growled into his coffee mug.

"Take that back, dick," Cash exclaimed.

"Or what?"

I slammed my fist against the table so hard the bowls bounced, spilling milk and frosted goodness everywhere. "Knock it off." I stood up with my now-empty bowl. "Both of you. Brett is Cash's friend, assholes, so treat her with a little respect," I reminded them as I walked over to the sink to rinse out my bowl. "I'm going to get my shit," I told them.

"Can I tag along?" Cash asked as he put his bowl in the sink. "I don't want to be here right now."

It would probably be a good idea if I brought Cash with me. He was friendly with Brett, she wasn't afraid of him, and he hadn't blown her off last night or ignored her since she dropped into his life. He also probably hadn't fucked another girl to try and get Brett out of his head only to have her there in his dreams naked and fingering herself while moaning his name, but whatever.

"I'm good." I surprised myself. I went to grab my jacket from the hook I usually left it on, only to remember that was why I was going back there in the first place.

"Use protection, boss man!" Jonathan teased as he bounded down the stairs. "Don't need you knocking anyone up today. One of you is more than enough."

Instead of snapping off some witty remark, I turned and walked outside to my bike. I had never let a girl get to me like this before, and there had been plenty of them. When I hit puberty, which was around five years ago, I must have grown a foot over the summer. I went from being a short, scrawny boy to a six-foot-five beast with broad shoulders, and a five o'clock shadow. My voice changed, my clothes got too small, and all of a sudden every girl in town was interested in me. I had no idea what to do with myself or how to react, but I learned damn quickly not to get attached.

I lost my virginity to Josie a month into our freshman year of high school. We were friends as kids because of our fathers, but I didn't love her. She claimed she had feelings for me, but I couldn't love myself, never mind her. She was always there when I needed a blow job or a good fucking, but she wasn't the only girl. Josie knew that and didn't get jealous because I always came back to her once the semen was drained from my balls. We were destined for one another whether I liked it or not, but I tried not to think about that most days.

I took the long way to Brett's, telling myself that I wanted to enjoy the cool October morning, but I was only lying to myself. I was avoiding the conversation. Avoiding having to see or speak with her again because the attraction I felt was stronger than anything I had ever experienced before. I was afraid of what might happen if I let my guard down for even one second around the purple-haired beauty, because it could mean disaster for both of us.

Chapter Five

Brett

I realized the moment my alarm went off the next morning that I had stayed up too late with Palmer the night before. She had bounced into my room the moment she got home and told me she had heard all about how Easton had stood up for me when Tate started to harass me. She wanted to know every little detail, especially the part about him giving me a ride home. I thought that Palmer might actually pass out when she saw Easton's coat sitting on my chair by the bedroom door.

The house was empty when I padded down the stairs in my blue overalls, ratty old Pink Floyd tank top, and old sneakers on my feet. Palmer was still sleeping while Ruby and Jennifer went out shopping, or at least that was what the text had said my mother sent. I heated up a cup of the now cold coffee and dug around in the cabinet, trying to find something to eat. I grabbed a frosted donut from the cabinet before I headed outside to the small shed Jennifer had let me use as my studio. I felt the urge to paint so badly it hurt, and I needed to get it out.

Last night kept running through my brain as I unlocked the door and stepped inside. The smell of oil paint hit me and I took a deep breath to take it in. The last piece I had been working on was still sitting on the easel, so I quickly replaced it with a plain white canvas. I could paint inside the house, but I didn't get the privacy or silence that I got here. The last place we lived I had to paint in my room, but this felt more like my own little sanctuary. I gathered my paints and brushes so that I could put them in order before I grabbed the elastic on my wrist to twist my hair up off my neck so that I could get lost in my work.

I zone out a lot when I'm painting, so I wasn't sure how long I was there before I was interrupted by a knock on the door despite having kept it open. I didn't turn around, figuring it was probably my mother coming to check out me now that she was home or possibly Palmer coming for more gossip.

"It's open!"

"Sorry to drop in unannounced, but I didn't have your number."

I nearly dropped the brush in my hand at the sound of Easton's voice. What the hell was he doing here? I whipped around which caused me to nearly spill the paint on the floor and met his emerald eyes. "What the fuck do you want?" The words were out of my mouth before I could stop them. The way his eyes traveled over my body made me wish I had covered up more, but it was too late for that now. I was sure that I was soaked in sweat and stunk like death warmed over.

"Wow, you painted all of these, Brett?" Easton's boots made a crunching noise against the wood floor as he walked closer to me inspecting one of my paintings. His eyes flicked back to me again. "These are really fucking good."

"Yes." I put my brush down. "You didn't answer my question." The spicy scent of his aftershave had replaced the smell of paint, and I found myself taking a small step back from him.

Easton laughed softly as I watched his eyes start to focus on the painting I had been working on. Shit, why didn't I do that in charcoal or a sketch where it wouldn't be out on display for the entire world to see? Fuck my life. He tilted his head. "You're not afraid of me, are you?" The way Easton stared at my painting was making my insides shake.

I'm goddamn terrified of you, I wanted to shout at him, but instead I just shook my head. "Why are you here? What do you want from me? Why did you ignore me for weeks only to suddenly act like some brave hero? Maybe you should—" My breath caught in my throat as Easton suddenly reached over to run his thumb lightly across my cheek before he wiped it on his faded jeans, leaving a trail of silver paint behind.

"That my bike?" He jutted his chin toward the painting I had just been working on. He leaned down to take a closer look and when I didn't answer right away, he reached out like he might touch it.

"Don't!"

Easton stood up to his full height, and I was sure his head would hit the roof. "Sorry." He brought his hand down over the back of his neck before he pinched it lightly. He was fucking beautiful with those sharp as all hell cheekbones and bulging biceps that looked way too mature for an eighteen-year-old boy. There was no doubt in my mind Easton Kennedy was built from every girl's wet dream.

"Uh, no. It's still damp," I muttered like a fool. *You know, just like my panties right now.*

"You enjoyed riding it?"

"Excuse me?"

"My motorcycle, babe, did you enjoy the ride?" Again he gave a small chuckle and Easton's hand came up to graze my chin as he moved my face to look at him. "You can say no. I won't be offended." His voice was sharper this time and I watched as he sucked on his lip ring. I wondered what it would feel like pressed against my mouth.

"It wasn't terrible."

Easton's eyes lit up as they moved to the painting again. "It's perfect, Brett. Looks like the real fucking thing." He tilted his head as he stared at it.

I was confused. Last night Easton seemed mad as hell at me, but right now he was acting like we were friends. "Why are you here?" I blurted out again and my breath caught in my throat when he turned to meet my gaze.

"My jacket."

My face fell and disappointment clouded my thoughts. "You came here for a fucking coat?" I threw my hands up. "Jesus Christ, you could have texted me for that and I would have gladly left it outside—"

Easton moved fast and before I realized it, he had me back against the wall. His breath came fast as he stared me down, his eyes never leaving my face. "You think I didn't think of that?" He growled deep in his chest and when he casually wrapped his hand around my throat just lightly enough to cause that ache to come back between my legs, I couldn't stop the moan that escaped from my throat.

"Let go of me," I hissed. "I swear to God I'll—"

"You'll what, Dorothy? Scream? You could, but do you think that Palmer is going to come to your rescue? Highly doubtful don't you think? And I don't see your best friend Cash around tp save you either."

I swallowed nervously as I stared up at him. "Please don't hurt me," I whispered and hated myself as tears filled my eyes.

Easton's lips twitched. "Babe, the only time I hurt a girl is when she begs me for it." He moved so that our noses touched before he ran it down my cheek. My entire body trembled at his words. "My jacket is all I came here for." He released me and I stumbled away from him. "Today." He sucked his lip ring into his mouth as he raised one eyebrow suggestively.

I sprinted out of the shed and back to the house. I didn't bother shutting the front door as I hit the stairs to grab that godforsaken leather jacket from my chair. When I spun back around Easton was already standing in the doorway. I shoved the coat in his direction, but once he grabbed it, he didn't move. His eyes slowly moved around my small, cluttered bedroom before he looked at me again. I still had a few boxes I hadn't unpacked which was my wishful thinking that we might not stay long.

"Thanks," he grunted and slipped the leather on.

"Leave, now."

Easton instead took a step forward. "You don't want me in your room, babe?" His eyes had grown dark with heat. "Or are you afraid of what might happen if I stay?" he teased. I went to take a step back, but his arm snaked out so that he could tug me against his hard chest. "You're not a virgin, are you, Dorothy?"

I shook my head as I clung to his arms. "No, of course not," I answered.

"You like fucking? You like having a cock buried deep inside that sweet little cunt of yours?"

I wanted to feel disgusted at his words with the way he spoke to me, but instead I felt my nipples grow hard inside my bra and white heat flare between my legs. "Yes." I licked my lips lightly.

Easton groaned softly as he let his hand drop to my hip. "You ever think about what I would feel like inside you?" he whispered. "How you would feel wrapped around my fucking dick as you rode me?" He dragged his tongue around my ear. "I bet you would feel fucking perfect, babe."

The whimper that escaped my mouth surprised us both. Then Easton suddenly released me. He stared at me for what felt like an eternity before he turned and marched back down the hallway.

No. He wasn't going to get away with turning me on like that and just fucking leaving. "Wait a second!" I called out and found myself chasing him down the stairs and onto the porch. "You came here to what? Get your fucking coat and tease me with your dirty mouth?" I exclaimed. "I'm not some whore, Easton. The words you say might turn me on, but I will never fuck you."

"Never say never, babe."

"Never."

Easton's eyes burned with anger. "Thanks for my coat, Brett." He glanced into the open door before he met my gaze again. "See you around. Good morning, Palmer." He turned and headed toward where his motorcycle was parked.

"What the hell did I miss?" Palmer's voice was full of confusion. "Why was he in your room?"

I wanted to chase Easton down again, but instead, I let him go. "He came for his jacket." I sighed softly.

"What?" Palmer shook her head. "I told Cash I would have you bring it on Monday. Which reminds me," she rolled her eyes. "You've been super friendly with him since you started school, but I don't understand why you won't give him your number. Please, for the love all God, can I give it to him so he'll leave me alone?"

I nodded as we went back inside the house. Not only was I confused as hell about Easton, but I was also ridiculously turned on. I wanted to hate him, but there was no denying the attraction I felt. I meant what I said though. I wouldn't sleep with him.

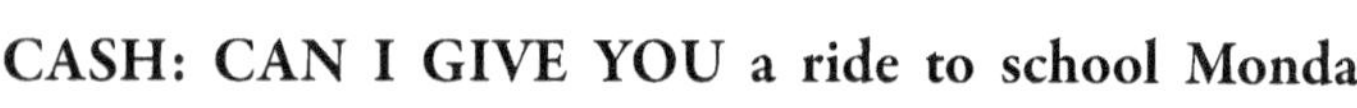

CASH: CAN I GIVE YOU a ride to school Monday morning?

Cash: I don't have a motorcycle, but Oz has a sweet Tesla that is way cooler.

Cash: I can bring breakfast if that would help.

Giving my cell phone number to Cash was a huge mistake. The second Palmer texted it to him my phone started blowing up and hasn't stopped since. I placed it face down on the table and watched it vibrate with every single message.

Cash: Are you busy later? I thought maybe you might want to hang out?

I rolled my eyes and stared across the table at Palmer who was busy stirring the spoon in her coffee. "This is your fault." I pointed to my phone as it buzzed again. "He's absolutely relentless."

Palmer smiled. "He likes you." She brought her mug to her lips. "But, you're like his best friend, right?" Her brows dipped as she drank her coffee. "You're more into Easton?"

Was she sniffing glue this morning?

"No." I groaned as my phone went off again. "And, no." I might find Easton Kennedy attractive, but that was far as that goes. "Jesus Christ." I grabbed my phone.

Brett: Yes, motorcycles are overrated, no, maybe.

I wasn't really a big texter, but I did it when I needed to. The second I hit send, I saw Cash had already read my message and waited for his response.

Cash: You're a woman of few words, cupcake, and I like that.

Brett: You just like women.

Cash: That might be true, but you're my favorite.

Brett: *eye roll emoji*

Cash: *tongue emoji*

Brett: You're insane, aren't you? Are you sure that you've been checked? Maybe the test was wrong. Might want to have that checked again.

Cash: Certifiably sane, boo, I promise you that.

"Why are you smiling at your phone like that?" Palmer interrupted my private conversation. "You look weird." She stood up to get more coffee.

"I have no idea what you're talking about."

"Right, okay."

I glanced back down at my phone. "Cash asked if I wanted to hang out tonight." I chewed on my bottom lip as I considered it.

"Don't do it." Palmer touched my wrist. "Look, I know you think he's nice, which he is, but those boys are... bad news." She sat back in her chair as fear glistened in her eyes.

I waved my hand at her. "Cash seems innocent enough."

"That's where you're wrong, B." That nickname she insisted on using for me wasn't as bad as I thought. Palmer leaned forward. "They're all—"

"Girls!" Ruby and Jennifer walked in the front door and interrupted our talk. "It's nice to see you two hanging out." That was my mother.

"Hi, Mom." I stood up and slipped my phone into my back pocket. "I was just going to work on my painting." I.e. I'm going to destroy the fucking thing because Easton Kennedy is a fucking dick, but I didn't say that part out loud.

Ruby caught me by the elbow. "One minute, sweetheart." She flashed a quick smile. "Who was that boy who brought you home last night? The one on the motorcycle?" Shit, I was hoping she had missed that part. Palmer's eyes went round.

"He's no one, Mom, don't worry. Just a boy from school. One I can promise you that I won't be seeing again."

"Just a boy that drives a motorcycle." Ruby sighed softly. "Brett, you know that I trust you, but boys like that only want one thing."

"Come on, Mom."

Ruby shook her head. "Don't 'come on, Mom' me, young lady." She narrowed her eyes.

"Don't worry, I won't make the same mistakes as you." I managed to yank my arm from Ruby's grip and started out the door. I could hear her yelling at me, but I ignored her.

She was the reason I was here in the first place. Besides, it didn't matter because Ruby never stayed mad at me longer than a few minutes. By tomorrow morning she'd forget what I had said and act like it never even happened. I grabbed my phone and shot off a text before I could change my mind.

Brett: Come get me. I need to get out of here.

Brett: Now.

Cash: I thought you would never ask, boo. I am on my way.

Chapter Six

Easton

When I got back to Oz's place, the party had already started. I was less than thrilled that I would have to put on a happy face, but it wasn't my house, so I couldn't complain too much. The street was lined up and down both ways with cars when I pulled my bike into the garage. I heard Josie's voice as I pulled the helmet from my head. I was in no mood to put up with her shit right now.

"Hey baby!" Josie purred as I walked from the garage. Today she was dressed in painted-on jeans with a low cut top that did absolutely nothing to hide her tits, and her hair was pulled up in a ponytail. My dick didn't even grow semi-hard at the sight of her.

I hit the remote on my keys to shut the door and slipped them into my back pocket. "What are you doing here?" I growled. I didn't even bother to stop as I headed inside the house. After Brett, dealing with Josie would complicate my brain even more and I thought about sending her home, but the thought of dealing with her father had me biting my tongue instead.

Josie had to run to keep up with me. "It's Saturday, Easton, why else would I be here? We usually spend the night together." She slipped her arm through mine, but I shrugged her off. Guess she already forgotten about last night and how I kicked her out of my room.

"Thanks, but I'm not interested."

"Are you feeling alright?"

The music was so loud when I stepped into the house it nearly made my teeth clatter together. I stopped to look around the crowded room which caused Josie to smack right into me before she managed to gather herself together and moved in front of me. I ignored her as I pushed past the kids from school, marched into the kitchen, and grabbed a red cup from the counter along with the bottle of vodka on the counter. I poured myself a shot, and gulped it down, followed by two more. My head buzzed lightly as I glanced over my shoulder just in time to see Cash walking in with his arm wrapped around Brett's shoulders.

What the fuck?

Brett was dressed in the same overalls from earlier with the ratty Floyd shirt. The overalls were just a little too big and hung down so that I could see a little bit of skin that the shirt didn't cover. The jeans had paint splattered all over them, but it didn't matter because Brett pulled that off. I had a feeling she could walk around in a garbage bag and make that shit look good. She looked shyly around the room before we finally made eye contact. The smile she had been wearing on her beautiful face disappeared and she leaned into Cash just enough for jealousy to spike right through me.

I couldn't stop the smirk that slid up my face before I turned and grabbed Josie's elbow to drag her downstairs to the finished basement where couples were already spread out everywhere. Some were just cuddling, but most were making out, and I was pretty sure that Jared Benson was getting a full-on blow job in the corner. The music was less yelly down here, the atmosphere more relaxed, and the crowd a hell of a lot thinner. I sat down on one of the empty couches so that I could pull Josie onto my lap.

Josie moaned softly as she adjusted herself so that she was straddling me. She slid her hands up my chest and laced them around my back just as I noticed Cash and Brett standing at the foot of the stairs. I let my teeth graze Josie's neck lightly as I kept my eyes pinned on the purple-haired beauty. She pretended not to see me, but her nostrils flared as I gripped Josie's hips and brought my mouth to hers.

I got lost in the moment as I stared at Brett, pretending she was the one dry humping me, not Josie while my tongue slicked together with hers. I wrapped my arm around Josie's waist to pull her closer, causing her to whimper into my mouth. Brett's eyes had grown dark, her eyes hooded and my cock twitched at the sight. When I finally pulled away from Josie, I winked. "What's wrong, babe, you wish this was you?" I teased.

Josie spun around to see Brett standing with Cash before she gasped. "Seriously, Easton?" She brought her hand up like she was going to slap me, but I caught her wrist. "Let me go, asshole, I'm not going to let you use me to make someone jealous."

"Stop it, you know you like it when I use you."

"Go to hell."

I only laughed as Josie jumped up from my lap and stormed up the stairs, making sure to bump into Brett on her way up. "What?" I asked Cash when he shook his head. Brett looked like she might follow Josie, but instead she stayed close to my best friend, and I wondered just exactly what was going on between the two of them.

Suddenly Jameson came bounding down the stairs. "We've got a bit of a problem." He glanced over at me before he realized Brett was standing there. He nodded at her.

"Who?" I kept my face void of emotion but my voice full of ice.

"Tate."

I quickly got to my feet. "Keep her here." I pointed at Cash as I looked at Brett who narrowed her eyes at me. "Don't give me any lip, babe, you know he's here because of you. Because of last night," I reminded her.

"You might need my help," Cash reminded me. "Is he alone?" he asked Jameson, who nodded. "Alright, cupcake, it's you and me," he teased before he grabbed her to sit down in the spot I had just vacated. I immediately felt the need to rip his fucking body apart, starting with his arms as he wrapped them around her frame, but when Brett shoved at his chest and moved to the cushion next to him I felt a little better although not very much.

"Let's go." I motioned for Jameson to follow me up the stairs. There was no need to push through the crowd of people in the kitchen because they just seemed to part for me like Moses and The Red fucking Sea when I appeared. We made our way through the room, and into the kitchen where Tate stood with a somewhat worried look on his face. I didn't blame him. On his right was Jonathan, and to his left? Mr. Nasty himself, Ozzy.

Tate held up his hands. "Hey." He flashed a brief smile at me. "I come in peace."

"That so?" I cocked an eyebrow as I sucked on my lip ring. "Don't recall seeing your name on the guest list, Taint." I let the nickname Brett used last night slip from my lips and watched the way his eyes went dark.

"You assholes don't seem to mind coming to my parties. You drink my beer without any problems." He raised his chin as if to challenge me.

Oz's body shook as he tried to control himself. "Well, that's because we're us, and you're..." He waved his hand in the air. "You, Taint." Shit, I guess that nickname was going to stick around.

"Don't fucking call me that," Tate hissed between clenched teeth.

I took a couple of steps forward so that we were now toe to toe. "Or what?" I saw the fear in his eyes. The way he refused to meet mine. "That's what I fucking thought." I realized that the music had stopped and when I turned around, I found my classmates all watching us. "Go back to your fucking party!" I barked out the order. "Have fun! Enjoy yourselves!" I whirled back around to the man of the hour. "You're going to regret this." I pointed my finger at him.

"This is because of *Brett,* isn't it?" The way he said her name sent shivers up my spine and not in a good way.

I stepped forward again and I expected him to move, but he stood his ground. "You fucking leave her out of this." I leaned down to get right in Tate's greasy face. "Remember what happened the last time you opened your goddamn mouth?" I warned.

Tate rolled his eyes, but then his eyes narrowed in on something behind me. "Speak of the little purple-haired she-devil." He laughed like that was the funniest thing he had ever heard before.

My fist connected with Tate's jaw, knocking him back. He didn't fall though and managed to put his hand up to try to stop the next punch from connecting with his body. It didn't work. I was faster, stronger, and my next punch hit went straight to Tate's stomach, this one knocking him right onto his back.

"You might want to fucking stay down, bro." Cash's foot came down on Tate's hand and the bone crunching underneath was loud enough to make anyone's stomach turn. Good thing the music had come back on to cover it up.

Tate let out a bloodcurdling scream as he pulled his hand away. "What is the fucking big deal? It's a joke!" He held his injured body part to his chest.

"A joke?" Jonathan mimicked. "I don't get the punchline."

Jameson joined his brother. "Neither do I. Explain it to us like we're stupid, man." He grinned like the joker on his craziest day.

"You're all fucking psycho!" Tate exclaimed. "What the fuck is wrong with you? You—"

I might have pounced on him if I hadn't suddenly seen a blur of purple out of the corner of my eye. I cursed Cash for not staying downstairs like I had told them, even though we had needed his help with Tate. "Don't—" She started to back away and then fled from the room. Shit.

"Take care of this," I muttered to my guys before I took off after Brett.

I wasn't sure where she had gone at first, but I caught a glimpse of purple hair as the back door slammed shut behind her. I pushed the screen open and watched as she stumbled down the steps, but managed to keep herself from falling onto the patio beneath her. "I'm going to follow you, babe, and when I catch you? Well, let's just say you might not like what I do to you," I called out.

Brett glanced at me over her shoulder. "Leave me alone, Easton!" She should be watching where she was going. I knew that Oz's parents were having some sort of new sprinkler system put in, so there were holes, and shit dug up all over their back yard.

"Watch out!"

Too little, too late. Brett tripped and face planted onto the grass in front of her. She landed like a sack of potatoes and I was afraid she might have broken something until she started to get back to her feet.

"Don't move," I instructed. "You could have some serious injuries."

Brett rolled her eyes. "I'm fine," she insisted, but winced as she put weight down on her right foot.

"That doesn't look fine to me." I attempted to wrap my arm around her waist, but she slapped me away. "I'm trying to help."

"Don't you think you've helped enough?" Brett glared. "Don't fucking touch me, asshole."

Guess I would have to do this my way. I ignored what she had just said and scooped Brett up into my arms bridal style which caused her to let out a squeal. "Just go with it, babe, because this is happening," I advised as I started walking.

"I fucking hate you," she seethed.

I winced slightly at the words she spat out, but I simply ignored them. I usually didn't care what people thought of me, but for some reason, I cared what Brett Cake thought. The girl with the purple fucking hair was already under my skin after barely two days. I wanted to keep her safe even if I couldn't have her. Even if she *did* hate me. Even if she ended up with my best friend. Speak of the devil—

"What the fuck happened?" Cash exclaimed as I walked back into the house. "What did you do?" He narrowed his eyes at me.

I ignored the last question as I started up the stairs. "I remember asking you to stay in the basement with your girl." Brett had her arms folded over her chest as I walked. "She somehow then ended up in the living room, and then I chased her into the back yard." I opened my bedroom door with my hip.

"Chased... why? Why did you fucking chase her, East?"

I placed Brett gently on my bed before I answered. "I don't know." Which was the honest truth. I guess because I was fascinated, scared, and curious all at the same time. "Stay." I pointed my finger which only caused rage to boil in Brett's eyes.

"I'm not a fucking dog," she reminded me.

"Please?" Cash asked.

"I hate it here." Brett folded her arms over her chest. "Can you just take me home?" She pouted her lips slightly which caused an ache to build in my dick.

I shook my head. "No." I reached for the foot she twisted. "Take off your shoe so we can take a look at it."

"Are you a fucking doctor now? When did you go to medical school?" She was such a feisty fucking thing.

I felt a smile tug at my lips. A real one and I tried really hard to fight it. "No, babe, but I've broken enough bones in my life to know if something is sprained or broken." I watched as she slowly looked around my room before she met my eyes again. I kept it neat and tidy in here because I liked things that way. Brett Cake was putting a major kink in my life.

Without a word, Brett reached down to untie her dirty Converse sneaker which she dropped onto my floor. "Happy, daddy?" She raised both eyebrows. "Not swollen." She wiggled it around, but I caught the slight wince. "It's fine, I can just ice it at home." I didn't miss the fact that she called me daddy, nor did my fucking dick as it plumped slightly in my jeans.

"No."

"No?"

I heard Cash mutter something under his breath and I shot him a look.

"Babe, you have no fucking choice." I was nose to nose with Brett now, and could smell whatever lotion she wore. It was intoxicating. I couldn't put my finger on what it was, but I wanted to lick every single inch of her body so bad it hurt.

Cash coughed. "Should I leave?" he teased. "I should leave." He started to walk backward out of my room.

"Don't you fucking leave me here, Cash!" Brett kept her eyes on me and we both heard the sound of the door shut. "Bastard."

"What's wrong, Dorothy? Afraid to be alone with me?"

"You fucking wish."

I chuckled softly. "Look, let me get you some ice, you can rest up, and then your boyfriend can take you home." I hated the way I sounded when I said that. I moved away from her before she could see my face.

Brett snorted. "Cash isn't my boyfriend." She eased her legs up onto my bed before she laid down. "Is this your room? Do you live here?" she asked.

I grabbed a plastic bag from the drawer by my bed as I walked over to the small fridge that I kept stocked with drinks and dug around for some ice. "Yes," I answered both questions. I slipped the ice into the bag and walked back to where Brett was. "Here." I held out my hand.

"Thanks." She placed the bag on her ankle. "Where are your parents?"

"Don't." I shook my head.

"I was just—"

"I know what you were doing, and I said fucking don't."

Brett threw the bag of ice at me which I caught in one hand. "You don't have to be an asshole about it, Easton." She jumped to her feet, but sat right back down. "I was just trying to make conversation, which clearly you can't fucking do."

I ran my hand through my hair. "Just... just... fuck!" I exclaimed before I stormed from the room and slammed the door, locking it behind me. I heard Brett yelling that I couldn't just keep her here like some sort of prisoner, but I ignored her and went back downstairs.

Chapter Seven

Brett

After Easton locked me in his room, I was furious! I yelled, screamed, and cried for what felt like hours, and when I texted Cash, he told me not to worry. It would only be until the party was over. The party I hadn't even *asked* to come to. When he told me he wanted to hang out, I thought it was just, you know, to hang out. Not some loud ass party that I didn't ask to attend.

I fell asleep at some point after the battery on my phone died. I was exhausted from the past couple of days and spread out on Easton's bed, which was amazingly comfortable. I had so many questions that he clearly didn't want to answer. So many things were fluttering around in my head about the mysterious boy that seemed to hate me when I woke up the next morning. Except this time I found myself in a different room with thick, massive arms wrapped around me. I slowly eased myself around to see who it was.

Cash.

I watched him as he slept for a moment before I reached up and ran my hand over his blonde hair. Why did he insist on throwing himself into my life? Why did he so desperately want to be my friend, my "bestie" as he put it? Someone like Cash would be easier to be with, date, and—

"You checking me out, cupcake?"

Oops, looks like I was busted. I blushed as his eyes moved over my face, and a smile spread across Cash's handsome face. "Maybe." I decided to go with it instead of lying. It wasn't like he was a horrible person, and he clearly liked me. I slid my hands up his chest so that I could link them behind his neck. "You like me, don't you, Cash?" I purred softly.

"Of course I like you. What kind of a stupid fucking question is that?" He rolled his eyes as he attempted to laugh it off. Cash's nostrils flared while he stared directly at my mouth. "You're just, you know, not my type." He licked his own lips nervously as he said that.

My brows dipped. "Not your type? Do you like blondes or something?"

His breath was coming faster now, and the raging erection he was now sporting told me otherwise.

"I'm gay."

"What?"

"Yep, that's it. I'm gay. Like, so gay. Gay, gay, GAY!" he sang loudly as he sprang up off the bed so fast he nearly fell onto his ass. I stared at him from the bed as he tried to justify himself.

Cash was lying to me. It wasn't just the fucking fact that his cock was giving him away, but he was now avoiding all eye contact with me as he babbled on about how much he loved men, dick, and assholes. I sat up on the bed and hugged my legs to my chest as I watched him throw his hands up in the air and talk about how much he enjoyed hairy balls. Ew, gross. Nobody liked hairy fucking sacks.

"Are you done?" I asked when he finally stopped to take a breath.

He blinked at me. "What?"

"I asked if you were done lying to me." I pushed my legs back down so I could swing them around the edge of the mattress. "Why are you lying to me? If you're not interested in me or don't find me attractive, just tell me. I won't be offended," I assured him.

"Brett, you're fucking gorgeous."

I rolled my eyes. "Right." I stood up to test my weight on my foot. "Add another lie to the mix." Last night I had twisted my ankle pretty good. Not enough to need to go to the doctor, but enough that I knew it would be sore for a day or two. I winced as I took a step, but managed to walk alright.

Cash shook his head. "Don't do that. Don't say stupid shit." He pinched the back of his neck with his hand. "It's just... I can't," he blurted out.

"Can't what?"

"Fucking hell." Cash sighed. "Easton doesn't want any of us to touch you." His eyes were guilty when he swung them up to meet mine.

"Easton?" I exclaimed. "Easton? Who fucking died and made him fucking king of me?" I was already headed toward the bedroom door when Cash caught me around the middle and swung me back around. "Put me down!"

Cash shook his head. "You can't go marching into his room guns blazing, cupcake, that's not how we do things around here." He rested his hands lightly on my shoulders.

"Easton is the boss around here, so we listen to what he says." He squeezed his fingers gently into my skin.

"I am the boss of me." I pointed at myself. "Do you understand? Me, not Easton fucking Kennedy." I was going to give that son of a bitch a piece of my mind when I saw him next. First, he locks me in his room and now he thinks he can just tell people to stay away from me?

Cash used his knuckle to tip my face to look up at him. His blue eyes had gone cold and the happy-go-lucky smile he usually wore on his face had completely disappeared as he pressed his lips together. "We're not exactly the nice guys I like to pretend to be, Brett. Hanging out with us could be bad for your health." His voice was hard when he spoke. "Easton meant what he said when he told Tate you're one of us, so you need to respect the boss man." He warned before he shook his head.

Goose bumps broke out on my skin as I tried to break free. This entire conversation had turned in a direction I had not seen coming. "I need to go home. My mother is probably worried sick," I whispered.

"I scared you." Cash suddenly realized. "Shit, cupcake, I didn't mean... I'm sorry." He pulled me to his chest and wrapped his arms around me. "Don't worry about your mom. She knows you're with me." He squeezed me.

"She what?"

"Your mom. I called her and told her you were spending the night with me. Oh, she was a little surprised, but once I assured her nothing nefarious was going on, she was fine." He chuckled softly. "Shower, cupcake?"

I shook my head in disbelief. Cash was all over the place this morning. Lying about not wanting me, telling me he was gay, which was also a lie, before telling me Easton didn't want anyone else to touch me, threatening me I think, and then telling me he told my mother I spent the night here. "We aren't showering together." I suddenly realized he had asked me a question.

"Of course not, boo." Cash released me. "Ladies first." He pointed toward the door to the right. "I have the softest towels, too. You're going to love them." He bopped the end of my nose with his finger.

I moved into the small bathroom off of Cash's room. It was nothing I would expect for an eighteen-year-old boy. It was extremely clean with blue, green, and white everything. I touched one of the towels hanging on the wall and fingered it, nodding my head. It was pretty soft. I stripped off my clothes and dropped them on the floor as I turned on the water before I stepped inside to pull the curtain back to give me a little privacy.

It was kind of strange that the boys all lived together, right? I mean, didn't they have homes of their own? I picked up the soap in the dish and brought it to my nose. Great, I was going to smell exactly like Cash did after this.

"Hey, I'm leaving some clean clothes for you. They're a little big, but you need something to wear." Cash's voice caused me to jump. "Take your time. I'm going to use Easton's shower really quick, but wait for me if you're done before I am." He shut the door loud enough for me to hear as he left.

I didn't waste my time in the shower. I actually wanted to get home as soon as I could. I had a little homework I needed to finish up as well as another painting I wanted to start. I dried myself off with the soft as all hell towels and wrapped my hair up in one before I stepped onto the bathmat. The clothes Cash had left for me were sitting on the toilet. He was right about them being too big. The boxers he left for underwear I pulled right up to my tits and the sweats he left hung off my hips no matter how tight I tied them. I decided to skip them and went with my overalls from yesterday. I didn't bother with a bra because I didn't have much to go with anyway, and the shirt he had lent me was altogether ridiculous as it hung straight to my knees, so I tied it around my side as best I could. Well, at least I wasn't naked.

Cash grinned at me as I walked back into the room. "Don't you look fucking cute?" he teased, dressed in nothing but a white towel wrapped around his waist. Just how many hours did he actually spend in the gym because his chest was ridiculously defined, his arms thick and toned with a little happy trail that disappeared under the fabric. "My eyes are up here, Brett," he joked.

Shit, had I been staring? I felt the blush that crept up my neck. "Thanks for the clothes," I muttered as I pulled my eyes away. "The sweats were a bit much though."

"Don't you two look adorable?" I turned to find Easton standing in the door with his hands gripping the molding above. "Having fun?" he growled.

"Bro, we're friends. You know me," Cash insisted.

Easton was still staring at me. "Why don't you get fucking dressed?" he ordered.

I glanced over at Cash as he began to dig around in his dresser, only to see deep, jagged scars dug into the skin of his back. When I met Easton's eyes, he shook his head.

"Let's go." He pointed at me and then the hallway.

"I'll wait." I folded my arms over my chest and sat down on the bed.

"Babe, don't be fucking stubborn we're going to get some breakfast." Easton sighed softly.

"And, I fucking said I would wait for Cash." I crossed one leg over the other. "You don't get to boss me around like you boss him around, Easton. I'm not one of your minions."

"Brett!" Cash hissed. "We talked about this." He had put on a pair of jeans and a Kingston Knights shirt similar to the one he had lent me. "Go ahead; I'll be down in a second." He jutted his chin toward the door.

I closed my eyes as I stood up like a spoiled child. "Fine," I grunted as I dragged my feet. I hated Easton. I didn't want to spend time with him, Ozzy, or the twins. It was Cash that was my friend. Why did he insist on forcing Easton on me anyway?

"Good girl," Easton teased as he followed behind me. "Sorry." He held up his hands as I whipped around to glare at him. "We have some fine dining planned for you, too," he added. "J2 like to go out to breakfast on the weekends when we have the chance so you're in for a real treat."

"Where we going?" I glanced over my shoulder as we headed down the staircase. I carefully eyed the downstairs and wondered where Oz's parents were and what they might do for a living. This place was furnished way too nice for my taste, but everyone was different.

"A little place called Chicks," Easton answered as he pulled his keys from his pocket. "Trust me; you are going to love it. The guys will meet us there," he assured me as he moved into the kitchen.

Shit, that meant I was going to have to get on that damn motorcycle again. I chewed on my bottom lip.

"I was a careful driver last time, right?" Easton must have seen the nervousness on my face. "Relax, babe, I won't kill you today." When my head shot up, he grinned at me, and I would be lying if the smile didn't make my stomach drop. Easton was fucking drop-dead gorgeous.

"You better not." I nudged his shoulder. "You're buying?" I asked.

He shook his head. "Fuck no, that's Oz's job. He's mister money bags. Come on." He dropped his arm around my shoulders before either of us realized it to ease me toward the garage and his motorcycle.

THE RESTAURANT WAS already packed when Easton pulled up on his bike, so I was glad that the twins were there in the back when we walked in. I was surprised to see Palmer there, too, with Oz sitting next to her. I thought she already had a boyfriend and wasn't she the one that had warned me to stay away from them in the first place?

Jameson grinned when we slipped into the round booth they had managed to snag. "Did you get any sleep last night?" He wiggled his eyebrows, but Easton reached over to punch him hard in the shoulder.

I rolled my eyes as I looked down at the menu in front of me and nearly sighed with relief when Cash squeezed in next to me. I don't know why I felt better with him there, but I did. It wasn't like I hadn't had friends before or boyfriends, but Cash was different. He draped his arm behind me and leaned over my shoulder.

"What looks good, cupcake?" He tugged lightly on the end of my ponytail. "Everything, right? Fuck, this place is amazeballs," he teased. "I'm getting my favorite though." Cash tapped the Belgian waffles. "With strawberries, and extra whipped cream," he added.

"That sounds good." I closed the menu to find Easton glaring at me with narrowed eyes. "What?" I scoffed. "You don't like waffles or something?"

"I like eggs and sausage myself, but that's just me," he grunted. I guess that fun guy back at the house was gone already. "You should try it sometime."

I shrugged. "If you bring your eggs and sausage anywhere near me, I'll bite them off and shove them down your throat." I flashed an innocent smile.

"Doubt you could get my sausage in your mouth, babe."

Cash snorted before he tried to cover it up with a cough when I kicked him under the table. "You're a real asshole," I hissed just as Oz snickered. "Something funny?" I narrowed my eyes at him.

"You two. Why don't you fuck and just get it over with?" He didn't lower his gaze, but kept his icy stare on me. "Right, sweetheart?" He clapped his hand down on Palmer's thigh, who looked horrified. I guess they were sleeping together now. I had so many questions since she'd given me the impression that she already had a boyfriend.

The waitress came over at that exact moment to take our order, and I recognized her as the girl from the party last night that was dry humping Easton when I walked into the basement. The one whose face he was sucking while staring at me. What were the fucking odds? She had long red hair that was pulled up into a tight bun on her head, big boobs, and the perfect fucking figure that she didn't bother to hide. I had time to read her nametag that said Josie as her big brown eyes were glued to Easton the entire time.

"Hey," she cooed softly. "You ready to order?" Her lips were lined with thick red lipstick as she continued to stare at her boyfriend, and she had yet to even acknowledge the rest of us.

"Excuse me for a second." I suddenly jumped from the table and ran toward the back of the diner where I assumed the bathrooms were.

I didn't hear anything else as I locked myself in one of the stalls. I don't know why I thought I belonged hanging out with Cash, or any of those boys when they could have Josie. I was never going to fill out that waitress uniform like she does or have red pouty lips or offer any of the things she did. I was so fucking stupid to think I was anything other than a friend to any of them, and it was only a matter of time before their eyes strayed to someone else. Someone like *her*.

"Open the door, Brett." Easton's voice caught me off guard and his boots appeared under the door. Why was he the one that came for me and not Cash?

"In case you can't read, this is the ladies' room," I pointed out. I should have pulled my feet up onto the toilet so he couldn't see me.

He wiggled the door. "Do you think I fucking care? Don't make me break it down, babe, because you know I will." His hand gripped the top of the stall.

I considered ignoring him, but I knew Easton would do exactly what he said. I reached over to unlock the door and the look on his face was not what expected. Anger rolled from Easton's body as he let his eyes move over my body and around the small stall. Then he stepped inside, sucking the air from my lungs and the small space.

"What the fuck was that?"

I shrugged. "Nothing. I didn't feel good and—"

"You're fucking lying," Easton spat. "Don't do that, Brett, not with me." He reached down to grip my chin in his hand so tight it hurt. "Talk," he demanded.

"The waitress."

"You mean Josie?"

I nodded as best I could with his hand on my face. "She just... I don't know." I wasn't used to feeling like I wasn't good enough for someone.

Easton knelt down in front of me not seeming to care that we were in a bathroom. "Are you comparing yourself to her because I wish you wouldn't." He ran his thumb across my bottom lip. "You're so much better than she is." His eyes went soft. "You are the most beautiful creature I have ever laid eyes on." Easton cupped my face with his hands. "Do you want to date Cash?"

"What?"

"It's a simple question, babe."

For some reason, that question sent my body into overdrive. My nipples grew into tight pebbles under my shirt while wetness I had never felt before slipped between my thighs. "He's my friend, Easton, nothing more." I swallowed hard.

"We're going to see Pearl Jam next weekend." His husked voice caused goose bumps to break out on my skin. "Would you like to go with us?"

When I nodded, that smile appeared on his face again. The one that made him light up like the sun.

"Good."

"Good," I repeated.

Easton held out his hand and when I just stared at it, he wiggled his fingers. "Come on, babe, everyone is waiting for us." He squeezed lightly when our palms met.

The only thing that I could think about was that I just agreed to a group date with Easton Kennedy as we walked back into the restaurant. That this man, this scary, but sexy man, had asked me out, and that I said yes.

Chapter Eight

Easton

I have no idea what possessed me to chase after Brett like that, okay, that wasn't true. It was the ass she had that wouldn't quit, and those fucking blues I couldn't stop thinking about. Or maybe it was the fact that she pushed when I pulled or that she zigged when I zagged. I knew getting close to Brett was bad news, but I couldn't stop myself from wanting her.

Before we got back to the table she instantly dropped my hand before anyone saw yet everyone shifted over so we could sit next to one another. I had a lot of questions for Ozzy, too, which I knew that he would ignore, but Palmer Wilson? She was way out of his fucking league. She was going to just end up hurt or worse.

"You two kiss and make up?" Cash pointed his fork between Brett and me before he stabbed it back into the waffles that looked to be at least six high. "Maybe a quickie or something?"

"Watch it," I growled as I watched Brett elbow him in the side. It still made me jealous even though I knew they were only friends. I couldn't explain why I was so much nicer to her when we were alone or why I had even invited her to the concert next weekend. Which reminded me. "Brett's coming with us to Pearl Jam."

Cash stopped with his fork halfway to his mouth. "Beg your pardon?" His waffle plopped back on his plate.

"I said—"

"We all heard what you said," Jonathan spoke up. "We're just interested in why."

Brett had started to cut up her food which looked very similar to what Cash was eating minus a few waffles. She stopped to look at me before her eyes rolled over to Jon. "Do you not want me to come? Am I invading your sausage fest or something because I certainly wouldn't want to intrude on that." She smirked as she went back to her food.

Jonathan blinked a few times before he went back to his breakfast. I was pretty sure that was the first time I had seen him at a loss for words.

Cash hooted with laughter. "Cupcake, you are my favorite person in America." He wrapped his arm around her shoulder. "I would kiss you right now if I didn't think Easton would punch me."

"I will rip your lips off, shove them up your nose, and pull them out your mouth." I swallowed a mouthful of food which was more than amazing.

"Thanks for that visual," Palmer commented.

I nodded. "That's how we roll, sweetheart, so if you can't hang with us, there's the door." I hooked a thumb behind me.

Palmer's brows dipped. "Don't worry, *sweetheart,* I can hang just fucking fine," she muttered under her breath loud enough for me to hear.

I opened my mouth to answer her, but caught the death stare Oz was giving me. "We have time to change that," I shot back before I looked back at Brett who was chewing her food, but watching me with her eyes narrowed, but she only dropped her eyes back to her plate.

"How do you like your breakfast, cupcake?" Cash shook his head at me just as Josie appeared around the corner swinging her hips before she placed her hand on my shoulder. Fuck, not now.

"Need anything else, baby?" She batted her over-coated eyelashes at me which only made my breakfast threaten to come back up. "What's wrong, Brett, don't you like your food? I'm sure that there's some—"

I shot out of the booth so fast Josie nearly fell over. "Mind your mouth, Silver," I warned as the entire diner went silent. My entire chest moved with each heavy breath. "Your job isn't to insult my fucking friends, is it?" My body shook with anger. "Is it?" I asked when Josie didn't answer me.

"No." Her voice was meek as she stared at me with surprise in her eyes.

I slammed my fist against the table. "I didn't fucking think so." Coffee, juice, and water slopped over the edges of the glasses. "Tell me then, what is your job?" I folded my arms over my chest.

Josie swallowed hard. "To, uh, serve food." Her voice was so quiet I could barely hear her.

"To serve food." When I realized I had an audience, I clapped my hands. "Good, now why don't you get us the fucking check, so we can fucking leave and you can serve the other fine folks that are waiting for you?" I dropped back down next to Brett who looked like she wanted to be any-where but here. "You alright?" I tilted her face to look at me.

"Sure."

"What did I tell you about lying to me?"

Josie was back with the check, which she quickly dropped on the table. "Um, I'm sorry," she muttered before she rushed back into the kitchen.

"Brett," I growled. "Don't you dare feel bad for Josie." I cupped her cheek with my hand, but when she pulled away, my body went tense. "You're mad at me? Is that what this is?"

She shrugged. "I can defend myself just fine, and you didn't have to do that. I'm sure your girlfriend was probably just—"

A laugh burst from my mouth when Brett called Josie my girlfriend. I couldn't stop it even if I had wanted to. "Josie isn't my girlfriend. She's just some chick I fuck. I'm not into monogamy," I assured her. One little lie wouldn't hurt I sup-pose, even if I didn't want Brett lying to me.

"You're a fucking asshole."

"I'm sorry, but have we not met?"

Brett's nostrils flared as she pressed her lips together. "This was a bad idea. Move. I need to get the fuck away from you." She shoved at me, but I stayed put.

"You said you could defend yourself, but I didn't hear you with Josie nor did I hear you defending yourself at the party with Tate. You're with us now, babe, so we're here to help you when you need it," I assured her and when Brett be-gan to climb over me, I simply grabbed her and pulled her down onto my lap.

"I don't want your fucking help," she seethed. "I hate you so fucking much," she reminded me once again.

I let a smile slide across my face as I heard the guys and Palmer start to get up from the booth. "You keep saying shit like that, but I somehow don't believe you." I watched the heat and anger that tangled in her eyes, and the way they became hooded with desire.

Brett tilted her head slightly so that her purple hair tickled my arm. "Easton, if you don't let me go I will scream bloody murder. And, this time someone is sure to come to my rescue."

She had me there.

I reluctantly released her so that she could climb from my lap, and I followed her out of the diner. Brett was already climbing into the back of Oz's Tesla with Cash which meant I was riding home alone. I didn't mind. I had somewhere to be today anyway. I shoved my helmet over my head, started the bike and took off without a second thought.

I DROVE THROUGH THE streets of our town as fast as I could without killing myself and tried to keep my mind blank. It was impossible, but it didn't stop me from trying. I kept seeing blue eyes, purple hair, and a kick-ass body. In all my eighteen years, I had managed to not have this happen to me. A girl who somehow embedded herself under my skin without trying and stayed there without either of us planning for it.

I slowed my motorcycle down as I got closer to Kingston Cemetery and killed the engine so I didn't bother anyone else that might be visiting. I stopped my bike right outside the gates so I could hop off and walk her the rest of the way before easing the kickstand up. Then I walked over to the headstone to squat down to run my hand over the tarnished letters. He deserved a newer, better, bigger one, yet I hadn't gotten that yet. I had grown to love this one for some reason.

"Hey, Pops." I eased myself down into a sitting position. "I, uh, think it's happening." My throat grew dry like it always did when I first arrived at my father's grave. The hurt that always hit me when I started to speak to him. I let my eyes move over the letters on his headstone before I spoke again.

Ralph Easton Kennedy, Jr.—Son, Husband, Father

"Remember you told me once that when I met her, I would know? That she would push every single button I had and yet I would still want more? That I would want to get to know her despite everything she threw at me? Like you were with Mom when you first met her?" I reached over to pull at a few blades of grass. "I think I met her." I looked around the empty cemetery. "Her name is Brett." I chuckled. "She has purple hair, Pops, can you fucking believe it? Just like they said she would." My eyes filled with tears as I reached up to touch the stone again. "She's fucking beautiful. God, her eyes are like the sky on a day without clouds. I just want to stare into them forever," I whispered as I let them fall.

It went like this every Sunday afternoon. I would cry like a pussy before I would get over it, and then tell my father shit I knew he would want to hear. I brushed my face with my palms once I got over myself. "Bike's running real good." I sniffed. "I take real good care of her," I continued. "I miss you," I added before I stood up. "I'll be back next week." I bent down to press my lips against the cold stone and headed back to the motorcycle.

I had one more trip to make before I went home and it was the one I always dreaded the most. It wasn't far from the cemetery and when I pulled up in front of the house I grew up in, I felt my blood grow cold. It had been my home for a short time and that was when my father had been alive. The moment Oz's parents told me I could start living with them, well, I jumped at the chance. I came by here only once a week only to make sure that Olivia, that would be my dear old mother, hadn't overdosed or choked on her own fucking vomit. I sighed as I tugged off my helmet and strapped it back onto the bike before I heaved myself from the vehicle.

The green paint on the ranch was peeling everywhere. The lawn was overgrown, the weeds out of control, and the windows covered with shades not letting an ounce of light inside. My mother was most likely drunk, high, or possibly both, but I figured I would take my chances as I walked up to the door and knocked. The screen was completely removed from the outside door, so I just reached right through and clipped my knuckles against the wood. When there was no answer, I did it again.

"Hold on, I'm coming," Olivia hollered as she got to the door. The sound of numerous locks being undone filled my ears before she yanked the door open. "Easton!" Her eyes flew open. "Sweetie, I didn't know you were coming. I would have—"

"Can it, Olivia." I pushed the door open and moved inside the house. She knew that I came over every Sunday because I did it every week since I moved out. "I didn't come here to hear your excuses." I looked around the small kitchen that was littered with empty bottles, beer cans, and God only knew what else.

Olivia tightened the tie on her bathrobe as she hurried past me. "I would have made you something to eat or picked something up." She threw a couple of cans into the garbage. "How are you, Easton?" She smiled faintly.

"Just wanted to make sure you weren't dead, Mother." I heard the sound of coughing come from the next room. "Is he here?" I demanded and when Olivia didn't answer, I growled. "I told you that motherfucker... you know what?" I threw my hands up in the air. "I didn't come here to fight with you."

Olivia put her hand on my arm which made my skin crawl. "Dan's changed," she lied. Every single time she told me that. And every single time? He fucking hadn't. He used her as much as she used him. "How are you?" She was going to try and keep me here as long as she could. She did it every week. "You can come back anytime you want. Your room is exactly the same." Which meant full of bugs, dirt, and whatever else might be living in there.

I shook my head. "Don't start," I warned. "You know I live at Oz's now. This place should be condemned." I pointed to the hole in the ceiling above the living room covered with a tarp. "Dad would be ashamed."

"Don't."

I squared my shoulders. This happened every single time. We would fight, yell, and I would storm out. "Goodbye, Olivia. I'll come by next week to make sure you're still breathing." I whipped the door open and strode outside without waiting for my mother to answer. When I got to my bike, I looked up to find her standing in the doorway, clutching her hands against her chest. I fucking loathed her.

Chapter Nine

Brett

When Palmer and I walked into the kitchen, Ruby was sitting at the table dressed in a ratty band shirt with her hair twisted into a French braid and her legs curled underneath her. My mother had me when she was twenty years old and sometimes she still passed for it. In fact, there were times when we were out that people asked us if we were sisters, and I knew that they weren't just trying to get brownie points.

Ruby looked up from the want ads, yes she still used a newspaper for that, and pointed to the chair in front of her. "Sit." Her eyes, the same exact shade of blue as mine did not look happy. "Where were you last night?" Ruby held up her hand before I could speak. "I know what I was told, but I want to hear it from you." She untucked her legs as she leaned back in the chair.

I didn't see Palmer getting the third degree. "A friend's." I pursed my lips. "Mom, Cash isn't like that," I insisted. "He's nice, he's sweet, and—"

"A boy."

"What does that have to do with anything?"

Ruby leaned forward. "Sweetheart, I love you. You know I trust you more than my parents trusted me at your age, and I know that you would never do anything stupid, but boys your age only want one thing." She pulled her feet out from underneath her and stood up. "You're grounded for a week."

"Mom!"

She shook her head. "Don't start, Brett, or you'll be grounded for two."

"That's not fair! I have plans next weekend with Cash," I exclaimed. "You could meet him, Easton—" Maybe that wasn't the best way to go about this because right now I thought Ruby's eyes were going to burst from her head, bounce onto the floor, and roll right out the door. "Please, Mom?" I wasn't against begging.

"That boy, Cash, the one that called me from your phone." My mother crossed her arms over her chest. "He's friends with the boy that drove you home on the motor-cycle?" I nodded. "Why these boys? Couldn't you just be friends with Palmer? Maybe the group of girls she hangs out with?" It almost sounded like she was going to cave. When-ever Ruby grounded me, it never lasted longer than five min-utes.

My brows dipped. "You know those girls aren't my kind of crowd. I wouldn't be caught dead hanging with the cheer-leaders," I reminded her.

"Shit." She sat back down and her shoulders slumped. "I want to meet them." I jumped from my chair and ran over to throw my arms around my mother. "That boy with the motorcycle had better not bring it because if he does, you'll be grounded for a month!" Ruby laughed as she hugged me back. "Jesus, Brett, you're lucky I trust you so much." She shook her head and then pulled back to look at me. "Can I ask you a serious question?"

Fuck. "Mom, do we have to do this?"

Ruby placed both hands on either side of my head. "Promise me, and I won't ask you if you're still a virgin, that you'll practice safe sex, sweetheart."

"Mother!"

"I'm dead serious, Brett. Boys like that will not stick around, and I don't want you to be a single mother like I was. You have so much potential, so much life ahead of you. You deserve someone who is going to love you like I do." She wrapped her arms around me again. "I know you hated having to move here, but I promise you this was for the best for both of us."

Which is what Ruby said last time, oh and the time before that, but I didn't say that out loud. "I know, Mom." I was getting good at lying to her about this since we had done it so many times. "Any luck finding a job yet?" I asked as Ruby pulled away to sit back down.

"I have a few things I'm going to look into." Ruby ran her hand over her hair. "I don't want to bum off my best friend forever."

"Ha!" Jennifer stepped into the room. "You know that you two can stay here for as long as you want." She winked at me as she moved around the table. "You and Palm have fun at that party? She said you went out to breakfast this morning?"

I could feel my mother's eyes burning into me.

"I have homework." I suddenly remembered. "I don't want to fall behind so quickly," I called out as I hurried upstairs. Palmer's door was shut when I walked by and I didn't know if she kept it locked or not, but I went in without knocking.

"What the fuck?" She looked up, horrified. She was laying spread eagle on her bed, naked, with her phone in front of her. "Brett, don't you fucking knock?"

Awkward.

I giggled. "Sorry to interrupt whatever this is." I waved my hand at her as I avoided looking below her neckline. "We need to talk." I raised my brows, straightened my shoulders, and let her know I wasn't going anywhere.

"Oz, I'll call you back." Palmer hit end on the phone before she tossed it on the mattress. "Mind turning around so I can put some clothes on?"

I did as she asked. "Maybe lock your door?"

"Maybe bite me?"

I shook my head as another laugh threatened to escape. I stared straight ahead at several photos Palmer had plastered on her wall. Several with her fellow pom-pom shakers, but one or two with a guy who she seemed pretty damn cozy with. "Who is that?" I tapped the picture.

"No one that matters. You can turn around now." Palmer was wearing an oversized Kingston Knights sweatshirt with black leggings. "Before you say anything else, Oz and I are complicated."

"I thought you had a boyfriend." I moved some of her clothes off the white wicker chair next to the dresser so I could sit down.

Palmer shrugged. "We broke up." She brought her hand up to her mouth and began to chew on her nail. "What's up with you and Cash?" She was trying to change the subject on me.

"Why did you tell your mother we went to breakfast?"

"Why do you hate Easton so much?"

I resisted the urge to scream in frustration. "You were the one that warned me to stay away from them, Palmer, do you remember that? Something about them being bad news?" I leaned forward. "Why?"

She shrugged. "No reason." Her eyes dropped to her bare feet. "Want to paint each other's nails?"

I moved from the chair onto the floor so that I was looking up at her. "Why did you say they are bad news? What do you know that you're not telling me?"

Palmer's eyes were wide with fear. "Just, you know, rumors." Her voice was a whisper.

"Spill."

Palmer wrung her hands together. "There was a boy, Adam, who went to our school. Freshman year. He was new, like you, and he must have been used to being popular from wherever he came from." Her voice shook slightly. "He wasn't a bad person or anything. He was actually really nice, but he didn't listen." Palmer licked her lips.

"Didn't listen? What does that mean?" My brows dipped.

"Adam was told not to try out for the baseball team, but he did. He was told to stay away from a few girls, but he didn't. Stupid shit like that. He kept showing up at parties he wasn't invited to, and I think that he thought it was just because he was the new kid, you know?" Palmer's teeth dug into her bottom lip. "He had an accident."

"What kind of accident?"

A tear slipped down her cheek which she quickly brushed away. "After practice one Friday night, they all went to Green Road to hang for one of Tate's parties. No one really knows the exact details, but the story goes something like this. Adam was invited by the boys, which made him think they were finally going to accept him into their little circle. The boys never accept anyone, never mind an outsider, and they were drinking, smoking, having a good time. Adam never made it home that night."

I swallowed as I waited for Palmer to finish her story as I ran my hand over her plush, pink carpet. "What happened?" I finally asked.

"They found him two weeks later wrapped in a tarp, covered in leaves and rocks, buried next to some dried up cornstalks."

Holy fucking— "You think Cash and his friends had something to do with that?" Why was she messing around with Oz if she thought they were capable of doing something like that? I got to my feet as I waited for an answer.

"I'm not sure, but they were the last ones that saw him alive that night."

"That's crazy."

Palmer shrugged as she fluffed her blonde curls behind her shoulder. "I'd say go ask Cash, but I don't think that's the best idea. There have been others."

"Others?" My heart had started to beat so loud I was pretty sure the entire house could hear it. "Other dead kids?"

Palmer shook her head. "More like accidents. There was Robby Green sophomore year, followed by Bill Smith a couple months later. Alex Michaels went missing junior year, and Dean Caser moved right before the start of this year because his dad got a new job, but the rumor was the boys threatened to break his arms, legs, and all his teeth." She stood up. "Don't say anything about this to Cash. I know you're besties now, but trust me. I'm saying that for your safety."

As if on cue, my phone buzzed in my back pocket with a text from my new friend.

Cash: How mad was your mom? Are you in big trouble or just a little? Still picking you up tomorrow, cupcake. *winking emoji*

I glanced up at Palmer to find her watching me with her eyes narrowed. "What?" I shoved my phone back into my pocket. "Don't worry, I won't say anything." I flashed a quick smile. "As long as you tell me about Oz." I sat back down on the carpet and crisscrossed my legs. I leaned my elbow onto my thigh so that I could rest my head on my hand. "Waiting." I sighed dramatically.

"Fine." Palmer rolled her eyes, but a smile began to tug at her red lips. "You're not going to believe this—"

THE HOUSE WAS SILENT again the next morning when I skipped down the stairs. I could hear Palmer moving around above me as she got ready for school, but I didn't want to keep Cash waiting when he came by to pick me up. He had said he would be here at six forty-five so I made to be downstairs at six-thirty so I could fill my travel mug, grab a donut from the package on the counter for the road, and stepped onto the porch.

My mind wondered for a second as I thought back to what Palmer had told me about her and Oz. Apparently she had only agreed to go to the party because some of her cheerleader friends had begged her to show up. Ozzy had said they could come along as long as Palmer did, and so she agreed. For them. At some point, I must have been locked in Easton's room at that point, one of those girls had suggested they play seven minutes in heaven, and Palmer ended up locked in a closet with Oz. Seriously, wasn't that the game you played in middle school? I stopped her at that point because I didn't want to know any more about her misadventures with Oz, but she didn't seem too upset about it. Especially if she was naked on her bed FaceTiming with him.

I took a sip of my coffee as I thought about what Palmer had told me last night about Oz. How he had hit on her a few times in the past, but she never thought anything of it until yesterday when she showed up to the party. She said she had no idea I was even still there until Oz told her I would be joining them for breakfast. Palmer wouldn't tell me if she slept with him or not, but by the way her cheeks reddened when I asked, I figured the answer could only be yes.

Just as Oz's eerily quiet, sleek, and shiny car slid up in front of the house, Palmer opened the front door to join me. She shrugged as she hoisted her bag over her shoulder, looking like she had just stepped off a runway dressed in a gray plush sweater, blue jeans, and a pair of Chuck Taylors on her feet. I was wearing black leggings, a T-shirt, and my hair pulled up into a high ponytail. I wasn't much for fashion, but I assumed that Palmer probably didn't have to think twice about stuff like that.

"Boo, I missed you!" Cash grabbed me the second I stepped onto the sidewalk, and swung me around before he crushed me against his massive chest. "You smell like heaven on a stick," he teased before he placed me back onto my feet.

I rolled my eyes. "You're an ass." I swatted at his arm when he tried to take my bag.

"Let me be a gentleman."

I sighed. "Fine." I shoved my bag at him as I watched Palmer slip into the front seat with Ozzy which left me in the back with Cash. J2 weren't there and I knew Easton would be driving his bike.

"A donut, cupcake?" Cash tapped the hand that had the breakfast treat in it.

"Don't approve?"

Cash chuckled. "No, but I hope you plan on sharing that with me."

"Don't eat that shit in my car," Oz growled, and I caught him glaring at me in the rearview. "It will only leave crumbs everywhere," he added.

I nodded. "Sure." He made me super nervous, and once again I was curious about what Palmer saw in him. He was cute, but almost a bigger dick than Easton. *Almost.*

Cash nudged my arm as he leaned closer. "Don't let his attitude fool you. He's a real pussycat," he whispered.

"I heard that."

Cash and I both giggled together like a couple of school-girls just as Oz pulled up in front of the school. I was almost disappointed that the drive was so quick, but that feeling quickly disappeared when I heard the distinct rumblings of a motorcycle pull up next to us. I watched in horror as a female climbed off the back of Easton's bike and removed her helmet to shake out her long red hair.

Josie. Didn't he tell me they weren't a couple? Why would he give her a ride to school? The cruel feeling of jealousy began to worm its way inside my head until I looked away. There was nothing going on between Easton Kennedy and myself. He was free to date, fuck, or hate whoever he wanted.

The only problem was that I wanted all three of those things to be me.

Chapter Ten

School was exhausting. I failed a pop quiz in algebra, which I tried to blame on Cash because he kept me out most of the weekend, but honestly, I waited until the last minute to do my homework so I was the one at fault. Easton made sure to ignore me the entire day, glared at me during the classes we had together, and when he sat down with Josie at lunch, I thought that Oz was going to have some sort of breakdown right there.

I tried to ignore him. I really did. Except it was nearly impossible to do. If I didn't see Easton's intimidating presence from the back of a room as I walked in, I was sure to catch a glimpse of him as I moved through the crowded halls with Cash to our next class. He was a six-foot-five mass of pure muscle perfection, and unavoidable not to notice.

By the end of the day all I wanted to do was go home and pass out, but because I hadn't driven myself this morning I was stuck waiting for Cash who had baseball practice. I was taken completely off guard when he told me that the five of them were on the team because honestly? None of them looked or played the part of athletes. Nor had Cash even mentioned it to me. Not even once.

Right now I was currently hunched over my sketchpad while I sat on the bleachers and waited. The baseball team was out on the field while they practiced, and I would be a liar if I didn't sneak a peek of them every now and then. Sure, all the boys filled out their uniforms, but Easton probably looked the best. Thick, muscled arms with ink curving around the skin that made me want to spend extra time running my hands and fingers over all the markings he felt he needed on his body. I noticed that he wore his cap forward while he practiced, as did the rest of his friends, and it was obvious the team looked up to him. Or maybe they were just as terrified of the guy as I was.

Occasionally Cash, who was standing behind first plate, would catch my eye, blow me kisses, or something lame like that. It was really too bad that he wasn't interested because he was going to make some lucky girl super happy. He was drop-dead fucking gorgeous, but in a completely different way than Easton. It was his happy-go-lucky friendly attitude that I liked the most about him, but his boy next door good looks didn't hurt either.

Oz was the pitcher, and even though I didn't know too much about the sport, I could tell he was good. The balls he threw seemed to nearly knock the catcher off his feet when they landed in his mitt as a hissing sound seemed to echo from the ball through the air. When someone actually managed to hit the fastball, the crack was louder than anything I had ever heard before. Did I mention Easton was the catcher? Right, so it was kind of surprising to see him nearly fall over when his friend pitched to him.

The twins were out in the field not too far from one another. I got the feeling they were kept close together on purpose, but they seemed to work well together when the ball came their way. They were focused, eager, and both of them hit the balls Oz pitched to them which only seemed to piss him off.

Across the field, I could hear the cheerleaders as they did their thing at their practice. Their loud and very obnoxious cheers were hard not to hear as they clapped their hands, waved their pom-poms in the air, shook their asses, and kicked their legs as high as their heads. More than once I caught Palmer stop and glance over at the baseball team as they practiced, but her attention would quickly turn back to what she was supposed to be doing.

"Is that us?"

I jumped at the sound of Cash's voice. He was sweaty, dirty, and in need of a shower as he stood above me looking at the pencil sketch I had been working on. Sometimes I just let my mind wander while I worked on my art and today was one of those days. I had drawn the baseball team, but it was mostly the five boys who were now my so-called friends.

Cash sat down next to me. "That's really good." He tilted his head. "Great job, boo." He pulled his hat off to run his hand over his damp hair before he pulled it back down again. "You're like super talented or something," he teased as he wrapped an arm around me.

"Ew, get off, you stink like ass." I shoved at Cash's chest only to have him crush me against his body.

He pressed a kiss on the top of my head as he chuckled softly. "I'll take a quick shower so we can get out of here."

Cash stood up. "The guys are probably done anyway." He nodded at Palmer, who was headed our way as he started to jog toward the school.

"Hey." She dropped down next to me, still in her cheerleader uniform. She looked around the empty field as she chewed nervously on her lip. "Did you hear about Tate?"

I shook my head as I continued to work on my sketch. "Can't say I have—" I stopped when I saw the look on Palmer's face. "What?" I closed my sketchbook. "Does this have something to do with them?" I jutted my chin toward the guys minus Cash as they headed toward us.

Palmer swallowed nervously. "Rumor has it," she whispered before she stood up to greet Oz. Was this about those missing kids thing again? Were they really capable of doing something like that? Or something much worse?

"What were you doing while we were practicing, babe?" Easton towered over me. "You seemed lost in that little pad of yours." He leaned closer. "Another picture of my bike?" he hissed between clenched teeth.

I glared up at him. "I painted over that." I hadn't, but Easton didn't know and I took pride in the way his eyes went wide. "Decided I should paint flowers and kittens instead. Much more my style." I smirked up at him.

"Liar."

"Prick."

Easton suddenly grasped both sides of the bleachers and pinned me between his arms. "Didn't I warn you about lying to me, Dorothy?" His breath was warm with a hint of mint against my face as he stared down at me.

"Why don't the two of you just fuck and get it over with?" Oz's voice sounded a hundred miles away.

A slow smirk started to spread across Easton's face before he grabbed the pad from my lap. "Let's just see what you were working on, shall we?" He stood up to his full height as he turned his back to me.

I was on my feet in a second, but it was no use. I couldn't reach Easton's hands even if I wanted to. "Give it back!" I demanded. "You have no right to look through my personal stuff."

"No, no, no, oh, what do we have here, babe?" Easton's brows dipped as he found my baseball sketch. "Is this, why yes? It's the baseball team. Is that me?" He pointed to the very obvious pencil drawing of him. "Pretty sure you have a crush on me."

"Pretty sure you're a fucking asshole." I put my hands on my hips.

He shrugged. "Never claimed to be anything else." He clucked his tongue against the roof of his mouth. "There's Cash, Oz, and the twins, too, but if you hate me as much as you say you do, why would you draw me?" Easton tilted his head.

"I fucking loathe you."

"There you go lying again."

"Easton!" The sound of Cash's angry voice caused us both to turn around. "What the fuck, man? I leave you with Brett for five minutes and you're terrorizing her like a kindergartener on the playground?" He held out his hand. "Give it to me."

Easton rolled his eyes. "Fuck off."

Cash's entire demeanor changed. "Give me the fucking sketchbook or so help me—"

"What, Cash? You'll hit me? You'll take it from me?" Easton snarled. "I'd like to see you fucking try." His greens moved to me. "I knew you were going to be fucking trouble." He dropped my sketchbook onto the bleachers where I had been sitting and started walking away.

A scream ripped from my throat when Cash jumped onto his best friend and knocked him to the ground. "You're not the fucking boss of me!" he exclaimed as he rolled Easton onto his back. "You don't get to disrespect Brett like that either."

"Get off." Easton pushed his friend off of him. "Are you fucking nuts? What is your damn problem?" He scrambled back onto his feet as he glanced between his friends before his eyes landed on me. "This is your fucking fault." He pointed a finger at me.

Cash blocked his view. "Leave her out of this," he warned before he took a step forward again. "You're just pissed because Brett isn't itching to have you get into her pants like all the other girls at this school. Newsflash, man, you're not the king god you think you are." As I peeked around his massive body, I noticed Oz flanked Easton's right side with one of the twins to his left and the other stood behind him.

"You sure about that?" Easton raised his chin. Desire burned deep inside my belly as his eyes roamed my body.

Cash wrapped his arm around me and crushed me against his side. "Brett's different, and you know it. You all know that." He dug his fingers into my skin. "If you don't like her, that's not my problem."

"I never said I didn't like her." Easton folded his arms across his chest. "Just that I didn't want her around because of exactly this reason." His eyes smoldered with disgust when they met mine. "Go ahead, tough guy, defend her all you fucking want, but remember who your real friends are." Easton turned and this time Cash let him walk away.

The twins and Oz were still standing there as well as a terrified Palmer, who looked like she wanted the ground to open up and swallow her whole from what she just witnessed. The last thing I wanted was to come between any of them, and if it meant I couldn't be friends with Cash, I would do that for him.

"Cash."

"Don't." Cash shook his head. "We should go." He dropped his arm from around my shoulders and avoided making eye contact as we walked to Oz's car.

NO ONE SAID A WORD the entire ride. Not even when Oz pulled up in front of the house or when I climbed from the car. I felt awful about what happened and I didn't want Cash to lose his friend over this. Why did these boys keep sticking up for me when I didn't ask them to?

"Hey, girls," Ruby greeted us as we walked inside. "How was school?" She gave me a side hug as Palmer went into the living room where her mother was sitting. The scent of my mom's famous meatloaf filled my nostrils, and my stomach growled, reminding me how little I had managed to eat today after the donut this morning.

"Exhausting," I answered and excused myself so I could lock myself in my room. I didn't want to make small talk with anyone right now. I threw myself onto my bed just as my phone buzzed in my pocket.

Cash: I'm sorry, cupcake *heart emoji*

Cash: Forgive me.

I sighed as I stared at my phone. Had they made up already or was Cash so willing to fuck over his best friend?

Brett: You don't have to apologize to me. You didn't do anything wrong.

Cash: *heart emoji* *smiley face emoji* *praying hands emoji*

Brett: Calm down, dude.

Cash: Can't boo, you're my favorite person right now.

Brett: As long as that doesn't mean you're screwing over your other friends for your new one. Can't say I'll be around forever.

I watched the little dots as I waited for Cash's answer, but it didn't come. I climbed off the bed to slip off my shoes and change into a clean pair of pajamas. I went into the small bathroom I shared with Palmer to pull my hair up into a messy bun so that I could wash my face followed by my hands, and when I went to grab my phone, I saw Cash still hadn't answered me. Great, either he was ignoring me or was trying to figure out how to word what he wanted to tell me next.

Dinner was amazing. Ruby knew how much I loved her meatloaf which I figured was why she made it. Palmer talked about cheerleading, and how she wanted to watch Oz play baseball on Friday not but due to the football team also having one she couldn't go. Then Ruby dropped the real reason she made meatloaf.

"I have a date tomorrow night."

I nearly choked on the mashed potatoes I had just swallowed. "What?" I croaked out as I reached for the glass of water in front of me.

Ruby smiled at me. "A date." She wiped her mouth with her napkin before she stood up. "I had a job interview today, which didn't go so great, but as I was leaving, I met this super nice guy named Chad."

Chad? No guy named Chad was nice. I stared wide-eyed as Ruby rinsed off her plate before she placed it in the dishwasher. We had been here for nearly a month. One month and she was already going on a date. Typical fucking Ruby Cake. She would date this guy, things wouldn't work out and I would end up having to leave my new school, my new friends, and my life would get uprooted. Again.

"That's great, Rube." Jennifer smiled happily at her friend. "Where are you going?" She did the same with her plate as my mother as I fumed in my seat.

"Not sure yet. Chad said he would call me tonight so we could make plans. Brett, honey, you're awfully quiet."

Palmer was watching me carefully across the table as she drank down the last of her water as I tried to control myself. I didn't want to blow up at my mother, but that was what was going to happen. I could just feel it. When Palmer shook her head, I pinched my lips together.

"Is that your phone?" Jennifer asked as we all heard ringing from the other room.

Ruby rushed from the kitchen and having lost my appetite, I quickly dumped my dinner into the garbage so I could head upstairs. This day just continued to get worse and worse as it went on, so when I flicked the light on to my room, I nearly fainted when I found Easton standing there.

"What the fuck?" I burst out.

He put his finger to his lips. "Shut the door, babe," he instructed.

"You can't just break into my house."

"It's not breaking in when you leave your window unlocked."

We stood there staring at one another until I finally shut the door behind me. "What do you want? Why are you here?" I folded my arms across my chest when I remembered I wasn't wearing a bra.

"To talk." He sat down on my bed and patted the spot next to him.

I shook my head. "No, no fucking way. Leave." I pointed toward one of the windows, not knowing which one Easton had climbed in. When he didn't move, I simply sat on the floor where I stood.

Easton chuckled softly. "You're going to make this hard for me." A smile tugged at his lips. "Fine." He nodded as his green eyes moved around the room.

Chapter Eleven

Easton

I watched as Brett slid down onto the floor in front of her bedroom door. "You're going to make this super fucking hard on me, aren't you?"

She was dressed in pajama pants with dinosaurs on them with a matching shirt. I hated to admit how fucking cute she looked. Her purple hair was pulled up on top of her head, and it took all I had not to push her down onto her back so that I could kiss those plump lips.

Brett glared at me. "You climbed into my room," she reminded me. "So, yes." She narrowed her eyes. "Couldn't you have just done this at school or something?" She leaned back against the door.

"No." I watched the way her eyes darkened, and it only made my need for her grow. "I wanted to do it in private. Without Cash, or Oz or Palmer around." I ran my hand through my hair and tugged on the ends. It smelled girly in here. Something I hadn't expected.

"Are you here to kill me?"

"What?"

"Simple question." Brett climbed to her feet. "Are you here to murder me? You're a serial killer, right? That would make a lot of sense now that I think about it." I watched in fascination as her perfect peach of an ass jiggled slightly under her flannel pants. My dick pressed uncomfortably against my jeans and I shifted, hoping Brett didn't notice.

I laughed. I couldn't help it. Loud, deep, and right from the pit of my stomach at her question. "No, babe, I can assure that I am not here to kill you." I ignored the serial killer part. Brett was staring at me now with eyes wide, her mouth slightly agape.

She tilted her head. "You can laugh?" she teased. "If I hadn't heard it myself, I might not actually believe it, but you can actually laugh. Like a real fucking human." Brett's lips turned up into a smile and when she moved to sit down next to me, I nearly flung myself from the mattress. Being that close to her was almost too much. The desire I had for this girl scared the shit out of me.

"You think I'm not human?"

Brett shrugged. "Maybe." She sucked in her breath when my hand came up to grip her chin so that I forced her to look me in the eye.

"I'm human," I assured her. "I have feelings just like you do." I let the pads of my fingers graze her soft skin.

"Wh... what do you want to talk about?" Her soft, breathy voice only made my dick harder. Brett raised her own hand like she was going to touch me, but I dropped my hand to the bed and watched the disappointment run across her face. I didn't like it, but I couldn't chance her touching me again. Not yet.

"This afternoon." I ran my hand through my hair again and tugged. It was a habit I had when I was embarrassed or nervous, which didn't happen often. "I'm sorry about what I did. About what I said, and I didn't mean to cause any problems between you and Cash. He's a good guy." I glanced over to find Brett watching me curiously.

"Easton Kennedy, did you visit The Wizard of Oz today to get a heart?"

"The wizard... are you making fun of me?"

Brett's eyes danced with laughter. "I'm only making a joke," she teased as she shifted her small body so that she was facing me and then tucked her legs beneath her. Whatever lotion or body spray she wore was driving me insane. "You know because you call me Dorothy and everything." She looked up at me shyly from under her lashes.

"You're saying that I'm the Tin Man?" I heard my phone ding, but I ignored it as I thought of Brett wearing ruby slippers and pigtails. Wait, did Dorothy have fucking pigtails? Didn't matter because all the blood had just gone straight to my fucking crotch now.

She stared at me for a second as my phone went off again. "Do you need to get that? Sounds like someone really needs you."

"No," I barked as I reached into my pocket to silence it. I couldn't stop myself from being so gruff with her. It was in my nature. I wasn't mister nice guy.

Brett dropped her eyes again. "Is this a truce between us or something? You're waving the white flag?" she whispered as she started to disappear from me again.

Fuck, no. I wouldn't let that happen. Not when Brett was starting to come out of her shell. I could see why Cash liked her so much. *Shit*. Before I could stop myself, my hands cupped Brett's cheeks so that I turned her face up. "Don't be afraid of me, babe."

Confusion flew through her eyes and a blush crept up her neck to cover her cheeks.

"You want me on your side." I leaned closer.

This time when Brett placed her hands over my wrists, I let her. The moment she connected with my skin it sent a raw, wild need through my body, and I knew Brett felt the same. Her pupils grew bigger, her eyes darker, and she licked her lips nervously as she continued to stare at me. I wanted to kiss her, but I was afraid if, I did I wouldn't be able to stop there, and that would be bad for both of us.

"I should go."

Brett didn't say anything as I climbed from the bed and headed to the window.

"Make sure you lock it behind me, babe." I winked before I pushed it open. "You never know what kind of monsters you can find under your bed if you don't."

"Easton." Brett stopped me when I was halfway down the roof over the front porch. I stopped and looked up at her. She shook her head. "What's with the lip piercing? You don't wear it at school and I just wondered—" She blushed as she blurted out the question and then she shook her head. "Never mind," she muttered before she shut the window. I heard the soft sound of the lock behind it.

I somehow managed not to kill myself as I hit the ground. My bike was parked right out front, although I didn't start it until I was halfway down the street. I found myself driving to my father's grave. I needed to talk to him tonight. He was the only person that would understand what I was going through right now.

"YOU LOOK UNUSUALLY happy this morning, boss," Oz commented as he looked up from his hard-boiled eggs. "You get laid last night or something?"

Jameson snickered. "You got in late. You go see Josie?"

Cash was standing by the coffeemaker with a cup in his hand, watching me with cold eyes. We hadn't exactly made up yet, but I had a feeling he already knew where I was. "He went to see Brett." He nearly slammed the cup on the counter. "Isn't that right?"

"I did." I grabbed the box of corn flakes. "Wanted to smooth things over with her for you." It wasn't a lie, but not the entire truth. I had to talk to him in private about my feelings for the purple-haired beauty.

Cash narrowed his eyes. "You're full of shit. You're trying to fuck her. Brett's too smart to fall for that," he warned.

"I'm not trying to fuck her." *Lie.*

"Not trying to fuck who?" Jameson appeared with damp hair.

"Brett," his brother answered.

"Cash's Brett? I thought you hated her?" He opened the fridge and pulled out a container of yogurt.

"I don't—" I shook my head as I sucked on my lip ring. "I know how much Cash likes her, and I went to apologize. To let her know she's cool to hang out with us. You, whatever." Also, I want to kiss her lips, stick my tongue inside her mouth, my dick inside her cunt, and have her ride me until she comes screaming my name. I also think she's the chick I'm going to spend the rest of my life with, but whatever. Something I could discuss with my friends at a later date. After I had put a ring on her finger.

Cash folded his arms across his chest. "Really?" He glared at me for what felt like forever before his usually happy smile returned. "Shit, man, you didn't have to do that. You could have just, I don't know, sent me flowers or something." He laughed before he moved over to slap me on the back. "Thanks," he added before he sat down next to me.

We bullshitted for a little bit longer before we headed to school, stopping to pick up Brett and Palmer on the way. Oz took his Buick SUV this time so there was room for all of us in the vehicle. Like the gentleman I was not, Cash climbed from the car to go get his bestie, but she seemed surprised to see me when she started to climb inside the vehicle.

"'Morning, babe." I nodded as Brett sat down on my right and what would be Cash's left.

"Uh, good morning." She blushed slightly. "I thought you drove your bike," she added before she leaned closer to Cash. Lucky bastard.

I shrugged. "Not always. There was also talk of rain today, so I figured why chance it." Another lie. Her every intoxicating scent hit me just then, making me what to run my tongue over her skin.

Cash was watching us with interest. If he thought I was flirting, I couldn't say, but I knew he would have questions for me later. I would answer them. I would tell him my intentions, too. He wouldn't like them, but he wouldn't stand in my way either. He casually dropped his arm over her shoulders. "We can switch seats." He grinned at me.

Fuck you, I mouthed.

"It's fine." Brett patted his leg. "Right, Easton?" She touched my arm.

"Right, babe."

The ride was short, and Cash practically dragged Brett out of the SUV by her hair. Too bad he didn't have his first class with her like I did. He could walk her there all he wanted, but her sweet ass was going to be sitting next to me in that room.

"Easton!" The sound of Josie's voice sounded like nails on a chalkboard, and I watched the way Brett's entire body went stiff. I was breaking it off with her for good tonight no matter what. I wouldn't do it here, not in front of the entire school because I knew she'd make a scene.

I casually turned around. "Not now," I hissed between clenched teeth as my friends began to move away. "I told you—"

Josie's red hair was a mess, her makeup smeared and her eyes red from crying. Shit, this wasn't good. "We have to talk." She hugged her books against her chest.

"What?"

"My dad—"

That bastard was always up to no good. "What about him?" In our town, this town, there were a lot of assholes, but Chad Silver was one of the biggest.

"He met someone." Josie sniffed. "He said that he thinks that she's the one this time, and he wants to marry her."

I laughed. "Sweetheart, what does that have to do with me?" The sound of the first bell had me start walking. I didn't care if I was late nor did the teachers because, duh, I was Easton Kennedy, but I had a girl waiting for me. "I don't care if your father marries the queen of fucking England." I hurried down the hall as Josie tried to keep up with me. She wasn't in this class.

"It's Brett's mother."

I skidded to a stop and slowly turned around. "Excuse me?" I narrowed my eyes.

"Look, I know you have a thing for that purple-haired freak, Easton, so you know; I thought you might want to know." She batted her lashes at me as I moved closer. "They apparently met at Jerry's Donuts yesterday. My dad was smitten, and asked her out. They haven't even gone out yet, but he's talking church bells, red roses, and white dresses." A smile tugged at her lips as a gleam appeared in her eyes.

"You're lying." I could tell by the look in Josie's eyes that she wasn't telling the truth. Maybe not about the date, but at least the marriage part.

"A little bit."

"We're done."

Josie giggled. "Are we?" She tilted her head. "I know so much about you, East, and your boys. You really think daddy is going to just let you—"

My hand was around her throat before I could stop it. Her eyes bugged slightly as she gripped at my wrist to try and get air. "We're fucking done because I said we're done. You stay away from me, my friends, and most importantly? Brett. If your dad dates her mother, that isn't your fucking problem. You accept it with open arms, do you understand?" I released her and Josie dropped to the school floor, coughing and gasping for breath.

"You're fucking crazy!" Tears spilled from Josie's eyes.

I glanced over my shoulder. "You don't even know the half of it," I warned before I headed down the hallway to the classroom and slipped inside. Mrs. Rhett hardly even looked at me as I moved into the back to take a seat next to Brett and behind Oz. My hands were shaking and when I looked over at Brett, she looked concerned.

Are you alright? she mouthed.

I gave a quick nod. No, I wasn't. It wasn't that I wasn't used to violence, but Josie's father was a scary bastard, and I would have to deal with what I did. There was no way that she would keep her fat mouth shut, not to mention there would be evidence. He wouldn't like that I attacked his daughter even if she provoked me. Or deserved it. Chad wouldn't accept the fact that I told Josie we were done either since he had once been my father's best friend and the two of them had made plans we had no control over.

I somehow managed to make it through class despite my phone buzzing the entire time. I knew who it was. I grabbed Oz before we went to our next class.

"Can I borrow your ride? I'll take good care of it. Have it back before the end of the day." I had to get out of here. And I would be taking Brett with me. Oz handed me the keys without asking why, but there were questions in his eyes. "Thanks, man."

I ran from the building without looking back and jumped inside the SUV without a second thought. I didn't have Brett's number, but I knew who did. I hoped that he would give it to me without being too much of a dick about it.

Easton: I need her number.

Cash: Go fuck yourself.

Easton: Come on, man.

Cash: Why? Where are you anyway? Class started.

Easton: Skipping. The number?

Cash: No.

Easton: Why not?

Cash: You're just going to use her like you use every other girl and then go back to Josie because you have to. Brett's different.

Easton: I know that.

The little dots told me that Cash was trying to figure out how to answer me. I knew he wasn't expecting that answer. I started the truck and headed toward the local supermarket in town to pick up a few things, and when I pulled into the parking lot, I had a response.

Brett's number.

Chapter Twelve

Brett

I found it strange when I got to my third period class that Easton wasn't there. He had looked a little nervous and maybe scared when he slipped into his seat late in first period, but said he was okay. I chewed nervously on the end of my pen as I listened to the teacher drone on until I saw my phone light up on my desk.

Unknown: Meet me out back.

Who the hell? I looked around the room, but everyone was busy pretending to pay attention.

Unknown: It's Easton.

Was he serious right now? What made him think that I was going to actually do that? And who the hell gave him my number? I glanced over to find Cash watching me. *That bastard.* How dare he give my number out to Easton without asking me first? My phone flashed again.

Unknown: Please?

Most likely this would continue until I either answered or went to talk to him. I shoved my phone into my bag along with my books and then excused myself from class, making an excuse about not feeling well. Then I walked to the back of the school to find Easton leaning against Oz's truck with his arms crossed over his chest waiting for me. His eyes lit up slightly when he saw me, and as he dragged them down my body I felt a slight ping of desire course through my veins.

"You're here." Easton's lips twitched in a half-smile as he reached for my bag, but I took a step back.

"What is this about?" My brows dipped. "What do you want?"

"I want to introduce you to someone." He took a step forward and this time I let him take my bag from my shoulder. "If that's alright with you," he added before he started to walk around the passenger's side of the SUV.

I hurried to catch up. "Do I have a choice?" I asked as Easton opened the door.

"You could have stayed in school."

He had me there. "Who gave you my number? Was it Cash?" I started to climb inside and squealed when Easton lifted me. I met his eyes when he sat me down.

"Yes, babe, it was Cash." His green eyes sparkled with something I hadn't seen before. "You're going to give him shit, aren't you?" Easton started to pull the seat belt on for me, but I stopped him.

"I'm perfectly capable of that, thanks. I'm not a child." I huffed before I snapped myself in.

"Never said you were, babe." The way Easton called me babe caused a lusty feeling of warmth to fall over my body, and I was happy when he shut the door so I could breathe, even for just a moment. Then he was climbing up next to me and starting the truck.

"So, where exactly are we going?" I asked once he started driving.

Easton glanced over at me. "Can't tell you," he said softly.

"Are you going to murder me now?"

"Are we back on the serial killer thing again?"

I turned my body slightly to look at him. "You have to admit this is kind of strange, right? You outright acted like you hated me, but now you're being surprisingly nice. So, yes. I'm back on the serial killer thing."

Easton chuckled softly. "Never hated you, babe, just don't like change." He kept his eyes on the road.

I rolled my eyes. "You could have fooled me. You chased me across Oz's back yard for God's sake." I sighed and brought my attention to the scenery as he drove. "You made me feel like—"

"Didn't I tell you I was sorry?" he exclaimed, and I noticed that his hands gripped the steering wheel so tight that they were white. "I meant what I said, Brett, too." Easton clenched his teeth together as he began to slow the vehicle. "I can be a real asshole, and you didn't deserve any of that."

I stared at him as the SUV came to a stop before I noticed where we were. "Are you sure about the not killing me part?" My eyes took in the sprawling greens, trees, and massive headstones that spread out over the cemetery.

"Positive." Easton yanked the keys from the ignition before he pushed open the door. He shot me a quick look. "I did say I wanted to introduce you to someone, and this someone is real important to me." He climbed from the SUV and opened the door behind him to pull out a picnic basket. What in the hell was going on right now? "You going to sit there all day, Dorothy, or are you going to come with me?"

I slowly unbuckled myself and climbed from the truck. "Did you actually bring that?" I pointed to the basket. "What are you up to, Easton?" I asked as he grinned.

That fucking smile was something to be seen. It made him even more attractive than he already was. The corners of his eyes crinkled slightly, and his entire face lit up like a thousand-watt lightbulb. I went slick and wet between my thighs despite myself.

"Not up to anything," Easton assured me, but I knew better. Especially when he reached for my hand, his long fingers wrapping around mine.

My breath caught in my throat, and I stumbled slightly only due to the fact that I continued to stare at him instead of watching where I was going. Flames flickered through my hand and up my arm as he tightened his grip on me. The ridiculous jawline, the soft scruff around his perfect face, his sharp cheekbones, and the permanent scowl he always seemed to wear. Except for now. Here was a boy that was perfectly perfect, but surely perfectly damaged. What had happened to Easton Kennedy to make him this way?

"Watch your step, babe." Easton winked as I caught myself before I tripped again. "What's going on inside that pretty head of yours?" he asked, which caused me to blush.

"What is this?"

Easton stopped and turned to look at me as he gently touched one of the headstones. "Dad, this is Brett." His voice was full of emotion.

My eyes went wide when I looked from Easton to the stone he was now looking at that read *"Ralph Easton*

Kennedy, Jr." written on it. "Hello, Mr. Kennedy," I whispered.

"Nah, call him Ralph because my dad would never be a mister." Easton chuckled softly, but I saw the pain in his eyes. The hurt, too. "He died when I was ten." His voice was thick with sorrow. "It wouldn't have mattered if anyone had been home because no one could have saved him."

Grief stung my heart when I saw the tears in his eyes.

"I thought, fuck, I don't know," he whispered. "Maybe this was a bad idea." He dropped the basket.

I touched his arm. "No, it's perfect." I wasn't sure why Easton wanted me to meet his father or felt the need to bring me here, but there was something he was afraid to tell me. Something he wasn't ready to reveal yet. "What did you bring to eat?" I asked as he continued to watch me.

"Just some bagels and cream cheese. Oh, and some juice."

"Sounds nice."

Easton's brows went up. "You think?"

I nodded. "I love a good carb." I fucking loved food in general.

Easton smiled as he reached for the basket. "Well, you're in luck, babe, because I got a dozen." He pulled out a blanket to spread on the ground. "I wasn't sure what kind you liked," he added.

I giggled as I sat down with my legs crisscrossed in front of me and let him take all the food out. No boy had ever done anything this nice for me before. I had a few boyfriends here and there, but none of them had planned a picnic or anything close to this. Not that this was a date, but still.

"So." Easton held out the bag of bagels. "Which one do you want?" he asked.

I grinned as I dug around for the cinnamon raisin. "I hope this wasn't the one you wanted." I watched the disappointment in his eyes. "We can split it," I suggested.

"Really?" Easton sounded like a five-year-old.

I nodded. "Of course, what kind of a person would I be if I ate the entire thing?" I started to split the bagel and held out half.

"Babe, you're a fucking dream."

I blushed. "Because of a bagel?" I avoided looking him in the eye until his hand gripped my chin to force me.

"Because of everything." His husked voice sent shivers through my body. Shit, was he going to kiss me? Did I want Easton to kiss me? He leaned closer and I licked my lips as I stared at him, at the lip ring that I clearly noticed he wore today, but then he dropped his hand and pulled away. Disappointed hit me like a brick. Maybe he only wanted to be friends.

"Brett." His voice was low when he spoke. "I want to kiss you. Believe me, I want to do more than just kiss you, but—"

I suddenly had lost my appetite as I smoothed cream cheese over my half of the bagel. "It's fine," I murmured.

"It's not fucking fine."

I glanced up to find anger rolling from Easton's body as he glared at me. "You have no idea how hard I have to control myself around you. If I kiss you, if I touch you, if I do anything... it's for your own safety that I don't." He growled deep in his chest.

Fear prickled over my skin. "What does that mean?" I whispered. "Why bring me here, to a place that means so much to you if you don't want to be more than friends?" I took a small bite of my food.

"I can't tell you that."

"Of course you can't." This was a bad idea. I shouldn't have come here. I should have stayed in school and stayed as far away from Easton as possible. I jumped to my feet. "Take me back to school."

"Babe."

"I'm not your babe."

Easton smirked at me. "Afraid you are." He was still sitting on the blanket. "Why don't you sit down and finish eating." I turned on my heel and started walking. "Brett, don't make me chase you again." He called after me. "Son of a—"

He grabbed me around the waist and swung me up onto his shoulder.

"Asshole, put me down!" I exclaimed as he carried me back to the picnic blanket. "I hate you!" I lied.

"You fucking love me," he teased before he placed me on my feet. "Sit the fuck down, Dorothy, or I will fucking tie you to a tree." Easton tilted his head. "The only time I want to tie you up is in my bed, when you beg me to." He gripped my chin again. "Ever had anyone do that to you before, or will I be the first?" When I didn't answer, he gave me his cocky smirk. "That's what I thought."

I hated how Easton made me feel. One minute I liked him with desire that drove me mad, and the next? It was pure hate. I hated how he turned me on with the words he said, the things he said were like nothing I had ever heard from a boy our age, and I'd be lying if I didn't want to try them. I sat down, but refused to eat anything else.

"We've already confirmed that you're not a virgin." Easton held out a small container of orange juice. "Take it, babe, please." He sighed softly.

"Correct, I'm not a virgin." I took the juice, but placed it next to me on the blanket. "Are you?" I knew he wasn't either.

"Funny." He snorted. "Lost that when I was thirteen. You?" His face grew dark with jealousy.

"Same."

"Really? What was the asshole's name so I can pay him a visit?"

I rolled my eyes. "We were kids. We had no idea what we were doing, Easton, and he hardly fucking had time to break my hymen before he blew his load in the fucking condom. We never spoke about it after it happened, and I moved a week later because my stupid fucking mother broke up with her loser boyfriend when she found him balls deep in our upstairs neighbor." I clapped my hand over my mouth. I hadn't meant to tell him all of that.

"Is that why you moved here?" Easton leaned forward. "Because your mother and her men trouble?"

"We move a lot because of that reason," I told him. "Why do you live with Oz?" I asked.

Easton's eyes narrowed as he pinched his lips together. "My mother isn't capable of taking care of herself, never mind me. After my father died, there were days I didn't eat unless Oz fed me and when his parents caught him sneaking extra food to school he told them why. They took me and

Cash in not too long after." My heart dropped at the thought of Easton suffering like that. What kind of a woman doesn't feed her own child?

"Easton, I shouldn't have asked that." I can't believe he answered.

"You didn't know and I wouldn't have told you if I didn't want to." He put his bagel down on a napkin. "Olivia's a drug addict, so she basically cares about one thing." He looked up at the sky before he met my eyes. "Why are you doing this to me?"

"I'm not doing... oh shit," I gasped as Easton pushed me over on the blanket.

Easton planted a hand on either side of my body. "You're in my head twenty-four hours a day, babe. I see your purple hair when I close my eyes, smell your intoxicating scent wherever I go, and all I can seem to think about is kissing your plump, perfect lips even though the moment I do, it will only put you in danger." He pressed his body against mine.

"Kiss me," I begged. "God, please fucking—"

Then I was lost in the moment as Easton's tongue slicked together with mine. I dug my nails into his back as heat rolled through my body, and I couldn't help but feel a grow- ing need inside me the longer the kiss went on. Easton wrapped his arm around my waist to pull me closer, pressing his impressive hard-on against me, and I moaned into his mouth as he ground against me. When I peeked out from under my lashes, Easton's eyes were hooded with heat and lust.

"So fucking gorgeous," he whispered against my mouth. "I could eat you with a spoon, you know that, right?" Easton's hand found my ass, and he gripped it tightly, and my insides went slippery. He stared at me with pure need in his emerald eyes, but suddenly he pulled away. "We have to leave."

"What?"

"Now, Brett, we have to fucking go." Easton began shoving things haphazardly into the basket without looking at me. "Come on, come on." He jumped to his feet and then grabbed me so that I stood up. "I'm not fucking around." Easton practically carried me to the black SUV where he threw the basket into the back as I watched from the passenger seat.

"Is everything alright?" I asked.

"Does it look like it?"

I shook my head, but didn't say anything else as I dragged my teeth across my bottom lip. I wasn't exactly sure about what had set Easton off back at the cemetery, but I preferred the friendly version to this one. I stared at my hands on my lap until he finally pulled the truck over and touched my arm.

"I shouldn't have kissed you." Easton brushed a piece of hair behind my hair. "Trust me, I wanted to, but the moment I did... there are things you don't know about us, me, the guys... shit." He smacked his hand against the steering wheel.

I shook my head. "You can tell me," I assured him. "Whatever it is, I won't judge you or say anything to anyone." I started to unbuckle my belt, but Easton shook his head.

"Don't." He glanced in the rearview. "I need to take you home."

"What about school?"

"I'm taking you home, Brett. End of fucking discussion."

My breath caught in my throat and I turned away. Tears stung my eyes, but I refused to let them fall. He wasn't a nice boy, he clearly didn't care about me at all and I shouldn't get involved with him. When he pulled up in front of my house, I reached for the handle to climb out.

"Brett, wait."

I turned to look at him. "Don't, Easton. I get it. Don't text me again." I opened the door and grabbed my bag on the way out, making sure to slam the door when I shut it.

Chapter Thirteen

I sat in the truck and watched Brett leave, feeling like a complete asshole. Kissing her was everything I had hoped it would be, if not more, but it was wrong. I had now put her in danger, and now I had to keep my distance like I had been trying to do from the beginning. Except—

"Fuck it." I jumped from the truck and found myself following Brett. She hadn't gone to the house, but instead to the shed I had found her painting in that morning, probably trying to hide from her mother so she didn't know she had skipped school. The door was open as I got closer and for a second I stood there watching as she gathered her paints together, the painting she told me she had covered up still sitting on the easel.

"I thought you turned that into puppies?"

Brett spun around with wide eyes. "Jesus Christ!" She laughed nervously. "You scared me half to death." She crossed her arms over her chest. "What do you want?"

I stepped closer. "I thought you liked me, babe, I thought we liked one another." When she didn't back away, I reached for her hand.

"I thought so, too, Easton, but you act like you like me one minute, and push me away another. I'm not a toy. I won't let you use me." Her chin trembled slightly as she tried to be strong.

Shit, Brett's mother. She had confessed to me, and here I was being just like the men her mother probably dated. "I need to protect you." I reached down to cup Brett's cheek with my hand. "Don't move away from me, babe, please." I wanted more than anything to kiss her right now. Kiss her until she couldn't see straight and so that I could forget everything.

"What are you trying to protect me from?"

My lips hit Brett's so hard that she might have fallen backward if I hadn't been there to catch her. Her lips tasted sweet as my mouth slid over hers while my fingers dug into her hips. I slowly moved my mouth down her jawline and angled her head to get better access to her neck. "You have no idea how crazy you make me," I murmured. "The fantasies I have had." Brett moaned as my teeth grazed her soft skin. "Tell me to stop, babe. Just say the word, and I will," I whispered.

"Keep going." Brett panted. "Do you want to—?" She blushed when I met her eyes, and it only made me want her more. She came across as so strong and confident, but right now she seemed shy, vulnerable.

I ran my thumb across her bottom lip. "Do I want to what, Dorothy?" I pressed my mouth against hers again.

"We can put a sheet on the floor," she suggested, and I swear all the blood rushed to my cock when I realized what she was suggesting. I let go of her so that she could grab one, and I closed and locked the door to the shed.

Once we were both sitting on the floor, I cupped Brett's face with my hands. "If at any point you want me to stop, babe, you only have to tell me. I don't want to do anything you're not comfortable with or that you don't want to do." I slid my lips across hers while slowly pressing my body against hers and leaning her back against the floor.

"Easton." Brett moaned my name as I kissed my way down her neck and found her collarbone. I glanced up to find her watching me with big trusting eyes.

I sat back on my legs and let myself take Brett in. She was perfection wrapped in a bow just for me, and I didn't feel worthy of her. I slowly started to raise her sweater up over her torso and when my fingers brushed her skin, Brett shivered at my touch. I stopped just below her bra line, my hands resting at her ribs. "Okay?" I asked.

Brett licked her lips nervously. "Yes." She smiled shyly. I leaned down to lightly press a kiss against her stomach and she let out a small gasp. I ran my tongue slowly around her bellybutton and I found her hands in my hair. "Oh, God," Brett whispered as I teased her.

I chuckled somewhere deep in my chest as my cock grew harder in my pants. I eased her sweater up over her tits and saw her hard nipples poking against her lacy bra. I dragged a finger over each one causing Brett to cry out and pull harder on my hair. I moved my arms behind her back to unhook her bra and gently pulled the fabric down on the cups to expose her perfect breasts. Then I took one pink little nipple inside my mouth.

Brett moaned my name on contact and arched her back up off the floor. I thought I would come in my pants at the sounds she made when I began to roll the other nipple between my fingers. "Oh, yes, Easton, yes," she murmured as I grazed my teeth against her skin. "Fuck, that feels amazing."

I groaned at her words and pressed my mouth against hers. "Fuck, you're making me so hard, babe." I let my fingers dance across her pussy. "Holy shit, you're soaking wet."

She had nothing on but those leggings girls insisted on wearing, and that did little to hide her desire now. Her hands fell to the button on my jeans.

"You first," I insisted and smiled when she pouted. "What, you don't want me to lick that sweet little pussy?" My brows dipped.

Brett dragged her teeth across her bottom lip. "Is that... is that what you're going to do?"

I lifted her enough to tug the leggings down and left them around her knees. "That was the plan, babe." I raked my eyes over her. "Has anyone ever done that to you before?"

"No."

I tucked my finger under her panties, and she whimpered. How was it possible? "You're going to like it," I promised as I eased myself down between Brett's legs so that I could bring my mouth to her pussy. I dragged my tongue over her clit and she cried out on contact. The sweet tanginess of her against my taste buds was overwhelming, and I couldn't help but flatten my tongue so that I could swirl it around to give her more.

"Oh, fuck, yes." Brett arched her hips slightly as I continued to work her over and I can't help but look up at her again. Those amazing tits with nipples harder than ever, her stomach concaved slightly and those perfect lips open slightly as she spiraled toward her orgasm. An orgasm that I was giving her.

I sucked and licked at her hard clit as I slowly began to ease one finger inside Brett. She was tight, really fucking tight, but her body easily sucked me inside. Her moans of pleasure turned into cries, and before she finally let go, her hand landed on the back of my head. Brett called out my name as she rode my tongue and nothing but need for this girl filled me. She was beautiful as she fell apart, her hair spread behind her and a flush covering her skin. When she started to sit up, I pushed her back down and covered her with her body with my own.

"Fuck, you're gorgeous." I slid my lips across Brett's as she smiled shyly at me from under her lashes. My heavy cock is pressed against my jeans, and as badly as I want to be inside her, today was not that day.

Brett grinned up at me as she cupped my face with her small hands. "Have you checked a mirror lately, Tin Man?" she teased. "I want you," she whispered and it takes all I have not to give in. Not to pull my jeans off, roll a condom on, and shove myself so deep inside her she feels me for a week. Or two.

The nickname she called me does not go unnoticed. "Not as much as I want you, Dorothy," I assured her. "But, not today. I have to go."

"What about you?" Brett grabbed my arm as I started to get up. "You just ate my pussy like a champ, and I don't get to do the same?"

My brows dipped. "Eat my pussy?" I chuckled.

"Eat your cock."

Fuck, that sounded so tempting coming from those lips. "Is that what you want?" I feel Brett's hand on my crotch, her fingers pressed against my dick before she finally started to unbutton my jeans. "Babe," I groaned as she slipped her hand down the front of my pants and squeezed. Shit, that felt good.

"Lie back," Brett instructed as she got onto her knees. "Let me make you feel good, Easton. Let me do to you what you did for me." She licked her lips, and I instinctively laid back down. Her small hand was warm around my shaft as she jerked it, and I couldn't help but shift my hips so that I could pull my jeans down.

"There." I brought my hands up behind my head. "I hope... fuck." I groaned as Brett made a fist around my shaft and pumped before she dropped her head to slowly run her tongue around the tip. Brett traced her tongue all the way down my cock and back up. Again, and again, before she finally wrapped her lips around the head to suck it down, making sure to keep that tongue of hers flattened against the length.

I watched wide-eyed as she sucked me. Brett kept one hand on my balls, squeezing gently as she ate my dick, and the other planted on my right thigh as she worked me over. I was fighting the sensation, wanting to hold onto it a little longer because I wasn't ready yet, but—

"Fuck, I'm going to come."

Brett didn't move, but instead took it all and moaned softly as I suddenly gripped her hair and wrapped it around my fist as I burst inside her hot mouth. I tensed and jerked before I slumped back against the floor where Brett cuddled her small frame against me. I wrapped my arms around her and pulled her closer. We stayed like that for a few minutes until I heard the sound of my phone buzzing in my pocket.

"Babe." I had to leave before they came looking for me, and I didn't want them to find me here. Not with Brett. "I have to leave." I looked down at her and she gave me a faint smile.

"I know," she whispered before she untangled herself from my arms. I watched as she pulled her leggings back up and got to her feet.

I shoved my dick back into my pants before I sprang up. "Wait a minute." I turned her around to face me. "This wasn't a one-time thing for me, Brett."

The look on her face told me she didn't believe me.

"Don't look at me like that." I used the knuckles on my hand to tilt her face up. "Babe, I—"

The sound of footsteps outside the shed made us both turn.

"I know you're in there, boy."

Brett's eyes went wide. "Who is that?" she mouthed as the handle rattled.

"I'll be out in a second, Chad, so give me a minute," I growled before I put my hands on Brett's shoulders. "Stay inside, do you understand?" I ordered in a hushed voice. "Don't come out, don't move, and do not look out the window. Got it?"

"Easton, what—"

I closed my eyes for a second. "Brett, this man is dangerous, just listen to me. Don't fight me or argue." My eyes flew back open and the fear I saw on her face was enough to make me hate myself. "Babe, I promise you'll be fine."

"You have five seconds." Chad knocked again. "One."

I balled both hands into fists. "Do not come out," I said again. "Lock the door behind me."

"Two."

I unlocked the door and turned over my shoulder to look at Brett. "Promise me."

"Three."

Brett nodded. "I promise."

"Four."

Fucker. I would break every bone in his fucking body. I ripped the door open, and slammed it behind me.

"You really had to come here?" I narrowed my eyes at Chad Silver as he tried to stare me down.

Gray-haired, with dark brown eyes, Chad Silver was the man who ran Kingston. Nothing happened in this town without his say-so. Or at least that's what he thought. He was richer than Oz's parents, but when his wife died during childbirth, he became a widowed bachelor with a daughter he spoiled rotten. He dressed in the finest suits, wore the most expensive shoes, and drove the best cars money could buy. My father had also been his right-hand man up until Chad put a bullet in his head.

Chad smirked. "Son, you put your hands on my daughter." He straightened his broad shoulders. "You know I can't allow that."

"Your daughter had it coming."

Chad's eyes grew dark. "My daughter is going to be your wife someday, or have you forgotten?" he spat.

Like hell I would marry Josie. That was a deal he had made with my father when I wasn't even old enough to walk, never mind make my own decisions. "So says you," I challenged.

I could see the wheels in Chad's head spinning as he tried to figure out how to handle this. He could try to roughen me up, he could have some of his goons come at me, or he could threaten Brett. I figured it would be the latter. He cracked his neck before he took a step forward. "Your father was a man of his word, boy, and you wouldn't want to disappoint him now, would you?" The evil gleam in his eye made me want to put my fist through it.

"Is that why you killed him?" I gritted my teeth as I stared him down. If Chad decided to try and come at me, I would win. I was bigger, and younger, but odds were he had his security clowns hiding somewhere around this house. He never went anywhere alone by choice.

Chad pursed his lips. "I want you to leave here and never come back. I don't want you to talk to her, look at her, or even fucking think about her ever again. Do you understand me, boy?" His eyes moved behind me. "It would be a real shame if something happened to her, wouldn't it, son?" A smile tugged at his lips.

"You touch her—"

"You'll what, boy? You threaten me again, and you'll wish you never fucking met her."

My nostrils flared and my blood roared through my body as I tried to control myself. I would tear limbs from

Chad's body one by one if he laid a finger on Brett. I opened my mouth to protest, but he only nodded at me before he turned and walked back down the driveway. My hands began to shake from anger or possibly fear. I had to get out of here. I had to talk to Cash, Oz, and J2 to let them know what happened. But first I had to try to explain to Brett why I couldn't see her again.

She opened the door when I knocked, but I could see she was scared. Her face was pale, and her eyes wide. "Who was that, Easton?" Her voice shook. "He said you were going to marry his daughter?"

"Josie's father," I answered. "Listen to me, you can't tell anyone about this." I attempted to put my hands on her shoulders, but Brett took a step back. "Babe, don't be afraid of me."

"You're engaged to her?" Her blue eyes were confused. "You told me—"

I cut her off. "No fucking way. It was something that Chad and my father talked about when I was born. I'm not marrying her," I assured her, but in the back of my mind, a little voice asked me otherwise. Would I really disappoint my father like that?

Brett searched my face. "You're going to tell me you can't see me again, aren't you?" She shook her head. "I think I met a nice guy, and then this happens." Tears spilled from her eyes and down her cheeks. "You should leave."

She was right, but I couldn't. I gripped her chin in my hand. "I'm not letting Chad scare me or you so easily, babe." I hated Brett like this. My cold, ice-like heart felt like it might actually break.

"You'd let him hurt me?"

"I'll protect you."

Brett looked doubtful. "You can't save me, Easton. If that man... wait a minute." Her eyes went wide. "Chad?" She stared at me. "My mother has a date with a guy tonight named Chad. Oh, fuck." She suddenly looked like she might pass out and I caught her right before she did. "I can't let her go out with him."

I smoothed her hair as I held her. "You have to, babe, because if he even thinks we had anything to do with that? He'll come after you, your mother, all of us." I pressed a kiss against Brett's head. "I need to go," I whispered.

"I know."

I helped Brett to her feet. "Don't come downstairs when Chad picks your mother up tonight. Lock your door, make sure your windows in your room are locked, and keep your phone charged."

When she nodded, I slid my lips across hers.

"I'll text you later," I promised. Then I opened the door to the shed and walked down to Oz's SUV, leaving Brett behind.

Chapter Fourteen

Brett

After Easton left, I couldn't concentrate on anything. I kept hearing what Chad had said to him ringing inside my head. "*You threaten me again, and you'll wish you never fucking met her.*" What kind of person says something like that? I couldn't just let my mother go out with him either. What if he did something awful to her because of Easton or me?

I spent the rest of the afternoon in the shed, even though I didn't get much work done. I checked my phone more often than I should, but I didn't hear anything from Easton or Cash and even though I tried not to be disappointed, I hoped that they were both okay. I thought about texting them, but I didn't want to be that girl either. I finally gave up and went inside around five because I knew that everyone would be home and probably wondering where I was.

Ruby was sitting in the living room when I walked in, and she waved happily to me when she saw me. "How was school?" she asked.

Did she not know I skipped? Did Easton have something to do with that?

"Fine," I lied. "I'm tired. I think I'm just going to go take a shower and maybe lie down."

Ruby stood up. "Are you feeling okay? You look awfully pale." She pressed a hand to my forehead. "I'm going to make a quick dinner before Chad comes to pick me up."

My stomach turned at the sound of his name. "I'm not hungry," I insisted. "You don't have to cook." Odds were I would just push it around the plate and not eat it anyway.

"Nonsense, honey, you need to eat. I'll make a quick pasta dish for you and Palmer. She should be along soon. Jennifer had to work late." My mother patted my shoulder before she moved to the kitchen.

I took a shower and stood under the hot water for what felt like forever. I was freezing and couldn't seem to get warm. I should be thinking about the fact that Easton finally kissed me, about what happened in the shed, how he made me come, and I did the same for him, about how he made me feel and told me I was gorgeous. Except, he was supposed to marry someone else, and I probably couldn't be with him in the way that I wanted.

Once I was done in the bathroom, I dried off and put on a clean pair of pajamas. This pair was blue with pink ice cream cones on it, and left my hair down before I went back to my room. I found Palmer sitting on my bed waiting for me, her arms crossed over her chest still dressed in her cheerleader uniform.

"What the fuck?" she hissed. "Where were you and Easton today?"

I couldn't tell her too much about this afternoon, especially the Chad part. "He kissed me," I blurted out, which caught her off guard.

"B, didn't I tell you he was bad news." Palmer chewed on her lip before she continued. "They all are," she added.

"This coming from the girl who seems to have no problem with Ozzy."

"That's different."

I put my hands on my hips. "How is that different?" I demanded. When she didn't answer, I shook my head. "I need to be alone," I told her.

"Are you okay?" Palmer touched my arm. "You don't look so good. Easton didn't force you or anything, did he?"

I sat down on the bed. "I wouldn't have done anything I didn't want to. There is a mutual attraction there, believe me." I blushed as my thoughts went to the way I made him come. "We messed around a little, too, but it wasn't sex or anything."

Palmer's brows dipped. "I've known Easton since we were kids, and the only girl I've ever seen him show any interest in, besides you, is Josie." She pulled at a thread on my bedspread. "I'm not saying that to try and upset you, B, I just wanted you to know. He's strayed before, but he always ends up going back to her in the end."

"Girls, dinner!" Ruby called from downstairs.

"Your mom is super awesome." Palmer smiled as she stood up. "This is so much better than all the TV dinners or cereal I end up eating because my mother doesn't cook much. Don't get me wrong, I'm not complaining about my mom, but she's not home as much." She skipped happily toward the door. "You coming?"

"I'm not hungry," I told her.

"What really happened?" Palmer asked just as we both heard the doorbell. "You know she's going out with Josie's father?"

I was going to throw up. The bagel I ate from this morning threatened to come back up, and I sprinted to the bathroom just in time as I heaved over the toilet. Then I pressed my head against the cool porcelain to relax.

"Sweetheart, are you alright?" The sound of my mother's voice washed over me. "I should stay home."

I shook my head. "Mom, I am old enough to take care of myself," I assured her. I tried to stand, but felt wobbly on my legs.

"Let me, Ruby."

No! I struggled in his arms, but he was stronger than I was.

"Relax, I only want to help you," Chad assured me before he placed me on my bed. "You should relax, Brett, you've had a long day." His eyes burned into me as I met them. "Don't want you getting sicker now, do we?"

Ruby appeared next to him. "I really should stay home," she whispered to him.

"We could stay in, watch a movie." Chad didn't take his eyes off of me.

My eyes fluttered shut after that, and I drifted off to sleep.

WHEN I WOKE UP A FEW hours later, I wasn't alone in my bed, and I nearly fell to the floor as I tried to get up. I flipped on the light, only to find Easton watching me with amusement and concern in his eyes. "What... how did you get in here?" My eyes took in his body, the bruising around his eyes, and the dried blood on his face.

"I made a copy of your key." He sat up.

"Are you hurt?"

"I'm fine."

I moved around the bed to get closer. I pressed my lips against his as my hands went to his hair. "What happened?" I whispered.

"Business, babe." His kisses were rougher than earlier, but I liked them.

I reached for Easton's shirt, but his hand landed over mine. "Let me make sure you're okay."

"Brett, I'm okay," he assured me.

"Please, Easton." I looked at him and he moved his hand away, letting me continue. I slowly pulled his T-shirt up over his head to expose his ink-covered chest and the hard muscles underneath. I touched his chest lightly with my hand before I pressed my lips against his again.

"Babe," East moaned softly, but he made no move to stop me. His green eyes were wide, watching me with hunger.

Then I kissed him all over. His chest, his arms, his neck, and back to his lips. I felt his mouth turn up into a smile when I met them again with Easton pulling me into his lap, pushing my legs around him so that I was straddling his waist.

"Feel better now?" Easton asked me, brushing the hair from my face. "Nothing is broken. Just a few bruises and scratches."

I nodded. "Yes." I touched his lips with my fingers and watched him break into a smile. A real smile, his entire face lighting up. I felt my insides melt and my pussy throbbed. "You should do that more often, Easton."

"What's that?" He kissed my fingers.

"Smile." My voice was breathy as he pulled one of my fingers into his mouth and sucked it lightly before releasing it slowly. I let out a soft groan. "It looks good on you." I could feel how aroused he was underneath me.

"Does it now?" Easton put his lips against my neck and licked up to my chin before he pulled back. "You look good all the fucking time." He ran his thumb across my upper lip. "Brett, if we do this... I may not be able to hold back."

"Then don't." I wanted him. I wanted Easton to fuck me. To make me scream out his name, to claw his back and beg for more. I took his hand and placed it against my chest. "I'm all yours."

Easton took one of my breasts in his hand and pinched the nipple between his fingers causing me to whimper softly. The thin shirt that I had on did nothing to hide the fact that both nipples were hard little stones. He leaned down and sucked one right through the cotton, teasing me until I thought I would come from that alone. I threw my head back, wiggling against his erection and only wanting more.

"Let's get this shirt off," Easton whispered before he practically tore it from my body. "Babe, look at me." His voice was low and when I opened my eyes, they were dark with desire. "You're absolutely beautiful." He grabbed the back of my neck to pull me in for a kiss, his lips hot against mine.

He pushed me back onto the bed so that he could pin my hands above my head and pressed his body against mine. I heard him whisper my name as his teeth grazed the skin on my neck before one hand dropped to my hips where he tucked a finger into the waistline of my pants.

"Please." I wasn't against begging, my pussy needed to be filled and I needed Easton inside me. I didn't want to wait; I wanted him to take me.

Easton kissed slowly down my neck, to my chest and between my tits, letting go of my hands, still keeping the one on my pajama pants. His lips were against my bare nipple now and I pushed against him, needing more. "Easy," he whispered, his fingers dancing against my heat. "Oh, Brett, you're so wet." He pressed gently against me and I cried out. He looked at me before he started to move down my stomach, his kisses like fire against my skin.

The feel of his lips against my skin drove me wild and I moved against him, before he pressed me back against the bed. "Easton," I said his name softly and his fingers dug into the waistline of my pajamas again before he finally just ripped them off along with my underwear.

"I told you that this wouldn't be gentle, babe," he warned me again, and then his finger was inside me, causing me to buck against him. I felt his breath against my clit as he pushed my folds open. "Fuck, you're beautiful."

I was going to explode. I didn't want it to end as quickly as it started, but the more he pushed his digit inside me, the more I clenched my walls around it. Easton put his tongue against my clit and gave it one lick. "Shit!" I whispered into the dark, clawing at his hair, and I felt another finger inside me, causing me to push against him. "Easton, if you—"

Too late, his lips were on me again and I exploded, my thighs tightening around his head, his hands gripping me, pulling me so I couldn't move. I saw stars as I lifted off the bed and when I was done, Easton licked every inch of me, before pulling me up into his arms.

"You taste amazing, Dorothy." He gave me little kisses and I could taste myself on him, the desire already building in me again. He put his hand over mine when I reached for his pants. "I need to be inside you." He climbed off the bed and removed his jeans, kicking them to the floor revealing he had nothing on underneath.

I stared at him, the sight of his erection, and how gorgeous he was. The perfectly muscled abs and the little happy trail that led down to his heavy cock. I watched as Easton slid the condom on his shaft before he caught me watching.

"Get a good look?" Easton grabbed me and pulled me up onto all fours. He pushed me down so that my backside was up in the air. He ran a finger over my slit. "Christ, you're dripping wet again." He growled deep in his chest. He grabbed my waist and pulled me against him as he reached for my nipple, squeezing it between his fingers. Without another word, he pressed himself against my entrance and eased himself inside.

I cried out into the pillow at the way Easton filled me. I had never felt so full before, and my walls pulsed and rippled around him as he began to move. He moved slowly at first while he made low grunting noises and it only made me want more. He gripped my hips, causing a sensation to slowly begin to build inside me that I had never felt before. I wanted him to fuck me like he said he would. I turned to look at Easton over my shoulder and saw his body already covered in a slight sheen of sweat.

"Don't hold back," I told him. "I'm not going to break." And then he grabbed my hair so that he could pull me up onto my knees.

Easton pulled me against him. "I told you I wouldn't hold back, babe," he said into my ear while he slicked in and out of me. "Touch your pretty little nipples," he demanded.

When I reached up to do what he told me, one of his hands gripped my neck lightly and Easton eased my head up so that he devours my mouth with his own.

"More," I begged him and he pushed me back down again so that my face was against the bed, his finger rubbing against my clit. I clawed at the bed as shivers began to consume my body.

Easton pulled himself all the way out of me and slammed back in over and over again before he pulled me back up on my knees. "Are you close, babe?" he whispered into my ear.

I moaned softly and pushed back against him, opening my legs, feeling his fingers dancing against my pulsing pussy.

"Tell me." He pushed me back down again.

"I'm going to come," I answered and I swear the orgasm stripped me of all control as I shook and convulsed beneath him. Easton shuddered against me with his face in my neck and his body against mine.

Easton slipped out of me and I heard him remove the condom. Then he pulled me close and wrapped his arms around me tightly where he buried his face in my neck. I wasn't sure how long I stayed awake so that I could listen to his breathing. I felt safer with Easton next to me even though I knew he was spoken for. That he was supposed to be with someone else.

Chapter Fifteen

Easton

I didn't sleep a wink. Believe me, I tried, but with Brett lying naked next to me, it was impossible. I hadn't come to her room to fuck her, but the moment she had put her lips against my skin, all of my restraint was gone. I had come there to make sure she was safe, and to keep an eye on her. I didn't trust Chad, and once Palmer had texted Oz to tell him Brett was sick, I knew that Chad would see that as her trying to ruin his date with Ruby.

I sat there watching Brett in the dark. The sun started to come up and there she was with her purple hair spread out on the pillow and her beautiful pale skin just itching for me to touch it. I resisted, but believe me, I wanted to.

I was going to ruin this girl and she had no idea.

I climbed from the bed as I started to hear movement inside the house. I wouldn't let her go to school alone, but I knew at any moment someone could walk into her bedroom and find me there. The door wasn't locked and I didn't want Brett's mother meeting me for the first time like this. I dressed quickly, only stopping to gently drop a kiss against Brett's head before I climbed out the window. I sprinted across the lawn and down the street where I had parked the car I borrowed from Oz so that I could send off a couple of texts.

Easton: I'm at Brett's. I'll be taking her to school this morning.

Cash: Seriously?

Easton: Deal with it.

Cash: You two a couple now?

Easton: Eat me.

Oz: I think that means yes.

Jameson: That was quick.

Easton: No one asked you, dick.

Jonathan: You kind of invited this on yourself, man, when you sent a group text to us.

Cash: I hope you used protection. Don't want any babies running around.

I rolled my eyes just as I realized I had better text Brett before she thought I had just left her without even saying goodbye.

Easton: I'll see you assholes at school.

Easton: Babe, I didn't want your mother to catch me in your room. I'll be picking you up this morning.

When she didn't respond, I hoped it was because she was in the shower and not because she was pissed at me. I started the Ferrari, one of Oz's, and eased it onto the street. I headed down the end of the block where I pulled a quick U-turn and headed right back to Brett's place so that I could pick her up properly. There was still no response from my girl—shit, was she my girlfriend now—so I climbed from the vehicle and walked up to the front door.

"What a surprise, son." Chad's voice caught me off guard. I hadn't seen his car, and I didn't think he would be up this early.

Yes, I knew he had stayed last night, too, but I didn't tell Brett that. When I slowly turned around, I found him sitting on one of the wicker chairs with a cup of coffee in his hand.

"What brings you here this morning?" He raised his brows as he brought the mug to his lips.

I clenched my teeth. "You know exactly why I'm here," I hissed.

"Do I?"

"Why are you here?" Like I had to ask.

"Son, I don't think that's any of your business." Chad smirked. "Didn't I tell you to stay away from the girl?" He started to stand, but the sound of the front door opening had both of us jumping. I didn't recognize the woman that stepped onto the porch, but I knew immediately it had to be Ruby, Brett's mother.

She had the small blue eyes, and the same small frame as my Brett, but her hair was dark and pulled back with a headband. It fell in soft curls down her back without a trace of gray or silver, nor did her face show any wrinkles. Ruby's eyes narrowed slightly as she took me in, the wrinkled clothes, the leather coat, and I'm sure the tattoos on my hands and neck were a sight to see, but when she smiled, it wasn't fake. Her eyes lit up like she was actually happy to see me.

"Now I see what all the fuss is about." She beamed. "I'm Ruby, Brett's mother. You must be—"

"Easton Kennedy, ma'am." I suddenly remembered my manners and stuck out my hand. "It's a pleasure to meet you. Brett has told me so much about you."

Her hand was warm, but strong when she took mine.

Ruby smiled. "I can imagine." She laughed lightly. "You're here to take Brett to school?"

I nodded. "Yes, ma'am, and I'm sorry that I didn't introduce myself sooner. That's not how I usually do things," I assured her.

"Oh, Christ." Brett burst through the door with her hair pulled back into a ponytail, dressed in tight blue jeans and an oversized sweatshirt. "Mom, we're leaving." She grabbed my arm. "Come on, Easton, you don't have to—" She stopped when she saw Chad sitting there and her eyes went wide. "What is he doing here?" she demanded.

"Brett!" Ruby exclaimed. "That's none of your business."

I hooked my arm around her shoulders. "Babe, your mom is allowed to have guests." I tried to speak to Brett with my eyes. Pleaded with her not to make a scene in front of Chad or her mother. Not now, not here, not today. I would fix all of this, but I needed time to do that first.

"Guests?" Brett blinked.

Chad got to his feet. "I understand that you're upset, sweetheart, but I'm not here to try and replace your father." I bristled at the affectionate term he used and turned to stare as anger rolled over my body.

Brett went stiff. "Replace my father? Are you fucking crazy?"

"Brett Marie Cake!" Ruby sounded horrified. "You are in so much trouble, young lady!" Her face had gone pale, and those friendly eyes from earlier were suddenly gone.

I had to get her out of here before she dug herself into a bigger grave. Or worse. "Brett." I started to drag her down the porch steps. "We're going to be late." I would have picked her up, but didn't think that would be appropriate in front of her mother.

Brett's nostrils flared as she followed me down to the car, and as I opened the door, I saw the fear in her eyes. She stared at me for a second before she climbed inside and folded her arms over her chest, waiting for me. I suddenly realized it wasn't just her mother or Chad that had set her off this morning. It was *me* she was really upset with.

"Babe, you know why I had to leave this morning." I climbed into the car just as Oz pulled up behind me. "Don't." I stopped her just as she put her hand on the handle. "Please, I'm sorry about leaving like that, but did you really want your mother walking in on us? What do you think would have happened?" My stomach twisted at the thought of her climbing into the Tesla with Cash.

Tears clung to Brett's lashes when she met my eyes. "I felt like trash when I found you gone," she whispered, and she shook her head when I put my hand on her cheek. "No, Easton, you can't just make everything fine by touching me or kissing me or—" She leaned her forehead against my shoulder.

"You're not trash, Brett." She sniffed softly. "Babe, your mother and Chad are watching us right now. I don't want her to come over, so can I at least start the car?" When she nodded, I smiled despite myself. I started down her street before I looked over to find her watching me. "What?" I asked.

"You called my mother ma'am."

"That's funny to you?"

Brett giggled before she sat back up to pull the seat belt across her chest. "Yes." She reached down and dug through her bag and pulled out some tissues before she wiped her face. "My mother is thirty-eight years old." She stuffed the Kleenex back into her bag.

"I'm really sorry that I left."

"It's fine."

I shook my head. "It is not fucking fine, babe, and I wish that I hadn't done it." I gripped the steering wheel between my fingers. "I could have at least left you a note, but I thought the text was better."

Brett stared at me. "You sent me a text?" She began to look through her bag again. "I didn't get a text from you, Easton, or else I wouldn't have been so upset." She pulled out her phone. "No, there isn't a text." She held her phone up to show me as I pulled into the school.

I stared at the texts I had sent her. She wasn't lying. "How is that... that, motherfucker." I slammed the palm of my hand against the steering wheel. "Chad must have deleted it."

"He came into my room?" Brett sounded scared.

I nodded. "There's no other explanation." I was going to fucking castrate that asshole just as soon as I figured out a way.

"He stayed over at the house, slept in my mother's fucking bed, and had the fucking nerve to go into my room when I was in the shower," Brett whispered.

Or when she was still sleeping or the brief moment I had managed to get a few moments of my own, but I didn't say that out loud. "Come on." I jutted my chin toward the school as I began to climb out of the car. I met Brett as she opened the door and grabbed her bag and dropped my arm over her shoulders. "You're safe with me, babe," I promised.

Brett slipped her arm around my waist like it was something that she did all the time. "I feel safe with you," she admitted. Did she notice everyone staring like I did? I raised my chin with just a little bit of pride as we headed inside the building, making sure to pull her as close as possible as we made our way through the crowded halls.

I knew that all of this was going to blow up in my face. That Josie was going to go running to daddy again, that Chad was going to make my life a living hell, but at least for this moment, I could enjoy feeling happy with Brett.

CASH KNOCKED MY SHOULDER before he swung his legs over to sit down at the lunch table next to Brett. "You two are the talk of the fucking school today." He grinned like the Cheshire Cat. "Seems you're the new power couple of Kingston High." He made kissing noises before he snorted and laughed like a hyena.

Brett's cheeks flushed pink as she opened her lunch bag. "You're an asshole." She rolled her eyes before she caught me staring at her. "What?" she asked.

I shrugged. "Nothing, just wanted to see what you thought about everyone talking about us." I wrapped an arm around her waist. "Now that everyone knows you're mine, I don't have to worry about them trying to date you." I winked before I dipped my face down to press my lips against hers.

"Yours?"

"Mine."

"Get a room," Jameson shouted as he dropped his lunch on the table. "Everywhere I go today, it's Easton this and Brett that. Since when do we live in a soap opera?" He chuckled as his brother sat down next to him.

I had never happier to see the cafeteria by the time lunch rolled around. I was exhausted from the lack of sleep from the night before, and I couldn't wait to see Brett again. I found her sitting at our table with Palmer on her left and an empty space on her right. I assumed it was meant for me, so I quickly moved across the room and sat down.

Brett smiled up at me as I tightened my grip on her. "Hey," she murmured as I tilted her face up to mine.

"Hey yourself," I teased before I brought my lips to hers. I didn't care that everyone was watching or that we were in the middle of the cafeteria. *Mine, mine, mine.* That's all I wanted everyone to know when they saw Brett Cake. That she belonged to me.

Cash narrowed his eyes. "We have a bit of a problem," he seethed before his angry eyes moved across the room and when I followed I found them staring at Josie. It caused every muscle in my body to go tense. But Brett seemed to be too caught up with Palmer to notice, which was a plus.

I raised my eyebrows. "Explain," I hissed between clenched teeth.

"Not here," Cash answered before he started to dig into his lunch.

Oz sat down at that point and by the look on his face, he had the same issue with Josie. "You're aware of our problem?" he mouthed before he turned to kiss Palmer on the lips.

"Everything okay?" Brett asked as I pulled my arm from around her shoulders. "You three seem super serious right now."

Cash nodded. "Sure thing, cupcake." He knocked my leg under the table with his foot and jutted his chin toward the door.

Principle Donovan walked into the room at that moment, and from the look on her face, it didn't look good. She glanced over in our direction, most likely to see if her son was still alive, or at least breathing, before she clapped her hands together. "Students, if I can have your attention?" Her voice was loud, powerful, and let everyone know she met business. When a hush fell over the cafeteria, she continued. "I wanted to take this time to speak to you all about a student of ours that is missing by the name of Tate Bernard."

Brett gasped next to me and when I glanced at her face, she had turned paler than usual. Her eyes met Palmer's, and both girls looked like they had just seen a ghost. I squeezed her hand gently, but her body went rigid and I wondered if someone had been talking to them about things they shouldn't. I knew it wasn't Cash because he knew better, so I wondered who else it might have been.

"Mr. Bernard was last seen by his parents on Saturday night," Mrs. Reynolds went on. "He went out to hang with some of his friends, but he never returned home. His phone was found outside their house, his car was still in the driveway, and no one has seen or heard from him since." She looked around the room again. "All they are asking right now is that if someone knows anything that they should come forward either to me, your parents, or to the police." Her eyes landed on her son again before she nodded. "That will be all for now." The room began to buzz with conversation that wasn't about Brett and me, but now I had a new problem on my hands.

I glanced around the table at my friends, who pretended to be just as concerned about Tate as everyone else. Brett was now picking at the sandwich in front of her and had grown unusually quiet, as had Palmer. "You alright?" I asked.

"Yes," she answered a little too quickly.

"What did I say about lying to me, Dorothy?"

Brett's blue eyes were full of fear when she dragged them up to mine. "Did you have something to do with Tate's disappearance?" Her hushed voice was quiet enough for only me to hear, but it sent a chill through my body.

I gave her a curt nod. "Who told you?" I removed my arm from around her waist and nodded toward Cash. When she shook her head, my brows dipped.

"I can't... I won't talk about it here. Not now." She looked close to tears and the last thing I wanted was for Brett to start crying in front of half the school because of me.

When the bell rang and we both stood up, I pulled her in for a hug. "You're safe with me, babe," I reminded her, but this time she didn't repeat it and she walked away with Palmer without looking back.

Chapter Sixteen

Brett

Easton told me had something to do with Tate's disappearance, and I couldn't stop shaking. What did that mean? Did he hurt him? Did he kill him? What kind of person was Easton Kennedy, anyway? He told me that I was safe with him and I wanted to believe it, but now I wasn't so sure. I wanted to say something to Palmer, but I couldn't. It wasn't something I felt comfortable doing, and even though she asked me numerous times if I was okay, I only nodded and said everything was fine.

I wrapped my arms around myself as I sat on the bleachers and waited for them to finish practice. I had homework that I should be working on or even sketches, but I couldn't concentrate on anything. I pretended to watch their practice, but averted my gaze when Easton glanced in my direction. I was scared. Scared of what he was going to tell me, of who he really was.

"Babe, you're ignoring me, and I don't like it." His voice was gruff. "If you have questions? I want you to ask me." He gripped my chin between his thumb and forefinger to force me to look up at him.

I drew a shaky breath and slowly let it out. "I don't want to talk about it," I whispered, which only made him crouch down in front of me and cup my cheeks with both hands.

"Don't do that." Easton shook his head before someone called his name, and he glanced over his shoulder. "We're not done." He stood up, but not before he removed his Kingston Knights hat and dropped it on my head. Then he jogged back onto the field with the rest of his team.

I thought it was a little ironic that just a few days ago this boy, no scratch that, *this man*, acted like he couldn't even stand the sight of me, and now he was acting like he couldn't stand to be apart from me. Did Easton really care for me, or was this some sort of game to him? Would I really have the nerve to ask him what happened to Tate, and how would I react to the answer that I was given? I had a feeling I wouldn't like it.

Palmer came bouncing over with her pom-poms in hand and sat down next to me. "You look funny." She tapped the hat. "So, it's like official then?" Her brows dipped as she turned to watch the baseball team.

"I guess."

"What's going on with you, B? You've been acting funny ever since lunch. I'm starting... oh shit." Palmer slapped her hand over her mouth. "Did he say anything to you?" She leaned closer as the boys moved off the field and went inside to shower before they headed home.

Except Easton was headed straight toward me.

"Hey, Palmer," Easton greeted us. "You ready, babe?" He held out his hand to help me to my feet.

I stared up at him. "You're not showering?" I asked.

"Later," Easton answered before he hooked his arm over my shoulders and began to lead me away from my friend. "Ask me," he grunted as we walked. "Go ahead, do it now before it's too late, Brett."

I shook my head. "How would it be too late?" I didn't want to ask because I didn't want to know. This was all too fucking crazy.

Easton sighed softly. "You already know that I had something to do with Tate's disappearance." He stopped just as we got to the car. "Something might come up that could prevent me from saying anything later on." He pinned me back against the vehicle by planting a hand on either side of me and raked his greens over my face.

"I don't want to know."

"Sure you do, babe, isn't that what you and Palmer were just talking about before I interrupted?"

I bit my lip. "Please, just take me home," I begged. "I don't want to think about any of this right now."

"He's not dead," Easton assured me. "Yet." A smile tugged at his lips as he brought them closer to mine.

A shiver ran up my spine as I stared up into his eyes. "Why?" I whispered as I heard the sounds of our classmates around us.

Easton chuckled, but it didn't sound friendly. "He disrespected me, my boys, and..." He moved closer so that his lips were right against my ear. "You." He pressed his hard body against mine. "I roughed him up a bit the last night before I came to your house and snuck into your room. He's been at our place since the party, hidden where no one can find him.

Don't worry, he'll get what's coming to him in the end be-cause they always fucking do." His voice was cold.

A sound that I couldn't interpret escaped my lips. "There have been others?" I already knew the answer to that. Palmer had told me about the missing and dead kids prior to my arrival.

Easton stood up and that angry look glowed in his eyes. "You could say that." He took the hat he had given me and put it back on his head. "We gotta go, babe, it's getting late. I need to take you home."

He tilted his head slightly before his mouth came crash-ing down against mine. The way his lips moved with such confidence, I wondered if Easton was trying to let me know that he wouldn't hurt me, but I wasn't convinced. I was terri-fied.

I didn't say much as Easton helped me into the car and closed the door behind me before he went around climbing into the car. I wasn't exactly looking forward to going home and dealing with my mother. I knew she was going to have some serious words for me about this morning, and this time she might actually ground me.

Easton reached for my hand once we're on the road and squeezed lightly. "Okay if I come by later?" he asked.

"Booty call?" I teased although I didn't feel like laughing about anything and he flashed one of those amazing smiles. "Sure, you can come over if you want."

"I'll use your window."

"Did you really make a copy of my key?"

Easton nodded. "That I did, babe." He slowed the car down and stopped in front of the house. "I'm glad I did though." He leaned closer to open the door. "I'll text you when I'm on my way over so you can unlock the window for me." Easton ran the back of his hand over my cheek and then slid his lips over mine. "Later, Dorothy," he whispered.

I resisted the urge to turn back around until I got to the porch and Easton was still parked there, which I assumed was to make sure that I was safe. I gave him a little wave and then unlocked the door to walk into an empty house. Where was my mother? The beep of the horn outside let me know Easton was gone, and I let out a shaky breath. I didn't want to be alone here. I hoped that Palmer would be home soon. I moved around the empty kitchen and found a note scribbled on the whiteboard by the stove.

Brett,

I've gone out with Chad this evening. You're grounded until further notice, and I mean it, young lady. There's lasagna in the oven.

xo

Mom

I was honestly surprised how my mother had gone this long without getting married. She loved the whole idea of being a housewife. Cooking, cleaning, and all that nonsense, but Ruby never could seem to find a guy that wanted to settle down with her. I figured it was because she was a little clingy and came on a little strong, but then again I couldn't be too sure.

I pulled the pan from the oven and then grabbed a plate from the cabinet. Then I cut myself a hefty portion of lasagna before I covered the dinner back up and put it back where I found it. I figured Palmer might want some if she came home before midnight, and then I grabbed my bag and head-ed upstairs to work on some homework while I ate.

I got lost in my homework, which was good for me. I had slacked off since I had gotten involved with Easton and com-pany, so I was happy to not think about him, Tate or Cash, or anyone for a bit. It wasn't until I heard Palmer and Jen-nifer talking downstairs that I realized I had been upstairs for quite some time. I glanced at my phone to see that it was nearly ten o'clock. Nothing from Easton, and it seemed that my mother was also still out.

I brought my empty plate downstairs to rinse off before I put it in the dishwasher. I said hello to Jennifer who was in the living room eating and then I knocked on Palmer's door on my way back to my room.

"Come in," she called out. She raised her brows when I walked in. "What did he say?" Palmer asked when I sat down on the edge of her bed.

Easton hadn't said that I couldn't tell her about it, but I figured that it was best if I didn't. So, I lied instead.

"I didn't ask."

"Why not?"

I shook my head. "I'm scared." I twisted my lips slightly. "Clearly they all had something to do with it, right? Not just Easton? I mean, what is he going to tell me? 'Yes, I had some-thing to do with Tate's disappearance. I killed him, skinned him, and I'm going to wear his skin like Buffalo Bill in *Silence of the Lambs*?'" The thought made my stomach turn, even though I was trying to make a joke.

Palmer snorted, but brought her hand up to her mouth. "That's not funny." She shook her head. "I tried to ask Oz about it, but he kept saying it wasn't any of my business and that I didn't want to be involved. Clearly that shows you the difference between the two of them." She sighed and dropped back on her bed.

"Easton said that he was going to come over tonight, but I don't think that's happening." I hadn't told Palmer anything about Chad or Easton or anything that had gone down yesterday or this morning. "My mother is on a date with Josie's father," I blurted out and watched as Palmer sat right up.

"Excuse me?"

I nodded. "Yep." I popped the P at the end. "It's weird, right? My mother thinks he's so amazing, but he gives me the complete and total creeps." I wanted so badly to tell her about how he threatened me, but I couldn't.

Palmer leaned forward. "What aren't you telling me?" she asked just as both of our phones went off. "That seems a little convenient." She pursed her lips together.

Easton: *Not going to be able to make it, babe. Something came up. I'll pick you up in the morning. Keep your windows and door locked.*

"He's not coming." My heart sank. "I don't know why I should be surprised." I stood up.

Palmer got to her feet and touched my arm. "I didn't want to upset you before, B, but Easton and Josie have been on and off since middle school." She swallowed nervously. "You're not the first girl that has caused him to stray, like I said before, but in the end, he goes back to her. He always goes back. No one ever seems to hold his interest like she does."

Tears hit my eyes before I could stop them. "How could I be so stupid?" I asked.

"You're not stupid, believe me. Easton is a good-looking guy, right? It's easy to fall for the looks, the bad boy thing he has going. I told you to stay away from them, right, and here I am doing the same thing. Jumping into bed with Oz the moment he looks at me." She laughed like it was funny, but I could see she didn't mean it.

I excused myself and went down to my room so that I could change into my pajamas and go to bed. I pushed open the door and nearly screamed.

"Don't freak out."

My hand shot up to my mouth. Why in the hell was Cash sitting in my room and how the fuck did he get here? "Do you have a key to my house, too?" I took a step back.

Cash nodded as he stood up and opened his arms. "Come here, cupcake." He wiggled his fingers. "What, you don't want to give me a hug? Are we not besties anymore?" He flashed me his happy-go-lucky smile, but I shook my head.

"Why are you here? Why can you come over but Easton can't?"

Cash sighed as he ran his hand through his blonde hair and down the back of his neck. "I can't tell you that, boo." He suddenly looked exhausted.

"Then you need to leave." I folded my arms across my chest.

Cash's brows dipped. "Not happening. Easton asked me to watch over you, so I'm fucking staying." He stood up.

I stared up into his eyes. "Where is he? Why didn't he tell me this himself, Cash? Just what the hell is going on? Is he with her?" I felt my heart seize in my chest as he wrapped his arms around me and pulled me tightly against his chest.

"Nice try, cupcake." He rubbed my back as he ignored my questions. "You're going to have to trust me," he added. I leaned my chin against Cash's chest to see a smirk on his face. "Please?" he asked softly.

I rolled my eyes as I untangled myself from him. "Sure." I wanted to, but I had so many concerns, questions, and doubts running around in my head right now. "I need to change, so, if you wouldn't mind turning around." I went over to my dresser to dig out a pair of pajamas.

Cash grinned at me and did as he was told. "You're hot, Brett, but you know I would never do my best friend like that. We trust one another. I wouldn't touch his girl, no matter what happened."

I finished putting on my bottoms, ones with cats all over them. "Is he off burying Tate under some lye or something?" I teased and watched as Cash's body went rigid. Guess I shouldn't make jokes about stuff like that.

"That's not cool, boo," he answered. "Can I turn around now?"

"Yes."

Cash had a serious look on his face when I met his eyes. "Cute." He pointed at my choice of pajamas. "Easton told you." He looked concerned.

"Well, he told me that you had something to do with Tate's disappearance, but not about where he actually is right now." I took a step forward. "You really aren't the good guys, are you?" I asked softly.

Cash's face darkened. "Didn't I already tell you the answer to that question, Brett? I'm not going to answer it again." He sat down on my bed and kicked off his sneakers as he made himself comfortable. "We've been responsible for taking care of the problems in Kingston. That's all you really need to know." He looked down at his hands before he met my eyes.

"Is that why Easton can't be here tonight? Because he's taking care of a problem?" I made air quotes around the end of the question. "Or is he taking care of the girl he's engaged to? The one he always goes back to once he's strayed?" I spat.

"Don't fucking do that."

"Why not?" My nostrils flared. "Because it's the truth?" I didn't like this version of Cash at all. The darkness that spread from his eyes, his face, and from his body was enough to make me realize he wasn't the nice boy he pretended to be.

His mouth twisted with hate. "Because you don't fucking know what you're talking about, cupcake. He doesn't have a choice in the matter. East's father made that deal, not him, and when his father tried to take it back, it was too late. Do you think he actually wants to marry Josie?"

I shrugged because I honestly felt like I didn't know the answer. I suddenly felt like I didn't know Easton or Cash at all.

"He hates her. He uses her for sex when he needs it, but that's it. Easton always knew there was someone out there that was his real soulmate, not her. His father told him that someday, when he met her, he'd know."

"You actually believe that?" I asked.

"Why do you think he acted the way he did around you, Brett?"

The laugh that burst from my throat surprised me. "You're full of shit." I shook my head, and when Cash stood up, I held out my hands to keep him at bay. "What are you doing?" I asked.

"I was going to hug my best friend, boo, but if you don't want me to, I won't." He sounded sad, like a lost little boy. "You want to know something about Easton? Something that he probably won't tell you?" He touched my face lightly with his hand. "He has a heart of fucking gold. Saved my ass more than once when we were kids when my pop was beating the shit out of me. It's why I do anything and everything he asks of me. I know you saw the scars that he gave me, but were too sweet to ask me about." He flashed a brief smile. "It's why I'm here tonight, to protect you because Easton asked me to come."

"Is that why you live at Oz's place?" I dared when he nodded I turned to make sure my door was locked and then faced him again. "We should probably get some sleep." Then I climbed up into my bed and stretched out.

"You're too good for us, cupcake." I heard Cash whisper before he clicked off the light and the bed dipped next to me. "You shouldn't be mixed up in any of this." He sighed in the dark as he pulled me closer to him.

"Your father really hurt you like that? Put those scars on you?" When Cash didn't answer, I figured he had either fallen asleep already or didn't want to answer, but then I heard him let out a long, slow breath. "I'm sorry, I shouldn't—"

"My father was a mean drunk when he wanted to be, which was all the fucking time." Cash's hand found my face in the dark and his thumb brushed my cheek lightly. "One night it was so bad that I thought he would kill me. The next day I could hardly walk, but somehow managed to get to school. Easton told me I could start hanging out with him at night if it would help, and not too soon after that, Oz's parents took us in."

"I'm sorry."

"Me, too."

I could see his blue eyes regarding me in the dark as he watched me. "You're loyal to Easton," I whispered and pressed a kiss against his cheek. "I'm lucky to have you as my best friend," I added and snuggled closer to him.

Chapter Seventeen

Cash was gone when I woke in the morning, but unlike with Easton, I got his text telling me that he would see me at school later. I showered quickly and then dressed in a pair of skinny jeans paired with a blue tulip blouse that made my eyes pop. I dug out my black boots that went almost to my knees and decided that I would wear my hair down for once as I hurried down to the kitchen with my bag in hand.

My mother must have still been in bed as I noticed the time was nearly seven. I wondered if I should text Easton just to make sure he wasn't running late, just as Palmer met me in the kitchen.

"Wow, you look like... nice." She grinned at me as she hooked her bag over her shoulder. "I'm getting a ride with Oz if you need one."

I was just about to tell her that I was getting a ride with Easton when my phone buzzed in my hand. I knew that it wasn't going to be good news.

Cash: Just kidding. You're with me this morning, cupcake.

Just at that exact moment, Oz's silver Tesla pulled up in front of the house and Palmer began to head outside. I either had to follow or drive myself. I pretty much knew how that would go if I tried to take my own car to school, so I followed Palmer outside.

"'Morning, boo, you look lovely today," Cash greeted me with his usual cheerful self, but when I didn't say anything, he quickly changed his tune. "Promise you won't get mad at me, Brett?"

I glared at him as Oz pulled away from the house. "I'm not promising you or anyone anything until I get some answers," I growled and turned away. I was hurt. It wasn't the sex thing that bothered me because I had used guys once or twice for sex myself. It was the fact that Easton acted like he liked me, and then he did whatever he was doing.

Cash glanced up at Oz for a second, who was watching us in the mirror. "Easton is engaged to Josie."

"What?" Palmer's head flew around so fast I thought it might fly off her shoulders. "Say that again?" she demanded.

My heart felt like someone had just squeezed it into a million pieces. "Tell me something I don't already know." My voice was unusually calm when I spoke.

"You—"

I held my hand up to stop Palmer from saying anything else. "Is that why he didn't come see me last night? Why he didn't pick me up this morning?"

When Cash nodded, I let out a loud, bitter laugh.

"That son of a bitch." Tears slipped from my eyes and down my cheeks, but I brushed them away.

"He did it for you, cupcake."

I couldn't even look at Cash. The moment the car stopped, I practically climbed over him to get out, and nearly smacked right into Easton and his fucking fiancée as they slid from the black SUV he had taken me in to "meet" his father in.

"Baby, you know how much I like it when you pick me up on your bike," Josie cooed happily as she jumped from the vehicle. "You know how everyone looks at us," she added as she came around to loop her arm around Easton's waist.

"You had to park here?" Cash hissed as he tried to block my view. "Have some fucking respect, dude." He really was a good person, or at least to me.

Easton didn't seem to even care that he had broken my heart. That he had lied to me after he made me promise not to lie to him. I pulled away from Cash and marched over to where he stood. "I hope you're fucking happy, asshole." I jabbed my finger against his chest. "I should have stuck with my first instincts about you." I turned, only to have him grab me and spin me back around.

"Remember what I told you," he growled as he brought his lips to my ear. "About lying to me."

"Fuck you," I exclaimed.

A smirk slipped up Easton's face. "Did that already, Dorothy." He let go of me before he moved back to drop his arm around Josie's shoulders. "See you around," he added before they both headed toward the school.

Palmer hooked her arm through mine. "Girl time, sorry." She practically dragged me into the building and straight to the bathroom. "You cannot let him win, do you understand?" She placed both hands on either side of my face. "Are they really engaged?"

I nodded. "Seems that way. Something to do with their fathers when they were kids, blah, blah, whatever. I don't know the entire story and I don't want to." The sound of the door flying open and smacking the wall caused us both to jump.

"You know that Easton doesn't actually like you, right?" Josie's eyes were full of jealousy as she swayed into the bathroom. "He likes to stick his dick in other girls, but in the end, he always comes back to me, Brett." She smirked as she pulled a tube of lipstick from her purse. "You're nothing special, and just because you shared a couple of nights together, doesn't make you any better than me. We're soulmates. Like Romeo and Juliet." She grinned as she leaned toward the mirror to apply her makeup.

Palmer and I glanced at one another before she stepped forward. "You know how that ended, right?" She snickered as Josie rolled her eyes.

"Uh, duh, doesn't everyone? They lived happily ever after."

"Bitch, they both died."

Josie spun around and pointed her lipstick at me. "Don't you call me names, you... you—"

I nearly jumped her so that I could rip every red hair from her head, but the moment I went to attack I was lifted up off my feet and over the shoulder of someone much bigger and stronger than myself who carried me from the bathroom.

"Are you crazy, cupcake?"

Cash.

For one split second I had hoped that it had been Easton, but no. I could see him outside the girl's room waiting for his rotten girlfriend, and the look on his face when he happened to look up was not a happy one.

"Put me down." I kicked my legs, and he spun me around and placed me on my feet.

"You can't do that. Do you understand me?" He looked almost scared. "We all hate her, Brett, but you don't just go and fuck with Josie Silver," he whispered. "Tell me you won't try that shit again."

"Fine."

"I need to hear you say the words."

What was so goddamn special about that girl? "I won't try that shit again," I grunted and wished that I could just go back to bed and forget all about this day. Better yet, I wished that I had never moved to this godforsaken town.

I let Cash walk me to first class which had already started and slid into my seat, which was now right next to Easton. He didn't even turn to look at me, but the scent of his aftershave hit me like a kick to the stomach. I glared at him, willing him to feel my hatred, my anger, and most of all my hurt, but not once did he even give one inkling that he even cared about me anymore. If he had ever cared at all.

The second the bell rang, I sprang from my seat only to have Jameson grab my elbow. "We like you, Brett." He dropped his hand, but stayed close to me as we walked down the hall. "Trust me when I tell you that this isn't a forever thing." He winked before he moved on to his class.

What the hell did that mean? Why did these boys talk like The Riddler from Gotham City all the time?

"My brother is right." Jonathan appeared out of thin air, scaring me half to death. "You fit right in, don't take any shit, and..." He looked around. "Easton really likes you."

"Could have fooled me."

He grinned. "Trust me, little girl, he's working on fixing things." He tapped the end of my nose as he hooked an arm over my shoulders. "He's doing what he has to do for you, but when it's all said and done?" He clapped his hands together, crushing me against him. "Boom, baby, boom!" Jonathan laughed as we walked into the classroom.

"You taking care of my girl?" Cash dropped into the chair behind me and I felt the pads of his fingers against my back. "Boo, you okay?" he asked before he rested his chin on my shoulder.

I nodded. "Never better," I lied as Easton walked in with Josie on his arm. If I survived this day, I wanted my straight jacket to be purple, to match my hair, and polka dots.

WHEN I WALKED INTO the cafeteria for lunch with Cash, he eased me against his body the moment he saw Easton sitting with Josie, Oz, the twins, and Palmer. Now she was eating lunch with us? No fucking way.

"You're hurt, boo, I get that, but remember what I told you this morning," he whispered into my ear as he steered me across the room.

For one split second, I saw a splash of rage in Easton's eyes, but it disappeared when Josie turned his face away from me and then pressed her lips against his. I pinched my mouth together in a thin, tight line and tried to ignore both of them.

Oz's eyes were wide as he watched Cash and I sit down. "Holy shit, this is going to be fucking good." He grinned and Palmer smacked his shoulder.

Cash opened his lunch and began to remove an apple, some sort of sandwich, a water bottle, chips, and a banana. "You want some, cupcake?" he asked before he handed me half his sandwich.

"So, are you two like a couple or something?" Josie blurted out.

I looked up to find Easton glaring at me with black hatred and the moment I opened my mouth, Cash's hand came up, turned my face back to his and his lips landed on mine. My eyes flew open wide as he kissed me with tenderness I had never felt before. He didn't try to use tongue or get aggressive, but when he was done, everyone in the entire room was staring at us.

"What in the actual fuck was that?" Easton growled.

"Oh, this?" Cash's arm came back around my shoulders. "Nothing, man. Just, you know, hanging with my bestie," he answered casually.

Easton gritted his teeth and when Josie put her hand on his arm, he shoved it away. "You and her." He narrowed his eyes at me as he raised his hand. "What's going on with you two?" He wiggled a finger between us. Easton actually snarled. Like his lip went up full-on Elvis style and everything. It might have been cute if it wasn't scary as fucking hell. "You just fucking kissed. On the lips," he reminded me.

Cash smirked and pulled me closer before he bit into his sandwich without answering. Why did I feel like Easton was about to beat the living hell out of his best friend?

"You're okay with that, Brett?" Easton turned his eyes on me again.

I picked at my sandwich with my finger. "Yes," I answered before I popped the bread into my mouth. "I mean, it's not like you and me—"

A scream ripped from my throat when Easton jumped from his seat and over the table to knock his best friend onto the floor, taking his lunch, and mine, with him.

"Get the fuck off of me!" Cash exclaimed as he pushed Easton off of him. "What is your problem?" He scrambled back up onto his feet as he glanced around the cafeteria to see everyone still watching.

Easton stood back up. "You kissing Brett, asshole!" He lunged forward, but Cash took a step back. "You don't get to do that."

"You don't get to decide that, Easton. I'm not yours."

Easton turned to look at me with pain written all over his face. "You are," he whispered as he swung around to make eye contact with me.

I stood up and put my hands on my hips. "Really? Is that why you blew me off last night? Why you didn't pick me up this morning after you told me you would? Why you're with someone else now?" My throat felt tight. "I'm no one's fucking property." My chin trembled as I saw the hurt and guilt flash in his green eyes.

"Babe." Easton's hand came up to cup my cheek and for a minute I leaned into his touch, but then he pulled away like I burned him.

I gathered up my things and hurried out of the cafeteria before the tears that filled my eyes could spill down my cheeks.

Chapter Eighteen

I saw red the moment Cash put his lips on Brett. I wanted to rip him apart limb from limb, starting with his fucking lips. I might have too, if Brett hadn't spoken to me the way she did. Who the hell did he think he was, putting his mouth on my girl like that? He knew that I was only pretending to be with Josie right now until I got everything figured out with her father. I wasn't sure how long that would take, but that didn't mean he could move in on Brett.

"You okay?" Oz asked as he joined me in the locker room before practice.

I bared my teeth. "What do you think?" I snapped.

Oz sighed and ran his hand over the back of his neck. "Look, man, you know he's only trying to get you to face your feelings for Brett. He doesn't actually like her like you do. They're fucking friends, nothing more. We all don't understand why you don't just tell Josie to go fuck herself? Who cares about something your dad agreed to when you were a kid?"

"My father was a man of his word, Oswald."

"I meant no disrespect, boss."

I stood up. "I know there was an actual contract that was signed by both Chad and my father, but for the life of me, I can't find it." I turned at the sound of the door opening behind us to find Cash and J2 walking in. I glared at my supposed best friend, who stopped dead in his tracks. "Don't fucking talk to me right now unless you want me to break both your arms and legs," I warned.

"I did it to prove a point." Cash crossed his arms over his chest and cocked an eyebrow.

A dark laugh burst from my throat. "Oh? And, what was that?" I scoffed as I yanked my shirt over my head to change into my uniform.

"That you love her."

A hush settled over the locker room as I continued to glare at Cash. He didn't break my gaze or back down when I took a step forward. In fact, a small smile tugged at his lips when he realized he hit the nail on the head.

"I don't love anyone," I reminded him and went back to changing.

"Dude," Oz hissed.

I blocked them out as I quickly got dressed so that I could head straight out to the field without them. I needed some fresh air, I needed a break from this, and I most certainly did not want to talk about Brett anymore or think about Cash kissing her again. Although I couldn't seem to block that from my mind, no matter how hard I tried. I was happy to find Coach Best already outside when I approached the dugout.

"Mr. Kennedy, that was quite the performance you put on this afternoon." He removed his glasses as he looked up from his tablet. "I need you to do some laps for me." He pointed toward the field. "Don't worry, Mr. Donovan will join you when he gets here. You two can talk out your differences then," he added.

I nodded. "Yes, sir." I dropped my glove on the bench and jogged out to the field without another word.

AFTER PRACTICE, I FOUND myself driving to Brett's place. I don't know why, but I wanted to check on her, and make sure she was okay. Cash and I didn't exactly make up during practice, but we didn't kill one another either. I knew things wouldn't be the same between us until I broke it off with Josie for good, and at least I had him around to make sure Brett wasn't alone.

I stopped my bike halfway down the street and then walked it the rest of the way so that no one would hear me. I had planned on just taking a quick look around the yard just to make sure that she was safe until I saw Chad's car parked in the driveway. That bastard was in the house right now, and there wasn't a damn thing that I could do about it. I clenched and unclenched my fists as I stared up at the house, trying to calm myself down before I did anything else stupid today.

"What the fuck are you doing here?" Cash's voice caused me to jump. I hadn't even heard him pull up. "Are you stalking Brett now?" he asked.

I shook my head. "Just wanted to make sure she was alright." I pointed to the blue Mercedes. "Which she clearly isn't with *him* here."

Cash grunted. "What would you do if he just walked out and saw you? You're supposed to be with his daughter." But I saw the worry in his eyes. "You should leave."

"Is she okay?"

"Don't."

I looked around the dark street. "Is she planning on going to the concert with us on Saturday?" I asked.

"If her mom will let her," Cash answered. "Look, East, I'm sorry about earlier." He took a step back when I turned to face him again.

I let my eyes wander again, but this time they went up to Brett's window. "You're right about me loving her," I said softly.

Cash gasped. "Fix it, man. Fix it so that you and she can be together." He knocked my shoulder with his. "You know that I would never go after your girl, right? I only kissed—"

I choked back anger. "Don't say anything else. I don't want to think about your punk ass lips on my girl, okay?" I tried to laugh it off, but jealousy gnawed inside me. "I'll go." I turned to head back to my bike. "Keep her safe for me?"

"Always," Cash assured me.

Once I was safely away from the house, I started my motorcycle and sped off into the dark, but I had one more place to stop before I finally went home. Before my father died, he had owned a fairly successful motorcycle shop that he had left to me in his will. When I graduated high school, it would finally be mine, but in the meantime, it was closed until then. People came by from time to time to make sure everything was maintained and kept neat like it needed to be, but it wouldn't officially open again until I had my diploma in my hand. However, that didn't mean I didn't have the keys to the place and couldn't take a peek around when I felt like it.

I hadn't been to Kennedy Cycle in a few months because it honestly hurt more than I wanted to admit. The smell of the oil when I walked in, the memories of hanging out and playing pinball while my dad worked on a Saturday afternoon were hard to take most of the time, but tonight I needed to force myself to deal with it no matter how awful it made me feel. I used my cell phone as a flashlight, unlocked the door, stepped inside the building, and headed straight to the back of the shop where my father's office had been where I began to dig through his paperwork.

THE SILVER HOUSE WAS dark when we pulled up in Oz's car the next morning. I didn't think for one minute that the place was empty or that they didn't have cameras watching our every move. I spent all night digging through my father's things until I found what I was looking for, and I had come home to wake up my boys, minus Cash since he was still at Brett's, to tell them to get their shit. We had a fucking job to do.

The house was set back from the road, with a long sprawling lawn, and a driveway that curled up from the street. I had no doubt in my mind that they were watching us behind cameras with guns aimed right in our direction. I motioned for Oz to follow behind me, and without a word, I headed straight toward the house. My hands were amazingly calm as I pulled the gun from my back pocket to protect myself. I didn't want to put a bullet in anyone this morning, but I would if I had to, and if I got shot in the process, it wouldn't be the first time. Oz and I both heard talking at the same time and stopped.

"This way," I mouthed and we began to move again.

Josie appeared on the front step dressed in skintight leather pants and a white sweater like she thought I was here to pick her up for school. Little did she know that this was the last time I would ever come to this house again. The last time she would ever speak to me or even look in my direction if everything went as planned.

"Get inside," I growled at her. I didn't need her getting hurt.

Josie pouted. "I don't want to be late... is that a gun?" Her eyes went wide with fright. "Easton, what are you doing?" she shrieked as I pushed past her.

"Put that away before you hurt yourself, son." Chad Silver was sitting on an oversized couch as I walked into the living room. "Then, take my daughter to school." He chuckled softly, but it faded when I dropped a yellow folder on his lap. "What's this?"

"My saving fucking grace, old man."

Chad dragged his eyes up to mine. "Are you serious right now?" He flipped open the folder and then ripped the pages in two and tossed it into the fireplace, where we both watched it go up in smoke. "There, all gone." He leaned against the couch. "Go now."

I cocked the gun. "Do you really think that I'm stupid enough to bring the original or not make a copy?" I exclaimed. "All this time I thought I had to marry your spoiled, rotten, bitch of a daughter because of some contract you and my father created sixteen years ago. But, the truth turned out to be if you or he died, the contract was null and fucking void."

Chad blinked calmly. "You'll marry her." He folded his arms across his chest. "Because if you don't, something terrible might happen to that little purple-haired girl you're so damn sweet on."

"I'll kill you."

"You wish."

I felt the cold metal against my lower back.

"See, son, I'm older, smarter, and much more experienced than you are." Chad stood up to grab the gun from my hand. "Your father stole something that belonged to me years ago." He paced around the room and spun back around to face me. "Your mother, Olivia, was supposed to marry me. We were in love. Had been for a very long time until good old fucking Ralph showed up." He glared at me with hate in his eyes. "Stole my sweet Olivia right out from underneath me." He dragged his teeth along his bottom lip. "Got her pregnant with you right after graduation, and so I did the next best thing. I pretended not to care, knocked up the first girl I could find, and then killed her."

"Daddy!" Josie exclaimed.

I almost felt sorry for her. *Almost.*

Chad shrugged. "Sorry, pooh, but it's true." He waved the hand with my gun in it around. "Your mother, on the other hand, was another story. I couldn't kill her because I loved her so much. I wish that I could take credit for her addictions, but Olivia did that to herself. The bullet in your dear old man was the icing on the cake for her though." He gave me a wicked grin. "I could have been your father. Imagine."

I felt frozen where I stood. There was no way that I would continue this game or marry his daughter. "You're not even half the man my father was," I hissed, and that wiped the smile from his face.

"You're going to pretend this shit never happened, Easton. You will fucking marry my daughter, or I will make sure you never see Brett Cake again. Do I make myself clear?"

I felt sick to my stomach. Here I thought I had a way out. A way to be with the woman I loved, and now I was just farther in the hole. I nodded. "Yes," I answered, although I had no plans to do anything he told me. I still had the original contract hidden, as well as several copies that I knew Chad would never find. He thought he was smart, but I was fucking smarter.

"Good." He nodded and then I felt a crack against my head and everything went black.

Chapter Nineteen

Brett

I stomped around the bedroom getting ready for school as Cash watched me from my bed. Yes, he had stayed again last night, but only because he had insisted. I had tried to get him to leave, considering what had gone down at school, but he wouldn't budge. Not even a little.

"You going to stay mad at me forever, cupcake?" he asked as I pulled a beat-up I Love NY sweatshirt on over my head.

I spun around and yanked my hair out from under the collar. "That might not be long enough." I pointed a finger at him. "You know, Cash, I thought you were different from other boys, but you're not, are you?" I asked.

"Is it me you're really mad at, or your mother?"

I stopped to stare at him. "Don't." I shook my head, but he was right. Last night my mother had dropped the biggest bomb on everyone when she came home and announced that she was marrying Chad Silver. Everyone had been shocked, but no one more than myself, and I told her if she thought I was going to move in with that bastard, she had another thing coming.

"Hey." Cash opened his arms. "Come on, cupcake, you know you'll feel better once you get your cute little ass over here." He wiggled his fingers, and I couldn't help but smile. When I stepped into his arms, he engulfed me in a hug that felt perfect. "I'm sorry." He squeezed me gently. "I shouldn't have kissed you or put you in that situation."

I pushed back to look Cash in the face and dragged the pads of my fingers across his forehead to brush a few blonde strands from his eyes. "You're lucky I like you so much, Donovan," I teased. "Do you think I can stay at Oz's if my mother actually goes through with this crazy scheme? I mean, if she marries Chad."

I felt his hands drop from my sides as he grabbed his phone from the bed next to him.

"What?"

"I gotta go, boo."

I saw the darkness in his eyes. The way his jawline hardened. "What's wrong, Cash?" I grabbed his elbow as he started toward the window.

He stopped and ran his hand over the back of his neck. "There's been an accident."

"What kind of accident?"

Cash shoved open the window. "Can't tell you that, cupcake, but as soon as I can, I'll let you know." He pulled his legs through and climbed onto the roof. "Love you!" he called.

"What kind of a best friend are you if you can't trust me with your secrets?" I called after him, but he only waved as he ran off to his car.

My mother had to know boys were hiding in my room at night and climbing out my window in the morning. We were making too much noise right now.

Palmer suddenly burst into my room. "Did you hear?" She's still dressed in her bathrobe. "Easton's been hurt."

"What?" I spun around to face her.

She nodded. "Oz just texted me that they went to confront Josie's dad this morning, and... why is your window open? It's freezing in here right now." She stared at me with concern in her eyes.

"Forget that, Palm, what happened to Easton?" I slammed the window shut and locked it.

Palmer shook her head. "Right, so they went to the Silver's place, but it didn't go as planned." She flipped through her text. "He's at the hospital now. They think it's a concussion."

That had to be the accident that Cash was talking about. What had happened to cause it, and why couldn't Cash tell me?

"Shit." I met Palmer's eyes. "Cash just ran out of here like someone lit a fire under his ass—"

"Cash was here? In your room?"

"Yes, he stayed last night."

Palmer's brows dipped. "Is there something going on between you and Cash that you're not telling, B?" She tugged the tie on her robe a little tighter around her waist.

"We're friends," I assured her.

She nodded. "Okay, let me get dressed so we're not late to school." Palmer flashed a brief smile before she hurried back to her room.

SINCE EASTON WAS THE one who was in the hospital, I would have thought the others would show up late, but Oz, Cash, and J2 were all no-shows for the day. I was surprised to see Josie walking the halls like nothing was wrong wearing a pair of leather pants that looked like she had to lie down to squeeze herself into while smiling and laughing like her supposed husband-to-be wasn't lying in a hospital somewhere hurt.

I tried not to worry about Easton, but I couldn't help myself. I hoped that the reason that he had gone to Silver's house wasn't because of me, but deep down inside my gut, I knew that it had to be. Sure, okay, maybe it was to pick up Josie, and bring her to school, but it was too early for that. I had texted Cash a couple of times, but I didn't want to be all crazy weird, so once I didn't get a response from him, I let it go. I figured he would get back to me when the time was right.

"Are you listening to me?" Palmer waved her hand in front of my face.

I blinked up at my friend. "Sorry, no, what were you saying?" I had totally spaced out.

Palmer folded her arms over her chest. "I was asking about the baseball game on Friday. Oz texted me that Easton wasn't going to be able to play."

"You've heard from Oz?" I asked.

"Sure, he's texted me a few times just letting me know that Easton was okay, but wouldn't be in school for a bit." She sat down at the desk next to me. "Shit, did Cash not tell you?"

Was Cash purposely not texting me? Or was I now just being paranoid? "Maybe Easton's still mad at him and didn't let him in the hospital room."

That was probably the case, right? Had to be. I could see by the look on Palmer's face that wasn't the truth at all.

"He's ignoring me on purpose," I blurted out. "The guy who went out of his way to be my damn friend is all of a sudden trying to not talk to me?" That made no sense. "What hospital are they at?" I suddenly had the desperate urge to go there. To make sure Easton was okay as well as Cash and everyone else.

"I don't know."

"Don't give me that bullshit, Palmer, because all of a sudden you and Oz are super fucking chummy, despite having told me that I should stay away from these guys." I shot out of my desk. "You're not telling me something." The sound of the bell ringing for the start of class didn't deter me. In fact, I grabbed my bag and headed for the door.

"Brett, where are you going?" Palmer called after me, but I ignored her. I would go to every single hospital in this state if I had to in order to find them.

TURNS OUT I DIDN'T have to. Cash's phone had died while they were in the waiting area, so he hadn't been able to text me back until he borrowed one of the twin's chargers. He texted me as I was leaving the school.

Cash: You left school? Cupcake, you can't do that
Brett: Where are you?
Cash: Can't tell you that

Brett: I'll drive to every single hospital if I have to.
Cash: *laugh emoji* No doubt you will, boo.

He finally told me, and don't worry, I parked my car so that I could text him back. When I stepped off the elevator onto the hospital floor, I found all four boys sitting around staring at the phones in their hands and coffees by their feet.

"How is he?" I asked and eight pairs of eyes swung up to meet mine.

Cash was on his feet first to grab me in a hug so tight that I swore he was going to break me in two. He swung me around before he placed me back onto my feet.

"He's resting. We didn't want to bombard him too much. Doctor said he could go home tomorrow," he answered before I felt a hand on my shoulder.

"We're glad you're here." Oz's voice was softer than normal, and when he turned me around, I was surprised when he pulled me in for a hug. "You should go see him."

"I don't—"

Jameson, or was it Jonathan, they really should wear nametags, nodded. "You should. It would totally lift his spirits." He flashed a quick smile. "He's bummed because he can't play in the game tomorrow night or for the next two weeks. Coach is going to be pissed."

His brother elbowed him.

I scrunched my face. "You think I should go in?" After yesterday, after everything, I wasn't sure I was ready to face Easton. I just wanted to make sure he was alright.

"Come on, cupcake." Cash started to guide me from the room. "You'll make Easton's day," he assured me.

The room was quiet except for the soft beeping of the heart rate monitor and the occasional drip of whatever happened to be in the IV bag that was strapped to Easton's arm. His eyes were closed, the lights off, and he looked like he might be sleeping as we stepped into the room. I hadn't been in too many hospitals and for that, I was lucky because right now I was getting an incredibly creepy vibe as I let my eyes move around the room trying to avoid looking at the boy in the hospital bed again.

"I can hear you assholes fucking breathing," Easton grunted, and when I dared look at him again, my heart ached. I hadn't noticed the hospital gown he wore when I stepped into the room, but it was white with blue dots, and for some reason that made this seem even more real than before.

"Someone wanted to say hello." Cash pushed me forward. "Thought it would make you feel better." He squeezed my shoulders. "Go on, cupcake, make yourself known."

Easton's eyes flew open. "Brett." My name came out as a whisper. "You shouldn't be here."

I glanced up at Cash who only squeezed me harder.

"But, I'm glad to see your beautiful face." He managed a weak smile.

"My mom's engaged to Chad," I blurted out for no reason.

Easton stared at me. "What?" He sat up just a little bit and adjusted the blanket.

"Ruby and Chad are engaged." I turned around to look at Cash again but he was gone, which left me alone with Easton. I twisted my hands together nervously. "He asked her last night and she, uh, said yes. I'm not living with that man. Do you think Oz's parents will let me live there with you guys or is that too much?" I took a small step forward. "Does your head hurt? What happened?"

Easton held out his hand. "Yes, a little, I tried to fix my problem, but it didn't go so well." He tugged me closer when I slid my hand into his. "I'm glad you came to see me, babe." He scooted over on the bed. "Climb on up and get comfortable."

"Is that a good idea? What if someone walks in?"

"So what if they do?"

I hesitated for a second before I did what he asked and Easton wrapped his arms around me.

"I'm sorry, babe. For what I did, for what I'm going to do, and for whatever happens next." His chest vibrated against my ear. "I'm going to find another way to fix it. I tried, but it backfired." He stroked my head lightly. "Turned out he and my mom used to be a thing before my father came along and ruined whatever they had going." Easton's voice sounded groggy, and I wondered if I should leave so he could rest. "He admitted to killing him, and to killing Josie's mother. Can you believe that?" He laughed, but it was bitter and angry. "I'll beat him if it's the last thing I do." He vowed as his breathing began to slow.

I glanced up to find Easton's eyes closed and knew that whatever medicine was in that pump attached to his arm had caused him to drift off. I knew I shouldn't stay here much longer because any moment Chad could burst into the room, but as I breathed in his scent, I couldn't help but wonder what was going to happen next.

"Cupcake, you need to bounce." Cash poked his head into the room. "Just got word Josie's dad is on the way over." He pushed the door open farther. "How about we go check out the cafeteria with the guys?"

I climbed off the bed, but not before sliding my lips over Easton's. "I'll wait for you, Tin Man," I whispered into his ear before I followed behind Cash.

Chapter Twenty

I didn't hear much from the boys for the next two days. I got an occasional text from Cash letting me know that Easton had been released from the hospital and was going home, but that was pretty much it. I thought it was odd, but I let it go, hoping that it was just because he was worried about his friend and nothing more.

When Saturday rolled around, I wondered if they were still planning on going to the Pearl Jam concert and if I should even bother asking my mother if I could go. She had plans to go wedding gown shopping with Jennifer, so I figured if I caught her before she left that would be a sure bet she would say yes in case things didn't go as planned while she was out.

"Good morning, Brett." Ruby smiled happily at me when I walked into the kitchen. "Big plans for the day?" she asked as she poured herself a cup of coffee.

I sat down at the table. "That's what I was coming in here to talk to you about, Mom. I was wondering if I could go out tonight. There's a concert that I wanted to go to." I chewed nervously on my lip.

"With Easton?"

"He'll be there, yes, but we're going with a few other friends."

Ruby tilted her head. "I don't like that boy, sweetheart. Chad said he runs with a pretty rough crowd around town, and that they get into a lot of trouble. That they might have even killed a boy." She paused to take a sip of coffee. "He said that his mother has a real drinking problem and that she might have had something to do with his father's death. He also mentioned something about him dating his daughter, so really if he's with someone else he shouldn't be seeing you, too. That Cash boy isn't exactly the best influence either, and those twins? I don't want you hanging out with any of those boys. Oswald is home alone all the time while his parents just jet all over the world? Who raises that child?"

My blood went cold as my eyes narrowed. "That's a lie," I hissed. "Chad is a liar, Mom, and he shouldn't talk about Easton like that. Cash is my best friend—"

"Good morning." The male voice behind me caused me to stop mid-sentence and turn around. Why was Chad standing in the kitchen in nothing but a pair of gray sweatpants? "Hello, Brett." He pressed a kiss to my mother's lips. "Are you going with Ruby to look at dresses this morning?"

I felt bile rise up in my throat as I stared at them. "No," I answered. "I have plans." I turned and rushed back up the stairs to my room before my mother could say anything to me, making sure to lock my door behind me. I had to get out of this house. I couldn't stay here anymore if Chad was going to be here all the time. I grabbed my phone and texted Cash.

Brett: Are you up? I really need you.
Cash: What's wrong, boo?

Brett: Can I come over?

Cash: Of course. You don't ever have to ask.

I took a quick shower, packed a quick bag, and hurried downstairs to run out to my car, happy to find my mother was gone as well as Chad, and when I pulled up in front of Oz's house, Cash was waiting on the porch. I had only been here once before, but I took in the size of the house, the six-car garage, and wondered where his parents were most of the time.

"Are you alright?" Cash asked as I climbed up the steps. He reached for my bag and I let him take it. "I have to warn you that Josie's here," he whispered as we went inside.

I stopped dead in my tracks. I hadn't even thought about that. Of course she would be here. Technically, Easton was her fiancé, and they were supposed to be a couple. "I shouldn't—"

Cash shook his head. "You should, cupcake," he assured me. "You're one of us now and you belong here. Come on." He guided me upstairs to his room where he dropped my bag on the bed. "Talk to me." He sat down. "Tell your bestie what's going on inside that pretty little head of yours," he teased with a half-smile.

I sighed as I began to tell him about Chad, my mother, and what had happened only a short time ago. "I didn't know what else to do or where else to go." I felt tears in my eyes. "I've never been in this situation before, Cash. My mother has had boyfriends before, but never has one of them been like this or has one of them asked her to marry him." I noticed the hardness in his eyes and the way his jaw was set. "Cash?"

"She said all that?"

I nodded. "That's what Chad told my mother. I have a feeling she'll believe anything that he tells her to believe." I watched as Cash stood up. "Wait a second. Where are you going?" I asked.

"Group meeting," he grunted. "You're coming, too, boo," he added.

I followed Cash out into the hallway where he knocked on four doors before he went downstairs into the finished basement and sat down on an oversized love seat before he yanked me down next to him. A few seconds later we were joined by J2, Oz, and finally Easton who looked surprised to see me.

"She can't be here." His brows dipped. "Babe, you can't be here. It's not safe." He dragged his eyes over to Cash. "Explain yourself."

Cash leaned forward. "Chad is telling tales out of school, boss," he snarled. "Tales about you, your family, and me. Telling Ruby things she shouldn't know. Isn't that right, Brett?" He nudged me lightly, indicating I should speak.

I glanced around the room at the boys who were all waiting for me. "Yes," I whispered. "Chad said some things that, uh—"

"It's okay, babe, you can say whatever he said. We're all friends here," Easton assured me, but the icy look in his eyes told me I wasn't going to like the reaction I got.

I licked my lips nervously as I began to tell them what my mother had said to me and repeated it to them. About the twins, Easton, Oz, and Cash. "I don't know how much Chad has told her, of course, but it was probably done to get her to not trust you and to get her to make sure I stayed as far away from the five of you as possible." My brain was starting to figure things out. "I'm eighteen, so she really can't tell me what I can and can't do."

Like where I lived, if it came down to it.

"He fucking said that?" Oz's eyes were dark with hate. "I'll kill him myself."

"Relax." Easton put his hand on Oz's shoulder. "We'll talk to him, don't worry. He knows he isn't supposed to talk about this shit until they're actually legally fucking married." He locked eyes with me. "Sorry, babe." He flashed a quick smile.

"Now what, boss?" Jameson asked.

Easton sighed and ran his hand through his hair. He still looked tired, but a little better than the day I saw him in the hospital. "We can't let him know we know about this yet." He stood up and then held his hand out to me to help me to my feet. "You holding up alright?" he asked as he pulled me against him.

"I guess."

"What did we say about lying?"

I rested my head against Easton's chest as I looked up at him. "How long, Tin Man?" I asked before he leaned down to slide his lips across mine. It sent my heart into a tailspin and blood burned hot in my veins.

"Don't lose hope yet, Dorothy," Easton whispered into my ear before he released me and left me standing there with Cash.

"Did he—?"

I shook my head. "Don't ask," I told him as I watched the back of Easton as he walked up the stairs. I could hear him talking to someone and then I heard Josie's voice.

"Does that make me the scarecrow?" he teased.

I tried to smile, but jealousy was already running ramped through my body as I pictured Easton kissing her, smiling at her, or worse. "You're more like my Toto," I assured him, but tears blinded my eyes.

Cash wrapped his arms around me and crushed me against his chest. "I know, Brett, I know," he whispered. "Give it time and Easton will figure it out. I promise." He squeezed me tight as I tried to be brave.

I hoped that he was right because my heart and mind couldn't take too much more of this.

I WAS ABLE TO AVOID Josie for most of the day by lying low with Cash in his room. We talked a bit about everything except the elephant in the room until he told me I could paint whatever I wanted on his walls. I dug out the paints and brushes that I had packed and began to move loosely over the wall until Oz burst in and started screaming about what his parents were going to think. I thought I was in serious trouble until I saw the smile on Oz's face that he was trying to hide.

"That isn't funny," I exclaimed as he threw back his head and laughed. "I thought you were going to kick me out!" I shoved the brushes into some water as he continued to chuckle at me.

"You should have seen the look on your face, B."

"No, you don't get to call me that. Only Palmer does."

Oz snickered. "Too late," he added before he ducked out of the room, mentioning something about getting ready for the concert.

Cash looked up from his phone. "We should probably think about changing and getting ready, too, if you're still going." He jumped up and tugged his shirt off like it was no big deal. Again I noticed the grooved scars on his back. "The room across the hall from mine is empty, so maybe you can have that one." He pulled a fresh shirt on over his head and then ran his hand through his blonde hair. "Although I'm sure you'll end up in Easton's bed soon enough." He almost sounded sad.

"What's wrong, Toto, you want me in yours?" I teased, but he only laughed. "How are you single?" I asked as his eyes grew wide and he winked at me.

"Why, Brett Cake, are you asking me out?" Cash teased, but then shrugged nonchalantly. "I don't know. Can't say I've met a girl that really makes my heart happy, you know?" He touched my face. "Not that you don't, but you and I were never meant to be more than friends, cupcake. I knew that the moment I saw you," he added. "When I meet her? I'll know she's the one I was meant to spend the rest of my life with."

"She's going to have to get through me first."

"I'm touched."

I wrapped my arms around Cash's waist. "I'm thankful I ran into you the first day I started school," I told him.

"Me, too." Easton's voice caused me to turn around. He was standing in the door and he gripped the molding above his head with sadness in his eyes. "She's gone, Dorothy," he added, which only made me run to him. "You got me all to yourself tonight." He tipped my face up with his knuckles before his lips met mine.

I sank into the kiss without even thinking about it. I didn't care that Easton was engaged to someone else right now or that I was slowly losing myself to him. Or that this group of boys were now becoming my family. *My home.* I felt safe with them. I felt like they were the only people who could understand me.

"Come on." Easton pulled away first but kept me close as we began to walk down the hallway. "You're riding with me to the concert tonight." He told me as we walked down the stairs. "I want to spend as much time alone with you as possible."

The way he said it almost made it seem like it meant something else, but I couldn't read anything in his face.

Palmer was in the kitchen with Oz when we got there, and I saw a quick look of surprise in her eyes that she tried to hide. I'd have to try to get it out of her later if we had a moment alone, but for now, I was just going to try and enjoy some time with Easton and my friends before we had to go back to school on Monday. Before I had to go back to pretending he wasn't mine.

Chapter Twenty-One

I let Brett do most of the talking on the way to the concert venue. My mind was elsewhere, and I was pretty sure that she knew why, too. Despite my feelings for this girl, how deeply I cared for her, and yes, I did love her. I was going to have to break it off with her until I figured out how to fix things. Tonight I only wanted to have a good time with her, but I had a feeling Brett knew things were not going to end the way we both wanted them to.

"You're quiet," Brett suddenly said. "Are you alright?" she asked softly.

I could feel her watching me with those eyes. "Never better, babe," I assured her. "You're by my side, what else could I want?" I lied.

I could think of a few things I could want, like Chad's head on a stake, his daughter far as hell away from me, and Brett in my bed forever. I didn't want to worry about one of Chad's goons catching us out tonight or what other lies he had been feeding Ruby about me and my boys, but it was still in the back of my mind.

"What did we say about lying, Easton?"

I chuckled at the way she turned things around on me. "My dad was a huge fan of Pearl Jam," I admitted. It was the truth and I loved them because of it. "What kind of music do you usually listen to? Please don't tell me it's One Direction or some pop shit like that," I teased.

"Something wrong with One Direction?" she challenged, but I knew she was only trying to get a rise out of me. It's one of the things I really liked about her. "I grew up listening to the music my mom liked. A lot of hair bands, but classic rock, too. Floyd, Zeppelin, stuff like that. Why are you laughing at me right now?" Brett asked as I pulled off the highway toward the venue.

I glanced over to find her glaring at me. Fuck, she was beautiful. "I think I just figured out where your name comes from." I turned right into the parking garage. "Did your mother name you after the lead singer of the band Poison?" I eased the SUV into a spot and turned to look at her.

"Yes."

"Guess it could have been worse," I told her. "You could have ended up being named Slash or Axl, right?" I teased.

Brett slapped my arm playfully which only caused my cock to push against my jeans. It had been too long since I'd been with my girl and I had refused to touch Josie even though she had tried. I made up an excuse that it was because of the concussion, but it's really only because I didn't want her. Josie had bought it, but that would only last for so long. I must have looked upset because Brett shook her head.

"I'm sorry, I didn't mean—"

"Are you flirting with me, babe?" I growled somewhere deep in my chest and watched as her eyes grew wide and the blue inside went dark. "Because I like it." I crushed my lips against hers and the sound of the moan that escaped her lips was enough to make me regret every decision I had made about breaking it off with Brett after tonight.

The sharp need for the kisses did nothing but make me want her more. Brett's tongue was wild inside my mouth, and as it rubbed against mine, I used a free hand to unhook my seat belt so that I could get closer. Brett's hands gripped my shoulders as I pulled lightly at her bottom lip and when someone knocked on the window I glanced up to find Oz and Palmer watching us.

Perverts.

"Jesus." Brett smoothed her shirt down as I noticed the pink of her cheeks. "We should probably go find our seats, right?" She looked at me shyly.

I smirked. "I'd rather make out with you, Dorothy." I winked as she unbuckled herself and then opened the door.

I didn't let her get too far before I caught up and grabbed her hand to lace our fingers together. I was almost thankful that the concert started once we found our seats. I didn't want to have to make small talk tonight. I wanted to sit, enjoy the music and be with Brett. Cash and J2 joined us a few minutes after the lights went down, but I almost didn't notice. I was too busy watching my girl as she enjoyed herself. The way she enjoyed the music, sang along, and danced around with Palmer when they really got into a song. When Brett eventually caught me staring at her, she blushed and shook her head, but kept looking back at me to see if I was still watching. Believe me, I wasn't the only one. Brett was hard to miss with that body, that ass, and the way she moved with the music. I eventually stood up, wrapped my arm around her shoulders and moved her closer to me just so that everyone knew that she was taken. At least for tonight.

After the concert, we all took our time walking back to the parking garage talking about the concert, how amazing it was, and how the band just seemed to get better with age. I made sure to keep Brett close, knowing that after this? Who knew where we would be. I caught Cash watching us, and the look in his eyes only made me hate myself even more for what I was about to do. Once Brett and I were alone again, I found myself wanting to make the night last a little longer.

"Are we going back to Oz's?" she asked as I pulled the SUV back onto the highway. "I don't want to be alone tonight." I caught the meaning in her voice and when her hand landed on my dick, I instantly grew hard.

"Babe."

"Tin Man."

I don't know why I liked it so much when she called me that. It wasn't an insult, not coming from Brett. "Tell me," I groaned as she palmed at my already growing hard-on. "Tell me what you want." I focused on the road in front of me, which wasn't easy.

Brett let out a soft moan of her own. "I want you inside of me, Easton. Even if it's only for tonight until you can truly be mine," she whispered and I felt like she knew what I was supposed to do tonight.

My heart ached at the thought.

"Yeah?" I felt tears burn my eyes.

"Yeah," she answered.

I glanced at her in the darkened vehicle. "Whatever Dorothy wants," I assured her as we drove back to Oz's place. If she was going to be living here now, we would have to get used to seeing one another and that wouldn't be easy either. I eased the SUV into the garage and Brett climbed up into my lap with big eyes full of desire and want.

My cock pressed against my jeans as she ground herself against me. "Do you want me, Easton?" she whispered as I groaned softly at her touch.

I gripped her hips. "You know I do." I slid my lips across hers. "Let's get inside so we don't get caught." I didn't have to say anything else. Brett knew exactly what I meant. It didn't look like anyone else had come home from the concert yet as we stepped inside the house and made our way upstairs to my room.

I pinned her against the wall as I brought my face closer to hers and slowly ran my tongue around Brett's lips before I slammed my mouth against hers. We kissed and pawed at one another, just standing there for what felt like forever. I sucked on her tongue and Brett bit down lightly on her bottom lip. She ground herself against me when I found her nipple under her shirt, my lips capturing her whimpers and moans.

I took a step back only so I could yank my shirt up off my head and watched as Brett did the same. She unhooked her bra and I groaned at the sight of her perky pink nipples that were just waiting for me to suck on them.

You're so fucking beautiful," I told her before I leaned down to take one in my mouth.

Brett cried out on contact and as my tongue swirled around the hard bud and her back arched toward me. She grabbed fistfuls of my hair and begged me for more. Whispered my name as I grabbed her so that she could wrap her legs around my waist and then I moved us over to the bed where I laid her down onto her back. The gaze she gave me was unsettling when I met her eyes. I kicked off my jeans as fast as I could before I helped Brett remove her own pants, and then I stopped to get a good look at her as she lay naked on my bed. Then I grabbed a condom from my nightstand and slid it on over my shaft before I climbed up on the bed.

I eased myself between Brett's legs and let the head of my heavy cock push at her damp entrance. "Ready, babe?" I moaned as she pressed closer. I gripped one of her hips and then I was all the way in. I gritted my teeth as Brett pulsed around me. I licked up her chest, throat, and then to her mouth as I slowly began to move.

I felt like I could lose myself in warmth and wetness, but I wanted this to last. I wanted to make love to Brett this time, not just fuck her. I wrapped an arm around her waist to pull her closer and Brett whimpered as my shaft slid over her clit with every thrust of my hips.

"You're perfect, babe," I murmured, bringing my lips to hers. "You're so fucking perfect," I whispered as she met my gaze.

"Fuck, it feels too good." Her hips arched against mine and I could already feel that fireball of bliss threatening to burst inside of me as a sheen of sweat began to build up on my skin. "Easton, I'm going to come," she warned me as her fingers suddenly dug into my shoulders.

The force of her orgasm caused her to shake underneath me and just as I thought I wouldn't be able to hold on any longer, my own release came on suddenly and I found myself crying out Brett's name as I spilled into the condom and I collapsed next to her. I didn't want to get up, but I knew I had to remove the rubber and wanted to make sure she was comfortable.

"I love you."

I stopped at the words that I heard Brett whisper as I had started to climb from the bed.

"I know that you probably don't feel the same or want to hear me say it, but I just wanted to tell you before—"

I silenced her with a kiss so hard that I saw stars behind my eyes. Brett had uttered the words that I had longed to say to her, but was too afraid. "I love you too, Dorothy," I assured her. "Give me a second." I jumped from the bed and came back with a washcloth so that I could help her clean up before I pulled the covers around us and pulled her close.

Brett loved me. She fucking loved me. Shit, that really put her at risk now. Not to mention what I was going to do to both of us tomorrow.

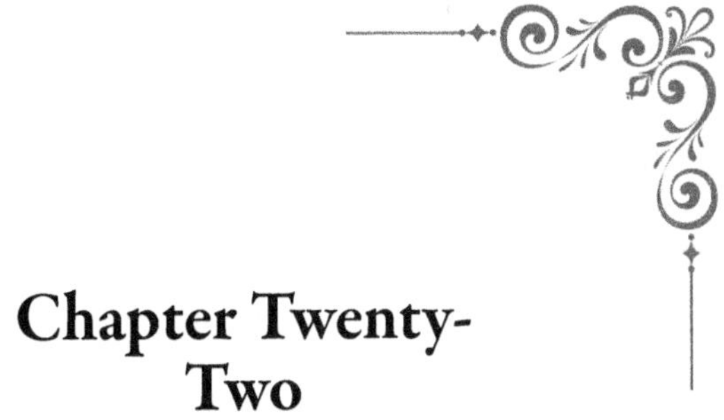

Chapter Twenty-Two

Brett

I knew that Easton was telling me goodbye last night. I knew that when I woke up this morning in his bed that I would be alone, but it still hurt more than I could imagine. The sheets were cold on his side of the bed which made me wonder if Easton had slept there at all, only to quickly push the thought from my head. He had been gentle with me last night, and tears burned my eyes as I climbed from the bed. I wondered if this would be the last time I had the chance to be in his room. I found my clothes in a neat pile on a chair and I dressed before I opened the door to leave.

The house was quiet as I walked down the hall to Cash's room, and I carefully pushed the door open so I wouldn't wake him. As I laid down next to him, he turned to look at me with sleepy eyes.

"'Morning, cupcake." He gave me a half-smile. "You okay?"

I shook my head. "No," I whispered and when Cash opened his arms, I happily moved into them so he could hold me. "It feels like someone just crushed my heart with their fist," I murmured against his shirt.

"I know," Cash said as he rubbed my back. "It's not forever," he assured me, but it still felt like it. He squeezed me closer.

I choked back a sob. "What happens if Easton can't change things, Cash? What if he ends up having to marry her, and I have to sit back and watch it?" I sat up to brush the tears from my cheek.

"Not going to happen, boo."

"You don't know that."

Cash sat up to face me on the bed. "Trust me. I've known Easton since we were in diapers. He wants what he wants, and he wants you. He is going to do everything in his goddamn power to not marry—"

The sound of girly laughter filled the hallway, causing him to stop.

"He won't marry Josie. I can promise you that."

The laughter started again, causing me to grimace as I pulled myself from the bed. "I should probably go home." I didn't want to be here if Josie was around.

"I thought you wanted to stay here?" Cash stopped me. "You're welcome to stay as long as you want, Brett, you know that. Oz was going to fix you up your own room just like we talked about." He tilted my head up. "You're safer here with us where we can keep an eye on you."

"My mother is going to flip out." I tried to smile. "You said the room across from yours, right?"

Cash chuckled. "Let me brush my teeth and I'll show you." He slipped into the bathroom and I heard the water turn on. I sat back down on the bed just as there was a knock on the door.

"Hey man, I was wondering... Brett, I didn't know you were here." Easton's brows dipped slightly. "You, uh, spend the night?" His eyes met mine as he pleaded with me to go along with his game.

Josie suddenly appeared by his side and he casually draped his arm around her like he hadn't spent the night in bed with me. It felt like salt in my already large wound.

"I did." I flashed a fake smile at both of them as my heart sank even further.

Josie tilted her head. "Seriously?" She looked doubtful as her eyes moved over me.

Cash slowly walked into the room. "What's up?" He looked between me and his best friend with the skanky red-head hanging off of him.

Josie was wearing jeans that looked painted on this morning, but the Knights shirt she wore looked suspiciously like Easton's.

"Boo, get over here." He grabbed me and yanked me up onto his lap as he sat down.

Easton pressed his lips together. "I needed to borrow your phone charger," he muttered between gritted teeth. "But, if you and Brett are busy, I can go bother the twins or Ozzy." He continued to stare at me even as I moved so that Cash could get up to get him the charger.

"Dude, I got you, don't worry," Cash assured him as he dug through his nightstand. "Just make sure to give it back, unlike the last time you borrowed it." He turned around with a grin on his handsome face. "I had to go buy another one because I think your little fiancée took it." He winked at Josie, making me want to rip her hair out.

Josie waved her hand in the air. "Did not." She rolled her eyes before she let go of Easton. "Speaking of phones, I think I left mine downstairs. Be right back."

I watched her bounce out of the room.

"You're fucking getting too handsy, man, back the fuck off," Easton warned and when I turned to look at him again, his green eyes were burning with anger.

"Re-fucking-lax," Cash hissed. "Get the fuck out of here before I kiss her again."

"Fuck off."

I stood up. "You're not making this easy on me, Tin Man." I licked my lips. "I have to watch you get all cozy with Josie, and you expect me to just sit back and watch? After last night?"

I gasped when Easton's hand came up to grip my chin.

"Last night was real, Dorothy," he assured me. "I fucking meant everything I said and did. Don't you forget it." He dropped his hand to his side. "Thanks." Easton grabbed the charger from Cash before he left the room, making sure to leave the door open as he went.

"That went well." Cash wiggled his brows at me. "So, that room."

"No, I'm staying in here with you."

"Cupcake, I don't think—"

I put my hand against Cash's chest right over his heart. "Please, just until we get all this shit figured out?" I pleaded with him.

"Boss man ain't going to like it much," Cash warned, but he let a slow, lazy smile spread across his face. "You're fucking bad, you know that?"

"You fucking love me." I giggled as he pulled me against him and hugged me.

Cash tickled my ribs, which only made me laugh harder. "You're lucky that I do. Why don't we go downstairs and see what J2 are up to? They usually like to either cook or go out on Sunday for breakfast. I thought I smelled bacon."

"Oh, you had me at bacon." I grabbed his hand as we started out of the room and hoped that my broken little heart could handle living here for however long I had to.

THE DINING ROOM TABLE was piled high with bowls of food. French toast, pancakes, eggs, sausage, hash browns, and bacon stacked up as we approached and I'd be lying if my stomach didn't growl just a little. It looked and smelled absolutely amazing.

"On your right, B," Jameson announced as he came in with a plate of what looked an awful lot like cinnamon bread. I was going to kill Palmer for coming up with that nickname the next time I saw her.

"Are you kidding?" Cash grabbed a piece and split it in half before he handed me one. "You two have really outdone yourselves this morning. What's the occasion?" he asked as I bit into the bread.

Jonathan came in with a pitcher of orange juice. "You don't know?" He glanced in my direction before he looked back at Cash. "I thought he told you."

"Who told me what?" Cash shook his head.

"You guys!" Josie squealed with excitement as she rushed into the room. "Look at what Easton just gave me!" She shoved her left hand out to show off a ring that was big enough to drag her down if she wasn't careful. "He said it was his grandmother's. Isn't it like the most beautiful thing you've ever seen?" Her eyes met mine for a brief moment before Cash yanked me from the room before I had a chance to say or do something I might regret.

"I had no fucking idea, cupcake," he tried to tell me. "You have to believe me. I never would have brought you down here."

Something between rage and jealousy threatened to burst from my body as images of the giant rock on Josie's finger dashed through my brain. How could Easton do this to me? "I hate him." Tears blinded my eyes. "He's a lying piece of shit, and I wish that—"

Cash crushed me against his massive chest. "There has to be a reason Easton did this." He tried to assure me, but my heart didn't believe it. "You can't go flying off the rails right now, Brett. Don't forget we're supposed to be a couple and you're not supposed to care about what he does." He held me tight as I struggled in his arms.

"I can't."

"You have to."

My entire body hurt right now like someone had used me as a punching bag. I was physically and emotionally drained. "I just... I just want to go lie down, Cash. I don't want to pretend I'm happy about anything right now." I glanced up and he ran the back of his hand over my cheek.

"I think that can be arranged, cupcake," Cash said before he scooped me up into his arms. I didn't even fight him as he started to carry me back up the stairs. "You feeling okay?" he asked. "You look awfully pale all of a sudden."

My eyes were really heavy, too. "I'm just really tired," I murmured and wondered if I would ever feel okay after today. Was this even real life?

"You with me, boo?" Cash's voice was slurred slightly, and I thought it almost sounded like he was underwater. But we weren't swimming right now. "Shit, what the fuck, Jameson." I heard him mutter. "Easton is going to fucking kill us all," he grunted as he placed me on the bed. He was muttering more things that I didn't understand, but I was so tired. One little nap wouldn't hurt me right now, would it?

No, I had to fight it. Something was wrong. It didn't feel right, and I felt myself topple from the bed onto the floor, causing pain to pierce through my entire body. I bit down hard on my lip to keep from crying out. It hurt, but it wasn't enough to make me stop trying to move. I dragged myself across the bedroom floor until I saw a pair of red heels standing in front of me.

Josie.

"Why can't you just stay down?" The voice sounded a million miles away. "God, you are just so annoying. Everything was fine until you got here and now you're trying to ruin everything." A hand gripped my hair and yanked.

"Let go!" I screamed and tried to reach up to get her to release me.

She ignored me. "You know, Brett, I didn't think much of it when you showed up at school. Except, I saw the way Easton looked at you. The way the boys just seemed to flock around you like some sort of golden queen or purple queen, might be more like it." Josie laughed bitterly. "What do you have that I don't?" She started to drag me across the room. "You don't need to answer that," she added as she suddenly released me and my head slammed against the floor.

My vision spun as I tried to get up. "You're fucking insane," I slurred.

"Maybe, but I got the man," Josie reminded me as she waved the hand with the massive ring on it in front of my face before she slapped me. "Don't think I don't know that he took you to that concert last night. Or that you slept in his bed." She shoved me so hard I might have gone over again if I hadn't grabbed on to the bed.

Where was everyone? Did they go out and leave me alone with this psycho?

"How?" I licked my dry lips. "Did you plant a camera in his room or something?" The sound of her maniacal laughter caused me to realize I was right. "Jesus Christ."

Josie jumped up and down like a little kid as she clapped her hands. How did she not fall over in those shoes? "Honestly, Daddy couldn't seem to take care of you since he's so caught up in your whore of a mother, so I had to take matters into my own hands."

"Don't call my mother—"

The loud knocking on the bedroom door caused me to stop. "Why is this door locked, Brett? What's going on?" Cash pounded on the door again. "I don't know, man, I didn't lock it. I knew she wasn't well, so I came to get you." He was talking to someone else. "Cupcake, stand back from the door," Cash ordered before it sounded like he tried to break it down with something hard and heavy. Probably his shoulder.

I squinted my eyes up at Josie. "Once he gets in here? You're really fucked. All of them are going to kill you," I told her.

Again, she slapped me across the face and I was just happy she wasn't punching me.

"Whatever you did to me or drugged me with is going to come out. You're going to lose everything. Easton isn't going to want to—"

Josie suddenly jumped on top of me and wrapped her hands around my throat just as the sound of crunching and splintering wood sounded in the room. Josie's hands and body weight were lifted off of me, and then Easton's voice was in my ear.

"I got you, babe," he assured me before I was transplanted to the bed. "Get that fucking cunt out of here before I fucking kill her myself," he growled before he smoothed the hair from my face. "Brett, talk to me," Easton ordered.

I shook my head back and forth. "Can't talk now... tired... Josie... crazy... sleep." I tried to get out the sentences that were running through my head, but I couldn't. Everything seemed to happen so fast, and I couldn't think straight.

"Someone call the doctor!" Easton roared, but he was still next to me. "You'll be fine, Dorothy, I promise," he tried to assure me.

Then everything went black as I finally passed out.

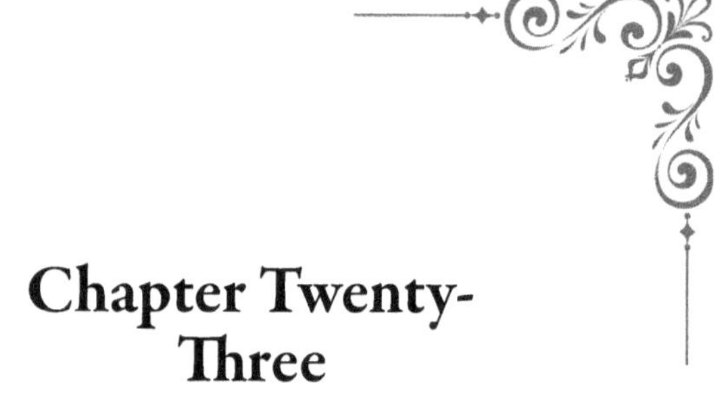

Chapter Twenty-Three

Easton

"What in the actual fuck?" I screamed the moment I stepped into the family room.

I wanted to castrate every single of these fuckers. All I asked was for them to take care of Brett and keep her safe while I wasn't available. And this was the goddamn thanks I got from my supposed friends? How did they leave her alone with Josie?

Cash lifted one eyebrow as he met my eyes. "You might want to calm your tits, bro. You were busy playing house with Annie Wilkes while I was trying to convince Brett that it was all an act. No one told me that you were going to put a ring on it today, or any day, for that matter. I didn't leave her alone; pretty sure that was you, correct?" I narrowed my eyes at him.

"That was an accident. Josie found the ring. What was I supposed to do? She thought it was for her," I told them. "Brett was in the house. She was safe." I started to pace. "I don't understand... wait a second." I stopped. "Where did the breakfast food come from? Did Brett eat anything?"

J2 shook their heads as Oz finally made an appearance by dropping into an empty chair. He looked like I felt with dark circles under his eyes, wrinkled clothes, and his hair a complete mess. "Sorry I'm late," he muttered before he took a sip of the coffee in his hand.

"That's not true!" Cash jumped from his spot on the sofa. "We split a piece of cinnamon bread, but I never actually ate it because I got distracted with Josie flaunting that damn ring." He spun around to glare at the twins. "What did you two do?" he growled.

Jonathan held up his hands. "Nothing, I swear! We didn't do anything, right?" He elbowed his brother who looked a bit more guilty, and a lot like he wanted to be anywhere than right here. "Jam, tell them we didn't do anything," he hissed between clenched teeth.

I slammed Jameson up against the wall before I could stop myself and listened to the clattering of pictures as they fell down behind him onto the floor. "Tell me what you fucking put in that bread before I cut you apart by piece by fucking piece." Our noses were almost touching I was so close to him and no matter how hard he struggled, I kept my hands pinned against his shoulders to keep him there.

"It wasn't something that could kill her, man, it was just a little—"

My fist made contact with his stomach and I watched as Jameson stumbled over in pain. "Why? Why would you do that? Why risk everyone else eating it, too?" I saw red as I stared at the boy who was supposed to be my friend.

Jameson clutched his belly. "I was going to accidentally drop it on the floor so no one else would eat any."

"Like that's stopped us before." Oz snorted, but looked away when I shot him a look.

My hand went through the wall before I could stop myself and I took a step back before I did much worse. I dragged my hands through my hair and yanked before I spun back around.

"Why?" I demanded.

Jameson glanced up at me. "Josie," he muttered before he dropped to the floor. "She said that if I drugged Brett, she'd leave you and we could be together." He closed his eyes. "Josie said she loved me, and that she wanted to be with me."

Jonathan stared at his brother like he didn't even know him. That made two of us.

"Josie is fucking nuts," Cash muttered just as the man we only knew as the doctor walked into the room. "What is it, doc?" He jumped to his feet.

"It was Benadryl," the doctor answered as he placed his bag on the floor. "Miss Cake will be fine once she wakes up. Probably a little groggy at first. It was a pretty big dosage, but she'll live."

"Deal with this." I pointed to Cash as adrenaline surged through my body before I ran up the stairs to my bedroom to get away from them. I would say something, do something, hurt them, or worse if I didn't calm myself down.

I stood in the doorway to watch her as she slept. Her purple hair was spread out behind her, and I wondered if Brett even knew what had happened? Did she even remember? I gripped the molding above me and closed my eyes.

"Easton?" Brett's sleepy voice brought me back to reality. "Where am I? What happened... oh." She must have remembered something because she shook her head.

I moved to the side of the bed. "You were drugged, babe, but you're going to be alright," I assured her. I placed my hand on her forehead. "I'm so fucking sorry," I whispered as I slid my hand down to cup her cheek against my palm. "If Josie hadn't found that ring in my drawer, if I had the balls to fucking tell her the truth instead of lying to her." I sighed softly as I stared at Brett's pale face.

She struggled to sit up. "Easton, no, this isn't your fault." She flashed me a smile that made my heart stop. "Don't do that to yourself." The heavy dark circles under her eyes told me there was still something left in her system. "Come lie down with me." She patted the mattress with her hand.

I didn't hesitate. I climbed up onto the bed with Brett and pulled her close so that my lips were against her hair. "It's taken care of," I assured her. I didn't want to get into the details with her yet, but Josie wouldn't be bothering anyone anymore ever again. "No one gets away with hurting my fucking girl." I squeezed Brett closer and when she didn't answer, I looked down to find her sleeping. "I love you, Dorothy," I murmured before I slid my lips across hers. I would have hell to pay for what I did to Josie, but I didn't care. Not anymore.

Cash knocked at the door. He ran his hand over the back of his neck. "I'm sorry to interrupt, but, uh, we got a big problem downstairs."

Every muscle in my body tensed up as I kissed Brett one more time, and then I eased myself from the bed so I wouldn't wake her. "Who?" I hissed through clenched teeth.

"You already know who," Cash told me as I made sure to lock the door behind him. No one was getting in there.

I did. I knew it would be Chad Silver coming to check on Josie and me. I also knew that he wasn't going to be too happy to find out that his daughter wasn't going to be coming home with him tonight after the shit she pulled today. I nearly put a bullet in Josie's head, but I held off on that. Oz's parents had a cabin that was about an hour or so from here that Chad would never think to check on. I had plans to stash her there until the time was right. I would let Chad think she was dead for as long I wanted to string him along. I knew he would try to move heaven and hell for his daughter, so I needed to keep something up my sleeve.

"Is he here?" I asked as we both took the stairs two by two.

Oz was waiting for us at the bottom. "No, but I can imagine he will be any minute." He glanced over at where Jonathan was standing. Alone. "He, uh, feels bad and wants to help in any way that he can." It was weird to see him there without his brother. I hadn't figured out what I wanted to do with Jameson yet.

"Of course." I gave a slight nod. "It's not your fault, Jon," I called out to him, but I saw the look in his eyes. The guilt he was carrying.

"Boss man—"

"No, no." I shook my head. "You didn't put your brother up to that." I gripped his shoulders. "He'll pay somehow, but not you. Got it?" I asked.

Jonathan blinked up at me with fear in his eyes. Was there something he wasn't telling me? "You should probably know that Jameson already alerted Chad to what happened here today." He swallowed and I watched his Adam's apple bob nervously.

"Where is she?"

I spun around at the sound of Chad Silver's voice. How the fuck did he even get in here? Jameson was a dead man when I saw him again. I bared my teeth as I watched him move around the room like he owned the place.

"You know damn well she isn't," I barked. "You have no right—"

A loud laugh cut me off. "I have no right to do what, Easton? A little birdie told me that you buried my daughter tonight. Is that true?" Jameson was already spilling lies he had known nothing about. Chad's eyes were dark and angry as he watched me. "What about your pretty little purple-haired girlfriend? Didn't I tell you to stay away from her, but I know for a fact that she's here. Maybe she knows something about Josie's disappearance? Or I could ask her mother." His eyes once again moved around the room before they landed on me again.

"You fucking leave Brett and Ruby out of this," I warned. "You touch a hair on either one of their heads and I'll slit your throat myself." His time as king of this town was going to end, and soon.

Chad clicked his tongue against the roof of his mouth. "You're the one that brought her into this, boy." He folded his arms over his chest. "If you don't bring Josie to me, I'll have to have someone else do it."

"Did you just fucking threaten me?" I snapped and took a step forward.

Chad hardly looked fazed. In fact, a smile slipped up his lips as his eyes moved behind me. "Nice to see you again, Brett." I swear the hairs on my neck stood straight up. "Surprised Easton didn't have you locked away somewhere today so he could keep you safe."

I spun around to find Cash already ascending the stairs to where she stood.

"Come on, cupcake." He nearly swung her over his shoulder to get her away from Chad.

"Is he going to hurt my mom?" Brett slapped at Cash's hands. "I can't live with myself if something happens to her." Her voice shook as she spoke. "What happened to Josie? Someone needs to tell me what's going on." Her eyes were wide with fright.

"Brett—"

I heard the sound of the gun as Chad held it to my head and Brett's scream of terror. "Best thing for everyone right now is to show me my goddamn daughter. If you can't?" He chuckled softly. "I guess I'll take Easton here in her place." He wrapped an arm around my neck and yanked me against his chest.

"Fuck you." I struggled, but it was useless. "I know Jameson told her she's fucking dead, asshole. That traitor sold us all out to save his own ass." I gripped the arm around me.

"Take me!"

"Brett!"

Brett shook her head. "Please, just don't hurt him." Tears streamed down her face as she rushed down the stairs. "I'll go in Josie's place if you promise not to hurt Easton. If you love my mother, and if Josie is dead, take me home with you. I can... I can try to be your daughter." Her eyes met mine for a brief second.

Fuck, I needed to tell her Josie wasn't dead. That I had stashed her away somewhere safe because I wanted to let everyone think she had split from Kingston, but if Chad hurt Brett because of me, I would never forgive myself.

Chad's grip loosened. "You promise to stay away from Easton and the rest of these boys?" he asked.

"Babe, don't do this," I pleaded.

Brett nodded. "I promise," she whispered.

Chad shoved me to the floor. "Okay, but if I catch you talking, texting, or sneaking around with one of them? The deal is fucking off." He held out his hand and when Brett took it, I felt like my whole world shattered.

Brett gave me one last look before I watched her walk out of the house with Chad Silver, leaving me sitting alone.

"You just let her leave like that?" Cash exclaimed. "We have to go after her. We can't let her be with Chad! He's fucking crazy." He sounded like I felt.

"What the hell?" Oz blinked in confusion. "I don't understand." He looked between the two of us.

I got to my feet. "We'll get her back. I don't know how, but we will. I love her and she loves me," I tried to assure them, but I wasn't so sure of the words that were coming out of my mouth.

Chapter Twenty-Four

Easton

The cabin was cold when I woke the next morning. I didn't even want to climb from the bed as I remembered everything that had happened yesterday. Brett was gone, and I had no idea where she was. She had left her phone in my room, so that was out, and when I had gone to Chad's house there was no sign of him or Brett. Ruby was gone, too, and that left Palmer and her mother in a panic when I told her Chad had taken Brett from Oz's house.

The four of us left that afternoon to get out of Kingston and hide Josie before Chad came back. It still sounded weird to say that, but Jameson was dead to me now. This was all his fault and I could see how terrible Jonathan felt every time I looked at him. I wouldn't be surprised if he eventually left, too, but that wasn't my concern at this time.

The cabin Oz's parents owned a few towns over where we sat around most of the night drinking and trying to figure out where Chad might have taken the two Cake women. As I finally managed to drag myself from my bed, I realized just how much I drank last night and stumbled slightly in the dark as I flipped on the light in my room. No amount of

227

fucking booze was going to bring Brett back to me. Only I was going to be able to do that, and everything was coming up dead ends.

I shuffled into the living room to restart the fire that had burned out during the night and found Cash glaring at me with his arms crossed over his chest.

"You're up early." The bruising around his eye looked pretty bad. I hated that I hit him. I hated that we had argued so badly that it came to that.

"Did you sleep at all?"

Cash shrugged. "A little." He watched me with narrowed eyes as I flopped down in the chair across from him. "You think of anything yet?" As much as I hated how he cared for Brett, I knew his feelings were not the same as mine.

I shook my head. "Of course not." The way we danced around one another was pussy bullshit. "Look, man, I'm sorry about last night. I shouldn't have decked you like that. Go ahead and take a shot at me." I totally deserved it.

Cash stared at me for a second before he let the usual grin that he carried around break across his face. "Thanks for the offer, but I'm good. It made me realize how much you actually care for Brett," he told me.

The moment Brett stepped out the door, Cash pushed me back against the wall. "What the fuck!" he roared. "You're just going to fucking let her go with Chad like that? Stop her!"

"You want both of us dead?" I shoved him back. "Don't fucking touch me."

"How can you say you love her?"

"Say that again."

Cash's blue eyes grew hard. "How can you say—"

My right fist made contact with Cash's left eye, and the sound that came out of his mouth was anything but human. He tried to hit me back, but I took two steps back before he had the chance. "Say it again, asshole, because I'll blacken the other eye just as fucking fast."

Oz stopped us both before I had the chance to hit my best friend again, and he literally dragged me from the room, screaming obscenities about how I would fucking break both his arms and legs if he ever dared look at my girlfriend again.

"I never thought we'd fight over a chick." I smirked and Cash chuckled softly. "I'd die for her," I added.

"You don't have to tell me that because you know that I would, too." Cash stood up. "Made some coffee. Want some?" He didn't wait for my answer, but instead shuffled into the kitchen, so I followed.

Jonathan looked up from his phone in his hand and nodded at me as I walked in behind my best friend. "Relax," I assured him, even though I knew he was probably texting his brother. They had some weird twin thing that I would never understand.

Cash glanced over his shoulder as he grabbed a couple of mugs from the cabinet and handed me one. "We'll find her," he tried to assure me, but it did nothing to calm my nerves. He poured himself some coffee before he took a sip. "Should we go check on Josie?" He asked. I opened my mouth to answer him, but that's when the ice man walked in.

Oz bumped my shoulder as he entered the already cramped room. It was hardly big enough for two large men, never mind four. "Did you drink all of the coffee or did you save some for the rest of us?" He grabbed a mug that read

"#1 Dad" across the front, which caused me to nearly choke. "What?" His brows dipped.

"Might want to rethink that mug," I spoke into my own.

Oz scowled. "You might want to rethink your face, dick, because you don't know shit about fuck," he barked. Something in his eyes said something I couldn't put my finger on, but I let it go for now.

Cash looked between the two of us as he eased himself into the chair next to Jonathan. "We're all on edge, boys, relax," he reminded us.

"Palmer said her mother is an absolute basket case," Oz grunted. "But she isn't going to the cops yet."

"Good." I sat down next to Cash. "Does she have any idea where they might be? Where Chad could have taken them?"

I had a few other guys looking into it, but the trail had gone cold the moment that asshole drove away from Oz's place. Like he disappeared into thin air. I watched as Oz chewed on his lip and stared at his phone.

"What's eating you this morning?" I leaned across the table. "You're acting fucking weird."

Oz glared at me. "Fuck off," he growled and continued to stare at his phone. "I gotta take a leak." He stood up and stomped from the room.

"Palmer's pregnant," Jonathan muttered the moment he was gone.

"*What?*"

Jon nodded. "Yep." He let the P pop as he nodded his head. "I don't think she wants to have the baby, but Oz does." He shrugged. "I'm not getting involved. We don't date for that reason. I hope that you're using a condom or that Brett is on birth control," he added.

I let the we part slide because it would take a while before he stopped using that. "That's not any of your business," I muttered, thankful that we used protection. Actually, we hadn't talked about any of that sort of thing. I would do whatever she wanted to do. I would fucking marry her if that was what she wanted.

"Wasn't she with Brantley what's his name before?" Cash asked softly. "What?" he asked when I turned to stare at him.

"You think she would do that? Palmer, I mean?"

Cash shook his head. "No, I don't. I was just asking." He stood up to move to the sliding back door. "I don't want to think about babies or Oz right now. That shit is fucked up."

Oz had said that things between Palmer were just casual fucking, but if he wanted to keep the kid, that clearly wasn't the case. I knew how he felt about his life, that his parents weren't around, but made sure he had whatever he needed. Maybe Oz wanted the chance to be a father so he could be a good father. The sound of the door opening caused everyone to stop and watch as our friends walked in.

Oz pointed a finger at Jonathan. "You're a fucking asshole." He marched past the rest of us without saying anything else and slid the door open to walk outside onto the porch.

I realized I should go talk to him, or at least try to.

"What do you think I should do, boss man?" Oz didn't even bother to turn around.

I shook my head even though he couldn't see me. "That's not for me to say." I ran my hand through my hair. "You love her?"

"Fuck if I know. We have fun together. I like her, and she's super cool, but she doesn't seem to care what happens to the baby." He sighed as he turned to face me. "How did you know?" He met my eyes. "That, you know, that you loved Brett?" His voice shook when he spoke.

I chuckled softly. "I wanted to fuck her and hate her at the same time, remember? She blew into school with that purple fucking hair, and all I wanted to do was kiss those bee sting lips until neither one of us could see straight." I surprised myself with the honest answer. "My dad once told me that the minute I met my soulmate, I would know. That she, or he, would turn my entire world upside down. Brett did that for me when I first saw her."

"Jesus Christ."

I nodded. "You need to talk to her in person when this all blows over. Don't do it over the phone, FaceTime or text. Girls don't like that sort of thing," I told him.

"Thanks, man." Oz's lips turned up into barely a smile, and I could see it in his eyes how much this was hurting him. Maybe the iceman was cracking. "Now, maybe instead of talking about my pathetic love life, we can put some brainpower into *yours* since that's why we came here in the first place."

I clicked my tongue off the roof of my mouth. "Why not." We both turned around as we heard Cash screaming and yelling. "Dude, what are you freaking out about?" I hissed.

"The castle," he blurted out.

I tilted my head. "Holy fucking shit," I whispered as I realized what he meant.

Oz looked between the two of us. "What?" He looked confused.

"My dad and Chad bought a place up in the hills when they were still buddies. They were going to share it, hang on the weekends, that sort of shit. It was this ridiculous place that looked like a castle, and—"

"You think they might be there?"

I squared my shoulders. "It's worth taking a look, right? I only went there a couple of times when I was a kid, and it was written into my dad's will that it would go to me when I turned eighteen. I had no use for the fucking place and planned to sell it when the time came. It's actually mine, but I've never seen a key or a deed or anything."

"What are we fucking waiting for?" Cash clapped my shoulder. "Let's go get your girl."

I held up my hand. "Not yet. We can't just go marching in there, guns blazing. We have to come up with a plan. We have to let Chad think that he won the game which also means we have to *play* his fucking little game."

"You want to just wait?" Oz's brows dipped.

Cash shook his head. "No fucking way, man. I don't like it." He pressed his lips together in a firm line. "I say we head over there, bust through the door—"

"I get it." I nodded my head. "I really do, bro, but if we do that, we put everyone at risk. Which means someone could get hurt or much fucking worse. I say we stay here for the day, the night, whatever, and go to school. Ignore Brett as much as it's going to kill us, pretend everything is fine, and put a plan together."

I licked my lips nervously as I thought about what not talking to Brett but seeing her would be like. My heart stuttered for a second in my chest. It would mean seeing other guys talk to her. Flirt with her, and the possibility of her doing the same right back.

Cash balled his hands into fists at his side. "I can't do that." He gritted his teeth. "Brett's my best friend, and it's already killing me not talking to her for this long. She's at school now without us, people are going to wonder why we're not there, why we're not talking to her, and start asking questions."

"We'll make something up."

"Like what?"

I chewed on my lip. "I'll start boasting about not being a one-woman guy. How Brett couldn't handle that. You're not her best friend anymore because you're my fucking best friend and you're on my side. Bros before hos, remember?" I hated that horrible cliché. "You know Brett will get pissed off, start a fight with me, and everyone will fucking hear it." I saw the fury in Cash's face. "Dude, you know I fucking love her, don't look at me like that." I knew he was about to flip his lid at me.

"I can't say shit like that about Brett," he whispered. "It will break my heart and hers."

Oz looked between the two of us. "What if I tell Palmer what we're going to do?" he suggested.

"I'd rather you didn't."

"East, you can't just sneak up on her like that."

I folded my arms over my chest. "We have to." I tilted my head. "Trust me." I glanced over to find Jonathan headed our way. "Okay boys, let's figure out our move for tomorrow and get ourselves ready." I flashed a quick smile as he joined us.

Chapter Twenty-Five

Brett

This "castle" that Chad had taken me to was cold, damp, and creepy as all hell. When we arrived Sunday afternoon, my mother was already there with a smile on her face like everything was perfect and nothing was wrong. I suppose she was just happy that she was living in her soon-to-be husband's house, but I refused to even crack a smile. I was told that my clothes and other belongings had already been brought to the home and placed in a room upstairs, but if the room wasn't to my liking, there were a few others that I could pick from. I didn't plan on staying long, but I kept that part to myself. I knew Easton, Cash, and the others would figure a way to get me out of here safely, but I hoped it wouldn't be long.

I stood and stared outside the window as I watched a heavy rain pour from the sky. Monday Chad had kept me home from school. He told my mother it would be a good way for us all to bond and become a real family. Did Ruby not know about Josie or did he never mention that he had a daughter?

My new cell phone that Chad had given me was sitting on the table by the bed and I picked it up just as a text came in.

Palmer: I'm not coming in there, but I'm outside when you're ready.

I was not allowed to give my number to anyone else, and if I did? Well, I didn't want to even think about what Chad might do. He had sworn to me he wouldn't hurt my mother, only Easton, but there had been a gleam in his eye that said something more, and the way his voice deepened as if he was hoping I would go against him—I shook my head as I tried to get myself together.

I had been up since four in the morning. Sleep hadn't been easy for the past couple of nights. I was worried about Easton, Cash, the others, and my mother. Not to mention Palmer and Jennifer. Palmer knew as much as I could tell her that would keep her safe, but I wasn't sure what Oz had told her. She hadn't mentioned him the last time we spoke which led me to think she was getting bored of him already or possibly she was just trying to keep herself and Jennifer safe.

As I headed down the stairs, I caught of glimpse of myself in the mirror at the bottom. I had dressed in a pair of loose jeans and paired it with the Knights shirt Cash had given me to wear. My hair was pulled back in a ponytail and I felt a slight pang of loneliness when I remembered it wasn't Easton picking me up. Was he okay? Was he worried about me? Or maybe he was going to sit back and watch everything play out first.

"Who is picking you up this morning?" Chad was in the surprisingly modern kitchen with a cup of coffee in front of him, reading a newspaper like it was in the fifties. I half expected him to have some sort of briefcase sitting at his feet, a cigarette hanging from his mouth while my mother pranced around the kitchen fixing his breakfast. His brows dipped only slightly when he took in my outfit.

I swallowed. "Palmer." I reached for the box of donuts I saw on the counter. "She's just outside, if you want to check and make sure." I hooked a thumb over my shoulder.

Chad's eyes grew dark just as Ruby seemed to float into the room. "Good morning, sweetheart." She dropped a kiss on my head, but she did the same to her boyfriend. *Fucking gross.*

"I'm out." I didn't bother to turn back around or return my mother's greeting before I dashed out the door and into the relentless rain. I managed to get completely soaked from head to toe before I got to Palmer's car.

She grinned at me. "Nice day we're having." She pointed to the two cups of coffee from Gerry's. "You're welcome," she added as I happily took one and brought it to my lips. The moment Palmer pulled away from the house, she shot a quick glance at me. "I'm pregnant."

I nearly shot coffee straight out of my nose but managed to choke it down my throat. I slapped a hand against my chest. "Oz?" I asked and she nodded.

Palmer pressed her lips together. "He's pretty pissed at me right now because I don't want to talk to him. We're hardly adults, B, and he wants to get married, raise the baby together..." Her voice trailed off as we pulled into the school parking lot. "Fuck," she muttered when we noticed the giant

SUV parked in the usual spot. "You okay?" Palmer touched my arm.

"No."

Would I ever be? I lost my boyfriend and my best friend in one shot. Not to mention two others that I considered brothers. I wasn't sure about Jameson yet. They must have been inside the building already because the vehicle looked empty.

"So, the baby… are you going to keep it?" I chewed on my lip, trying to change the subject.

Palmer shrugged. "I don't know." She let out a long sigh. "We should go inside while the rain has let up a bit," she suggested.

We both ran inside the building only to come face to face with Easton, Cash, Oz, and Jonathan standing around like they might have been waiting for us. Something told me they had. The four of them stopped talking the moment their eyes fell on Palmer and me, but I quickly looked away. It hurt too much to even be this close.

"What's wrong, boys? Cat got your tongues?" Palmer poked the bears.

Oz snorted. "No, sweetheart, we were just watching the show." He elbowed Jonathan as his eyes nearly burned through Palmer.

Palmer threw her arm over my shoulder. "That so?" She raised her chin. "What show is that?" she asked.

"Let's just go," I nearly begged. I wondered what everyone in school was going to think about this now. It was bad enough about what had happened with Cash in the lunchroom, but now it was obvious they were all angry with me. That I was no longer part of their crowd.

"Oh, what's wrong, Brett?"

I bristled at the way Cash said my name. When I met his eyes, I saw nothing but contempt and anger behind his sky-blue eyes and there was no trace of a smile on his face. "None of your fucking business," I sneered.

The four of them started laughing like I had just told them the funniest joke in the world, which only caused hot tears to burn my eyes. A few classmates had stopped to stare, stopped to listen, and I knew by noontime, another rumor would have spread through Kingston High like wildfire. I was no longer protected by Easton's boys and no longer part of their group.

Easton stepped forward with dark, mad eyes. "Where did you get that shirt?" He ran his finger up the front of my chest and over my chin. Up my face and around my head before he grabbed my ponytail so hard I saw stars. "If it's mine, I want it back. You don't get keepsakes, babe." Green eyes searched my blues.

"It's not—"

"It's mine." Cash stepped in. "I'd make you give it back now, but no one wants to see you walking around naked." That caused another round of laughs from the other two behind them. "You had better wash it, dry it, press it, and bring it back tomorrow, woman." His words were coated with venom.

I hadn't even realized Palmer had walked over to Oz and they were talking in hushed whispers. My chin trembled with fear and embarrassment as I brought my eyes back to

Easton and Oz. "Fine, I don't want the stupid thing anyway," I hissed between clenched teeth. "It only reminds me of the fool I was."

"You were easy prey, babe," Easton sneered.

Cash nodded. "They always are, bro." They high-fived just as the bell rang for first class.

I didn't wait for Palmer, but instead rushed down the hall so I wouldn't be late, and slid into an empty seat. I didn't care who it belonged to. I couldn't sit with Easton or Oz. They came in behind me, but I kept my eyes down when they passed by my seat. I knew it was Easton by his scent and when I noticed the boots on his feet.

I tried to slow my breath as roll call started, only to have the door open for a latecomer. There was a collective gasp from the entire room and when I looked up, I did the same. Tate Bernard stood there looking like he had gone more rounds with Conor McGregor than possible and lost. One eye was swollen shut while his upper lip looked like it might have been busted open. His nose was covered with bandages indicating it was broken, and as he walked forward to hand our teacher a note, I noticed a slight limp.

I immediately spun around to find Easton watching me. His nostrils flared only slightly, but he gave me a quick, but sharp nod before his eyes went back to the front of the room. He hadn't killed Tate because he was here in front of us. He did that for me.

"Mr. Bernard, I wasn't expecting you today." Mrs. Rhett's eyes were wide.

Tate shrugged. "My mom wanted me to get back before I missed any more school," he answered, and then he looked at me. His beady eyes narrowed into slits before they went wide with fright when he noticed Easton and Oz in the back.

Mrs. Rhett nodded. "Well, take an empty seat and get comfortable."

Tate shuffled down the aisle farthest away from me, but not too close to Easton either. I had so many questions, but I knew they wouldn't be answered. Not if I wanted everyone I loved safe.

"SO," PALMER WHISPERED as we sat down to eat lunch. "There's a rumor going around about Josie." She bumped my shoulder. "Did you hear?" She grinned.

I shook my head. "Do I even want to ask?" I could only imagine what the Knights had said to get this going. I had thought she was dead, like Tate, but after this morning I had my doubts.

"She ran off with some random sugar daddy she met online."

"What?"

Palmer nodded. "A few of the cheerleaders were talking this morning when I got to class." She giggled softly as she opened her water bottle. "Not to mention how Tate just showed up out of the blue like that, which is fucking nuts. Do you think Easton did that for you?" Her brows dipped as she stared at me.

I rolled my eyes. "Why aren't you sitting with Ozzy?" I asked as I watched the Knights out of the corner of my eye. Jameson was nowhere to be seen today which made me wonder where he was. He might have drugged, but I was still curious.

"Don't try to change the subject." Palmer took a sip of her water. "We're not a couple, B, besides, who would you sit with?"

"I could make new friends."

"Like who?"

I dragged my teeth across my bottom lip as I glanced around the room. "I don't know," I answered just as Tate approached the table. He looked nervous, scared, and possibly mad all at once.

"I wanted to tell you I was sorry, Brett." He kept his eyes glued to me as he spoke in a low tone. "About, you know, the party at Green Road, and then for being rude at Oz's place. It was wrong, and I'm sorry I disrespected you." He stared at me like he was almost looking right through me as he planted a palm against the table like he needed to steady himself.

I waved my hand in the air. "It's fine," I assured him. "No big deal."

Tate looked like he wanted to be anywhere but here. "Okay, sure." He nodded before he slowly walked away.

Palmer wrinkled her nose. "That was fucking weird, right?" She asked.

I nodded. "Totally—" I realized Tate had left something behind when he put his palm against the table. I quickly grabbed it and pulled it to my chest. When I looked over at Easton's table, he glanced away from me. "I need to go to the bathroom."

I grabbed my bag, left my lunch, and hurried off to be alone. Once I locked myself in a stall, I opened it to find twelve words that made everything feel a little better.

While I was in love, I was the happiest man on earth.

Tears streamed down my cheeks as I stared at the paper in front of me. He had quoted me something from The Wizard of Oz. Something small, trivial maybe, but it was enough to let me know he still loved me.

"You okay in there, Dorothy?"

I jumped at Easton's voice. I hadn't heard him come in or even realized he was there, but I saw the boots under the door, his ink colored fingers above the stall door which caused a sob to escape my chest. "I can't do this," I whimpered softly. "It hurts too much."

Easton gripped the door tighter. "It's not forever, Dorothy," he whispered. "I can't stay here because if someone catches me and word gets back to Chad... well, you know." He chuckled, but it was bitter and angry.

I sat there while Easton left the room. Listened to the sound of his feet as he walked away and the way the door slammed shut behind him before I shoved the piece of paper he had given me inside my bra. I knew that was the safest place for it and that Chad wouldn't think to look there. I washed my face with cold water, fixed my hair, and somehow managed to get to my next class on time despite the feeling of hopelessness I felt in the pit of my stomach.

Chapter Twenty-Six

I somehow managed to get through the rest of the week. It wasn't easy, but life went on. When I got home on Tuesday night, after Easton's note and after Tate showed up at school, I cried myself to sleep. I needed to keep him safe. I wanted to make sure Cash wasn't going to be hurt or Oz or Jonathan for that matter, so in order for that, I had to stay away.

Wednesday morning I walked in to find Easton with his arm around another girl by the name of Abby Greene. He looked bored, but she looked over the moon delighted. I felt more than humiliated, but pretended not to care, and instead marched past the five of them, Abby included, to class with my heart breaking into pieces which I know I left on the floor behind me. I knew Easton was playing a game for everyone to see, and I had to play along, but it didn't make it hurt any less.

Thursday afternoon I came home from school to find my mother surrounded by wedding cake samples which she insisted I try with her. Each one tastes like bitter cardboard that got stuck in my throat when I swallowed and had to

245

wash down with a glass of water. I honestly couldn't tell the difference between the first one or the last one, but Ruby wanted my honest opinion, so I went with the chocolate cake with the peanut butter filling and white frosting because I knew it was what she would want.

Friday was another baseball game, which I knew Easton couldn't play in, but would be at because he would want to support his guys. Palmer didn't have a football game to cheer for and wanted to go to be there for her man. Yes, they were back together and still trying to figure out what to do about their situation, and so I went with my friend to try and have a normal high school night out.

I dressed casually in a purple sweater, hip-hugger jeans, and a pair of black boots. Instead of pulling my hair back, I left it down, which was something I didn't do often, but tonight I wanted to do something different. When I slipped into Palmer's car, she stared at me wide-eyed.

"Wow." She grinned at me. "I almost didn't recognize you, B." She winked. "I see what you're doing."

"I'm not doing anything." I pulled the belt over my shoulder.

Palmer puckered her lips. "Right, okay." She nodded.

"Look, I changed my hair back to its normal color. What's the big deal?"

Palmer glanced to her left before she pulled the car onto the road. "You look like a completely different person." She looked up into the rearview. "Why?"

"Why what?"

"Why did you change your hair back?"

I sighed and folded my arms over my chest. "My mother is getting married," I muttered.

"That fucking bastard." Palmer scowled. "He told you to change your hair back to brown for the wedding?" She shook her head, and I watched as her blonde curls bounced naturally against her shoulders. "He threatened you."

I shrugged. "All he has to do is mention Easton's name, and he knows I'll do it." I looked out the window as she eased into a parking spot. Nothing in this town was far from the school. "He could ask me to swallow fire or else he'd burn Easton alive, and I'd do it."

Palmer laughed bitterly. "Don't give him any ideas, B, Jesus." She touched my arm. "I'm sorry. I know this has to be hard and I know you can't really tell me too much about it, but I am sorry."

I flashed a quick smile. "I know," I told her.

We were able to find a couple of empty seats together on the bleachers, and I could feel the eyes on me as we sat down. My hair, which I had been dying strange and fun colors since I was a young teen, was now its normal shade of chestnut brown. I had had a few inches trimmed from the ends, but it still hung to almost my waist in a straight line. I hadn't wanted to change it back, but, like I told Palmer earlier, I had no other choice. I somehow managed to ignore the stares, whispers and everything else as the game started and the boys, minus Easton, ran out onto the field.

Palmer was way into the game. Yelling and screaming when Oz struck someone out, which was most of the time. The same when he was up at bat and hit the ball. And I might have found her obnoxious if I didn't find it cute with how proud she seemed to be of her boyfriend. Cash was up to bat next, and when the ball hit the bat, the crack was loud enough that I knew he hit a home run. I might have cheered along with Palmer if it didn't hurt to see my best friend run around the bases one by one until he hit home again. It wasn't until he turned around and looked up into the crowd to zero in on me that I felt a little better.

Palmer's elbow hit my side. "They do miss you." She giggled.

"I'm going to get a hot chocolate." I suddenly needed to get away from the game. "Want one?" I asked, and when she nodded, I took off down the bleachers to get some.

It wasn't too busy at the concession stand now since everyone was watching the game. I ordered our drinks and paid, only to nearly plow right into someone on my way back.

"Sorry, didn't see you there." The voice was deep, but friendly.

I glanced up for only a second, but the eyes were soft and brown. "It's alright," I answered.

"You must be here for the opposing team because I don't recognize you from my school."

I took a step back to get a good look at him. Dirty blonde hair, big brown eyes, and a splash of freckles across his nose. He was tall with broad shoulders, but not as tall as Easton or Cash. He had a friendly smile on his face and his chocolate brown eyes danced with happiness as they moved over my body.

His grin got bigger. "Spencer Pearson." He held out his hand, and when I realized I didn't have an empty hand, he took one cup of hot chocolate from me. His hand swallowed mine.

"Brett Cake."

Spencer dropped my hand just as fast as he took it. "I think I heard my friends calling me." He started to walk away, but I caught up with him. "You can't be seen with me, Brett." He glanced around, but no one was even there.

"Why not?"

"The Knights."

Now I was really confused. "The Knights?" I asked as Spencer suddenly stopped so he could turn to face me.

"Uh, yeah, Easton and his boys." He scratched the back of his neck. "No one is supposed to talk to you." I watched the way he turned red under the lights.

I resisted the urge to throw the hot drinks at him because one, I was cold, and two, it would be a waste of money.

"That didn't work out for me." My throat felt tight when I spoke those words. "Easton and I are no longer together." Like he cared.

"Those guys are fucking scary, okay? I knew if I even dared look at you wrong, I would get my ass handed to me. Look at Tate," Spencer reminded me.

"How do you know so much?" I blurted out. "You're from Weston High, right?"

Spencer nodded. "Small towns talk. Tate was seeing a girl from my school. Word got around that he gave you shit at his party, and that the Knights didn't want anyone messing with you because you were one of them. Which was unusual because they didn't normally take in outsiders." His eyes moved behind me for a second. "But, you're not with him anymore?" he asked.

"No." I felt my phone buzz in my pocket. "I have to get back." I realized Palmer was probably worried about me.

"Are you... never mind."

I tilted my head. "Am I what?" I asked.

Spencer glanced down apprehensively, and I realized he was nervous. Was he actually blushing? "Are you going to the after-party? I mean, it's Tate's party, but—"

"Are you asking me to go with you?"

Spencer dragged his foot against the asphalt. "I think so."

"I'll meet you there," I said, and then walked past him without looking back.

I instantly felt guilty because I was in love with someone else. Someone I was supposed to be waiting for, but that someone was actually dating someone else, too.

Palmer looked relieved when I sat back down. "There you are! I started thinking something happened... wait a second. What happened? You look funny." She peeled the lid back to take a sip and her eyes rolled slightly. "It might be cheap shit, but it tastes fucking good." She moaned.

I wrinkled my nose. "Things I don't want to see or hear." I rolled my eyes. "I have a date."

Palmer nearly spit hot chocolate out of her mouth. "Say that again?" Her eyes were as big as saucers.

"I have a date."

Palmer stared at me for what felt like forever. Her nostrils flared as she pressed her perfect red lips together. "Explain," she finally said and folded her hands on her lap.

I shrugged. "Nothing to explain. I met him getting hot chocolate. He's from Weston." I finally took a sip of my drink. It wasn't so bad.

"Weston?"

"Look," I sighed softly just as someone from the other school managed to hit the ball. "Easton is seeing Abby." I used air quotes around the seeing part. "I can at least play my part, right?" I watched her shake her head.

"This is not going to go well for whoever he is, B, I can promise you that." Palmer finished off her drink. "This guy is going to end up hurt, or maybe worse," she reminded me.

Just at that exact moment, we won the game. The boys beat Weston 18-6 and Palmer suddenly rushed down the steps to get to Oz, which left me by myself. I saw Easton come out from the dugout where he had been standing just as Abby came down to greet him. He seemed relaxed about the entire situation as he pressed a kiss to her forehead before he met my eyes. I tried to look away before he caught me, but I wasn't fast enough. Easton's eyes were almost empty, but there was a slight flinch when he realized I saw him.

I sat back down on the bleachers as I waited for Palmer. I knew that Oz would have to shower before he would head out, so it wouldn't be too long before she would come back to find me. I happened to look down to see Spencer headed my way about fifteen minutes into my wait.

"Hey, I know you said you'd meet me there, but you want to ride over with me?" He looked around nervously, like maybe one of Easton's friends would jump out and drag me away.

I nodded. "Sure, let me just text my friend to let her know that I went ahead without her." I slipped my phone out of my pocket as I stood up. "Thanks," I added as we began to walk down the steps.

Spencer was quiet as we walked to his car, but he stopped to open my door and shut it behind me. When he climbed behind the wheel, he coughed nervously. "You're sure this is okay? I mean, I don't want to piss anyway off." He bit his lip nervously.

"You have nothing to worry about," I promised.

He started the car and seemed to relax as he started the drive to the party. "Where did you live before Kingston?" Spencer asked as he flipped on his right blinker. "I have lived in Weston my entire life. My family travels in the summer to Cape Cod, but that's the only other place I've been. Pretty boring."

"My mom wanted to move back to her hometown." I kept it simple because I didn't want to get into anything tonight. I didn't know Spencer at all, and I figured I could at least make a new friend.

He nodded. "Cool, cool, cool." He was nervous. I could see how his hands shook when he reached to turn the heat up or when he turned the music down. "You have any siblings?" He was trying to keep the conversation going, too.

"No, you?"

"One older sister, one younger brother."

I felt almost relieved that we had arrived at the party, but not so much when I saw the big black SUV parked in the grass. There were tons of other cars spread out through the field, but that was the one that stuck out the most. How did they get here so fast? Unless Easton was driving that and Oz was driving his Tesla?

"You're close to them?" I asked as we climbed from his car.

Spencer laughed. "I wasn't always so close with Lena, but now that she's at college, we're cool. Reid is five years younger than me, so he's alright, but sometimes annoying. I'm the middle kid, so I think that sometimes my parents forget about me." He dropped into step with me.

The party was jamming as we grew closer. Crowds of kids from school standing around a few bonfires holding plastic cups of beer. I immediately regretted coming to this thing because I wasn't big on parties, and I could see Easton standing with Abby, his arms wrapped around her small frame, his tongue shoved down her throat.

"Hey, you uh, want something to drink?" Spencer asked as he spotted the keg.

"Yes, thank you." I flashed a quick smile.

Spencer went off to get us both some beer which left me alone and as I wrapped my arms around myself I wondered how long I would be able to stand being here. I moved slowly over to where Spencer had gone and when he saw me, his face lit up like a sunrise. He was cute, but I would never feel anything for him.

"Here." He held out the first cup to me before he started filling another one. I had half of it gone before he finished filling it. "Wow, you like to drink?"

I shrugged. "No, but I feel like tonight is the night I start." I glanced over at Easton again, only to find his angry glare watching me. Good, now he knew how I felt.

Spencer caught the look. "You want to leave? We don't have to stay." He was probably the world's kindest boy, but he wasn't going to be the one for me.

"Now, you two should stay, relax, have a good fucking time." Cash's voice boomed loudly. "Isn't that right, cupcake?" He slapped a hand on Spencer's back. "Who's your friend, Brett?" He tilted his head.

"Knock it off, Cash." I drained the rest of my beer. "Spencer, don't listen to him." I needed more booze.

Spencer looked like he might actually faint. "I could leave," he whispered.

"We're just getting started." Jonathan had joined us.

Easton and Oz were now behind them. "That's right, Spence," Easton growled. "Pull up a fucking chair, dude, because the night is just fucking getting started."

Chapter Twenty-Seven

Brett

I saw fear rip through Spencer's eyes the moment Easton spoke. This was what he was worried about, and I had told him not to. That I was no longer part of his entourage, although not exactly true, I didn't think the boys would cause a scene in front of everyone. Not when it would get back to Chad.

"Don't do this." I glanced up at Easton to find his eyes focused on me with black hatred. "You have no right—"

"I have every right," he cut me off. "To do whatever the fuck I want, Brett, so I'll stop you before you can say anything else. Did you forget who I was or do I need to remind you?"

Spencer looked between the two of us. "She... she told me you weren't together anymore." He was looking for help from me. "Right, Brett? Isn't that what you said?"

I took a step forward only to have Cash block my path. "We're not together anymore. You made that clearly obvious to everyone on Tuesday morning. You're over there playing fucking tonsil hockey with Abby, so why can't I have a little fun?" I demanded.

Easton's nostrils flared. "Fun? You think what I'm doing is fun for me?" he roared and before I could stop him, his hand was around my throat and he shoved me against the nearest tree. "Don't fucking test me, babe, because you will not win this. I don't know what you think you're doing with this guy, but it ends now. Do you understand?" The grip he held around my throat was tight enough to scare me but not enough to keep me from breathing.

I brought my hand up to his and kept my eyes glued to Easton's. "Nothing was going to happen," I assured him. "Nothing—"

"That's not the fucking point, Dorothy."

"Then tell me what it is."

Without hesitating, Easton slammed his mouth over mine and I could feel the anger, hunger, and lust behind it. As he slipped his tongue between my lips, he used the hand around my throat to tilt my head up slightly. I moaned softly as I gripped the front of Easton's leather coat to keep from falling down and when his free arm snaked around my waist, I could feel his erection pressed against my belly.

"Mine," Easton growled before he suddenly shoved me away and took a step back. "Does everyone fucking understand that? It doesn't matter that we're not together anymore. Brett Cake is fucking mine. If any of you assholes think you're going to touch her, you're going to have to get through me first!" Then he turned around and slammed his fist right into Spencer's face.

"Easton!" I screamed so loud I was pretty sure my mother might have heard me back at the house. I grabbed his arm as he hooked back to take another swing and his elbow hit me in the chest, sending me to the ground.

Cash pulled me up by the armpits. "Should have thought about that before you brought another guy here, boo," he said casually. I shoved my best friend away only to come face to face with Easton.

"Are you alright?" His brows dipped as he searched my face. "I didn't mean for... did I hit you?"

I shook my head. "I'm fine, Easton, please, stop this." I lifted my hands to touch his face but he stepped back.

"Let's go." He jutted his chin at his friends. "We're out." Easton turned to Spencer, who was holding his hands to his nose. "Stay away from her." He warned as he pointed a finger at him. "Lesson learned, right?" Spencer's brown eyes moved to me and back to Easton again before he gave a quick nod of his head.

I waited until Easton and his Knights left the party before I moved closer to Spencer. "I'm so sorry," I whispered. "Let me take you to the hospital."

"I'm good, Brett, just stay away." His eyes told me everything I needed to know. He was scared to be near me, and I would never speak with him again.

"Spencer—"

"I said stay away!" he cried and started walking away from me.

How the hell was I going to get home? I had gone to the game with Palmer, come to the party with Spencer, and now I was pretty much stuck. I began to slowly walk toward where everyone had parked, only to see the black SUV waiting up ahead.

"Need a ride, cupcake?" Cash was leaning against the side with his arms crossed over his chest.

"Is that such a great idea?" I was just as pissed at him as I was at Easton, but I would be lying if I didn't miss him.

He shrugged before he gave me that playful smirk and opened his arms. "I fucking missed you," he whispered just as he wrapped me in his tight hug and squeezed me so tight I nearly couldn't breathe. "Ozzy is going to give you a ride in the Tesla with Palmer." Cash dropped a kiss on top of my head as I noticed the silent silver car pull up next to the truck.

"Get in the fucking truck, Brett." Easton's deep voice caused me to jump. I didn't even know he was still here and when I looked over at the truck, I saw him sitting in the back watching me. He opened the door and pushed it open. Cash gave me a lopsided grin before he released me so that I could climb up inside.

I stared at Easton nervously as he looked me over. "You're pissed," I whispered into the darkness.

"What the fuck were you trying to pull tonight?" For such a big guy, Easton moved faster than I anticipated and pinned me against the door. "Were you trying to make me jealous?" He ran his index finger down my cheek. "I'm a little confused about why you would bring that asshole here. Why you would bring another guy to a party that you knew—"

"I didn't know you were going to be here!" I exclaimed as tears spilled down my cheeks. "How do you think I feel, huh? Seeing you with someone else? Her touching you? Your lips on hers? Your tongue down her throat? I have to pretend that I don't care because you love me, but it kills me, Easton. It breaks me into tiny pieces just thinking of what else you might do with her." I turned away so I couldn't see his face.

"Don't look away from me."

"Don't tell me what to do."

Easton's hand gripped my chin and twisted it back. "Do you think I would fuck someone else, Dorothy?" His hostile glare was hard as daggers. "Is that what you fucking think?" His voice shook with emotion. "When I was a kid, maybe five or six years old, Kingston had its usual spring carnival. You're going to love it, trust me on that, but there was this one booth that was set up with tarot card readers and mediums, bullshit stuff, right?" Easton loosened his grip on me and slid his lips across mine. "My parents thought it would be fun to have their cards read." He ran his thumb over the dampness on my cheek. "I was just a kid, but was fascinated by the lady who sat there telling my mom all these things about her future."

I shook my head. "Why are you telling me this?" I asked.

"If you let me finish, babe, you'll understand." Easton chuckled as Cash knocked on the window to let us know our time was up. "The tarot reader turned over one of her cards and then looked at me. She told me one day my favorite color would be blue because of a girl's eyes, and purple because of her hair." He sighed softly. "I'm sorry I hurt you, Brett."

His lips met mine again and this time the kiss was soft, slow, and so erotic it took all I had not to beg him to make love to me.

"Time's up." Cash opened the front door. As Easton helped me from out of the vehicle another car pulled into the field. "Who is... oh shit," he hissed as I saw Jameson climb out.

"Get lost, asshole." Easton stepped in front of me as his former friend headed toward us. "Unless you want to end up with a few broken bones or worse tonight," he added.

Jameson kept moving. "I thought the two of you were supposed to be broken up or something." A smirk pulled at his lips. "At least that's what Chad said. Oh, are you sneaking around? I wonder what would happen if he found out you were lying to him." His eyes glittered with hate.

"Relax." Cash pressed a palm against Easton's chest. "Piss off, traitor, or I'll take care of you myself," he warned.

Jameson looked unfazed. "I think you need to let me take Brett home." He folded his arms across his chest as Oz walked across the field. "Because even if Palmer is in the car? Chad's going to be suspicious." He raised his eyebrows as he waited for one of them to answer.

"Jameson is right," I spoke first. "If Chad sees Oz in the car with Palmer, he's going to question everything I did tonight. If I come home with him?" I jutted my chin at Jameson. "He won't care."

"I don't fucking like it," Easton growled. "He drugged you once, who's to say he won't do something worse?" He glanced between me and his friends. "No fucking way."

Cash nodded his head. "It's actually not a bad idea, East." His voice was low.

Easton grabbed my hand and pulled me against him. "You lay a finger on her... if one hair is out of place? You're a dead man." He glared at Jameson before he tilted my head up to look at him.

"Wouldn't dream of it, boss man." Jameson flashed a knowing smile. "Shall we?" He held his hand out.

Easton cupped my head in his big hands. "I love you," he mouthed before he released me and I slowly moved toward Jameson, making sure to ignore the outstretched hand.

I was afraid to look back as we walked to the car. Afraid that I would say fuck it all because I knew what that meant. I knew it meant Chad would hurt my mother, hunt us down, and probably kill us. I didn't want that for Ruby or my friends, so instead I did what I thought was right. Even if it broke my heart.

"Heard you brought someone from Weston to the party tonight." Jameson snickered as I climbed into his car. When I didn't answer, he sighed loudly. "You're going to ignore me the entire ride?"

"It's a short drive I think you'll survive."

Jameson tapped the steering wheel. "She speaks." He chuckled to himself. "You know, I do like you, Brett, but sometimes we do stupid shit for love. As you already know." He started the car and swung it around so he could pull out of the field face forward. "I was stupid to think that Josie actually liked me, but pussy makes you crazy."

I pressed my lips together and looked out the window into the dark. "Are you like Chad's errand boy now or something?" I asked, but when he didn't answer, I turned to find him gripping the steering wheel with a force so strong I thought he might rip it right off.

"I regret what I did." Jameson's jaw clenched tightly. "My brother won't speak to me now, and I'm like the plague in school because of it. I thought that maybe, just maybe, if I could get you on my side—"

"What?"

Jameson flipped on the right blinker as he slowed in front of the house and then pulled into the driveway. "It was the biggest mistake of my life." He stared straight ahead as he spoke. "I'm truly sorry for what I did to you, Brett, and if I could take it back I would." Jameson bowed his head. "I have lost the trust of my friends, my brother, and everyone I cared about, and for what? For a girl who didn't love me."

I watched Jameson while he spoke and watched as silent tears slipped down his cheeks. I was angry at him because all of this was his fault, but I could see he was in as much pain as I was.

"What are you doing tomorrow?"

He turned to stare at me with curiosity in his eyes.

"My mother and Chad are having an engagement party." I chewed on my lip. "I thought maybe if you weren't busy you'd like to come."

"Like, as your date?"

A smile began to slip up my face. "Yes, as my date," I told him. "Party starts at six o'clock, so don't be late. Make sure that you wear a nice suit, too, and, oh, I'm wearing red, so if you want to match or whatever." I started to open the door, but when I saw the look on Jameson's face, I stopped.

"Easton's going to hear about this. That's why you're asking me to be your date, so that he can use me as his fucking punching bag. He'll come in there guns blazing, but you have no idea how powerful Chad is, Brett. Easton might be the prince of Kingston High School, but Chad? Chad is the fucking king of Kingston. He's a smart man and has his eyes and ears everywhere." His voice trembled as he spoke.

"You don't think that Easton's capable of taking Chad down?" I asked softly.

Jameson smirked. "If anyone can, it's Easton, but trust me when I tell you that Chad won't go down without a fight. He'll try to take everyone with him... including your mother. Think long and hard about what you're doing because you could end up losing everyone tomorrow."

I pressed my lips together. "I don't have much of a choice," I whispered as I thought about everything that had happened this week. "Will you be here tomorrow?" I turned my body to face him. When Jameson nodded, I pushed the door open again and climbed out of the car before I stuck my head back inside. "Thank you." Then I shut the door and hurried inside the house to find Chad waiting for me.

"Who was that?" he asked as he lifted his wine glass.

"Jameson," I answered.

"Really?" Chad's brows dipped. "What are you up to?" He leaned forward across the table.

I gave him my best smile. "Nothing. We ran into one another after the baseball game and got to talking. He gave me a ride home. Just a couple of friends trying to catch up. Nothing more." I began to walk toward the doorway. "Oh, he's coming to the party tomorrow night as my date," I added before I ducked from the room so that Chad couldn't say anything else.

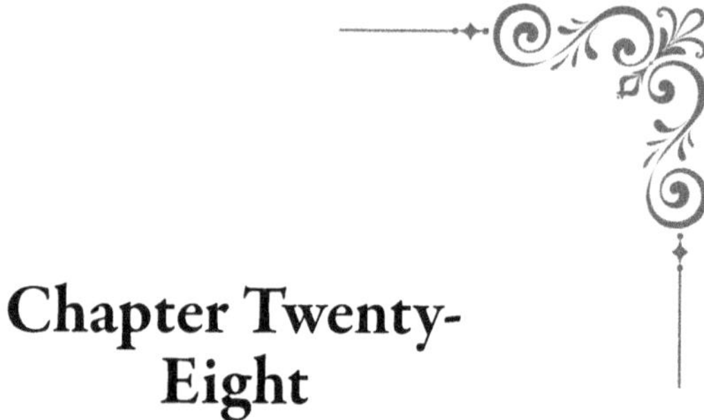

Chapter Twenty-Eight

Easton

I paced the floor of my room most of the night. After I watched Brett drive away with Jameson, it took all I had not to follow them and make sure she was okay. That rat bastard had no right to be within ten feet of her. He had a point about Oz bringing her home. It wouldn't have looked good, and I hated him for being right. I think I might have gotten two, three hours of sleep tops before I climbed from my bed and dragged myself downstairs.

My boys were sitting around the kitchen table staring into the cereal bowls. Things didn't feel right since Brett left. She was one of us, part of us now, and we missed her. I poured myself a cup of coffee and sat down next to Cash.

"You look like shit, boss," he commented as he pushed a box of frosted flakes toward me. "Eat something."

"Fuck off," I growled and ignored the food. "I'm not hungry."

Oz grunted. "Got something important to tell you, boss, so brace yourself." His eyes were icy when I looked up.

"Palmer's having twins?"

I was in no mood for any bullshit today. I was supposed to pretend not to care about Brett when I was outside this house. I had made plans with Abby to take her out tonight so it looked like we were actually seeing one another, but I was regretting the decision. What I really wanted to do was go into that castle, guns blazing, and take my girl home with me.

"You're a fucking peach this morning." Oz dumped the rest of his bowl into the sink. I had noticed he hadn't been eating so great lately, and I knew exactly who was to blame. "For your information, Palmer told me that Brett asked Jameson to come to the engagement party tonight." He squared his shoulders.

I choked back anger that threatened to explode inside me. "What?" I gritted my teeth together as I tried to wrap my head around what Oz had just told me. "Why would she do that?" I turned to look at Jonathan, who shook his head.

"I haven't spoken to him, East, I have no idea." His eyes were wide with fright.

"Maybe she's doing it for you," Cash suggested.

I stood up so fast I knocked the chair over. "How is taking someone else to her mother's engagement party for me? I warned her what would happen, didn't I? She saw first fuck-ing hand last night—"

Cash put a hand on my shoulder, but I shrugged it off.

"Fuck you! Don't touch me! None of you know what I'm going through right now!" I roared. "Text Palmer and find out what Brett is trying to do." I pointed a finger at Oz.

"She doesn't know, man, I already asked. She said Brett only said Jameson was coming to the party, and that was all she could say. Chad's probably reading her texts, so she has to be careful what she says to anyone." Oz shrugged.

I ran my hands through my hair and pulled on the ends. Brett was up to something. Did she want me to know so that I would show up? What would that prove? If I started something at her mother's party, Chad would fucking slit my throat. Unless I slit his first.

"Boys, get your best suits ready because we're going to a party tonight." I felt a big, wide smile on my face as I realized what I was about to do.

"Easton, no." Cash shook his head. "He'll kill us all."

I grinned at him. "We're going to fucking kill that bastard first. So get your shit ready." I turned to look at Oz and Jonathan. "All of you," I added. "We leave at seven." I clapped my hands together.

I was going to get my girl back tonight and I would kill anyone that dared get in my goddamn way.

THE PARTY WAS IN FULL swing when we rolled up at nearly seven-fifteen. For one split second as I stared up at the sprawling castle, God that thing was ridiculous compared to the rest of the houses in town, I was hit by a brief memory of when I was a child. Running through the halls with Josie, no not Josie, because this girl had dark hair and she had red, while she giggled and laughed hysterically.

"I'm going to catch you!" I assured her as she ducked behind one of the many Knight replicates that stood throughout the house. "You can't hide from me." She giggled again. "You know what happens when I find you, right?"

A hand waved in front of my eyes, snapping me out of the memory, but I knew who that little girl had been. It had been Brett. I could see it so vividly in my mind. Her blue eyes as she turned to look over her shoulder at me, and that wicked smile on her face.

"Boss man, you okay?" Oz's voice boomed loudly in the car and I tried to focus my attention back on the task at hand.

"Fine."

Jonathan spun around from the front seat to look at me. "You look like you've seen a ghost," he commented. "You sure you want to do this?"

"You guys know I used to come here when I was a kid, right?" I murmured as I checked to make sure my pistol was in my pocket. "I always had foggy memories of playing with a little girl and just assumed it was Josie." I glanced over at Cash who was fixing his tie. "It was Brett." I watched as my best friend's hand stopped and he slowly moved his eyes toward me. "Dark hair, blue eyes. Who else would it have been because it sure as hell wasn't one of you ass clowns."

"Holy shit." Cash's shoulders slumped forward.

A knock on the window of the Tesla caused us all to jump and when I saw it was Jameson, I narrowed my eyes. We had come here for a reason and he was part of it. He took a step back as we all climbed from the car, and I saw the fear in his eyes as I cracked my neck from side to side.

"This does not make us square." I pointed a finger at him. "You tried to kill my girlfriend so as far as I'm concerned you're fucking dead to me."

"She's waiting for you." Jameson looked up at the castle and back at me. "She knew that you'd come tonight. I can sneak you in."

Oz shook his head. "No way. You're not going in alone." He put a hand on my shoulder. "We all have to go inside together because we don't know what Chad has planned."

I heard him, but all I could do was stare up at the window where I knew Brett was.

"Go home, boy!"

The voice had all of us spinning around and I bristled at the voice. "Fuck you, old man!" I answered back. "You got something that belongs to me, and I plan on taking her home with me tonight." The floodlights came on at that moment, leaving us all blinded.

"I think you underestimated me, Easton," Chad called out and the sound of bullets sent us all running for cover.

I hit the damp grass hard and felt something ding my shoulder that felt like it might be a bruise or a slight bee sting on my shoulder. I put my hand up and felt a warm liquid against my palm. Shit, that bastard fucking shot me! It wasn't bad enough to keep me down, but it hurt like hell and now I was even more fucking pissed off.

"Where did Jameson go?" Cash asked as he came up next to me. "Shit, did you get hit?" He pointed to my arm.

I nodded. "I'm fine." I noticed someone crawling across the lawn in front of me and landed on my stomach to stop him.

Jameson turned to see it was me. "Let go, man. Let me go distract Chad." When I continued to hold on to his legs, he started to kick back and one foot landed right on my nose.

I heard the sound of the bones as they crunched beneath his shoe and the strong smell of copper blood invaded my senses.

"No!" Jonathan exclaimed when he realized where his brother was going. He jumped up to take off after him, and that was when the second set of bullets went off. We watched in horror as Jonathan fell onto his back and stayed down.

Oz's eyes were wide. "We're getting fucking murdered here, boss! Two guys down now, and if we're not careful—"

The sound of the explosion threw us up and flat on our backs causing me to cry out in pain. That didn't stop me from jumping onto my feet again though. I couldn't see or hear anything with the flames and smoke swirling through the air, but I knew we had to get out of here before the cops showed up. Oz was farther than I was, but I saw him sitting up and looking around. Cash was also on his feet and his mouth was moving, but I couldn't hear what he was saying with the ringing in my ears. Holy crap, Brett!

I started running toward the burning building without a second thought. Oh, fuck, what if she was dead? I would never fucking forgive myself. Someone hit me head-on, and when I looked down, tears sprang into my eyes. She was covered in soot, and her dark hair was a mess. I could see that she had been crying because her cheeks were wet, and the beautiful red dress that clung to her curves was ruined, but Brett still looked beautiful to me.

"Let me go!" She struggled against me.

"It's me, Dorothy."

Brett dragged her eyes up my chest and to my face before her face completely crumpled. She might have collapsed if

I hadn't caught her. "Easton." She sobbed against me as I hoisted her up despite my own wounds. I winced slightly at the pain in my arm as I managed to get us to the car at the same time as Cash.

"Let me." He held out his arms, but I shook my head. "Just open the door," I ordered and he did as I asked. I groaned softly at the pain as I bumped my shoulder climbing into the vehicle and balanced Brett on my lap, who was staring at me wide-eyed.

"What happened to your face?" she asked.

"Jameson." I swallowed as I thought of my friend lying out there and I had to fight back tears again. "He was trying to go save his brother, and I tried to stop him, so he kicked me." I bit down hard on my lip.

Brett reached up to touch my face lightly. "Are... are they dead?" she whispered and when I nodded she began to cry. "This... it's all my fault." She shook her head. "I shouldn't have invited Jameson to the party. He warned me—"

"Ssshhhh." I pressed a finger over her lips. "Don't cry, Dorothy." I glanced up as Oz jumped into the car and we could all hear the sounds of the sirens as they began to get closer.

"Chad took my mother." Brett hiccupped as her crying began to get worse. "Do you think he'll hurt her, Easton? He said he loves her, but I never believed it. I thought that he was up to something the entire time and tonight only proves that. There were people inside that house. People he claimed were his friends!" Her eyes were wide with fright and I could see that she was on the verge of hysteria until her eyes rolled slightly and she slumped in my arms.

Cash looked at me, Brett, and then back at me again. "Did she just pass out?" he asked. "Doc?" he asked, and I gave him a brief nod.

We were all going to need to see the doc tonight. I had a broken nose, my shoulder felt like it was on fire, and I could see blood splattered on Cash's arm. I wasn't sure if he or Oz had any injuries, but they would need to get checked out just in case. I leaned my head back against the seat as Oz headed toward the cabin to keep us safe for at least the next couple of days. Chad would be lying low, too, since he knew we would end up coming for Brett soon. He would be coming for all of us soon.

Would Chad kill Ruby? I wasn't sure, but I knew he would try to hurt everyone we loved in the meantime. That meant Palmer and her mother would need to be checked out. I knew we should check on Cash's parents and Oz's as well, "Oh shit." I sat up, trying not to jostle Brett in my arms. "My mother," I barked out.

Cash glanced at me curiously. "What about her?" he asked.

"We have to check on Olivia just in case... I don't think Chad would actually hurt her, but he might. To get to me because he wants to get to me because of Josie." I shifted Brett's weight to my non-injured arm. I needed to figure out what I was going to do about my now ex, but I could do that later.

"On it." Cash started texting on his phone and I sighed softly. I had just declared war on a man that I knew I couldn't beat, but I wouldn't wave the white flag. Not even if he put a bullet in my head.

Chapter Twenty-Nine

Brett

I woke up covered in sweat in a dark room that smelled funny and I had no idea where I was. The scent of fire penetrated my skin and hair, which brought back the events of last night causing a sob to escape my throat. I jumped from the bed and moved blindly to try to find a light, the door, or both. My hands wrapped around the handle, so I yanked the door open and nearly fell into the hallway.

"Easton!" I screamed his name as loud as I could. "Easton!" I cried out again when I didn't hear him. I heard the sound of feet on the floor and then he appeared above me with white gauze wrapped around his nose.

"Why are you out of bed?" He went to pick me up, but I slapped at his hands. "Don't do that, Dorothy," Easton scolded. "Let me help you back to bed."

I felt my chin tremble. "How could you leave me by myself like that?" I whispered, and this time when Easton bent down, I let him scoop me up into his arms. "You left me alone in a strange place after what happened. I had no idea if you were dead or if Chad had come to get you or me." I stared up at him as he placed me back onto the bed. "I want to take a shower. I need to get this stench off of me." I folded my arms across my chest.

Easton sighed softly as he eased himself down next to me on the bed. "Babe." He smoothed the hair from my forehead. "I'm sorry that I left you alone. I just got up to go talk to the guys for a minute, check and make sure that my mother was okay. Chad is not getting into the house without anyone knowing. We have eyes everywhere." He tilted my head. "You can take a shower anytime you want, babe. I'll show you to the bathroom." A faint smile appeared on his lips before it disappeared.

"Do you still love me?" I blurted out.

Easton's eyes grew dark. "How can you ask me something like that?" he growled.

"Let me come with you." Suddenly sleep was the farthest thing from my mind when I remembered what happened and I sprang up from the bed. "I don't want to be alone right now." I grabbed Easton's hand.

"Brett."

"Please."

"Alright." He nodded his head. "I have some boxers that you can put on until Palmer gets here with some clothes. I sent her shopping." He opened up a drawer on the dresser and began to dig around. "Here, babe." Easton held out a pair of black underwear for me and watched me pull them on over my own panties. "Hey." He flashed a quick smile when I met his eyes. "Come with me."

I followed Easton out of the room and reached for his hand as we moved down the hallway. He stopped outside a room and knocked on the door. "You up?" he asked before he pushed the door open. Inside the room were two twin beds and there were bodies lying on each one buried under multi-colored blankets. "Guys, show Brett here you're not dead."

Jameson and Jonathan both sat up which caused me to gasp. "Holy... how?" I covered my mouth with my hand.

"Bulletproof jacket," Jonathan answered before he looked over at his brother. "Same as him."

Jameson grinned. "That's right." He started to pull his shirt up, but Easton coughed. "Sorry, dude, I was just going to show her the marks on my chest to prove that even though I didn't get shot like you, I still have some marks."

My head whipped around. "You were shot?" I exclaimed.

"Hardly, I was grazed." Easton glared at Jameson before he met my eyes. "Babe, relax, I'm fine. Just a broken nose," he added.

"Why didn't you tell me?"

"For this reason."

I moved closer. "You could have been killed," I whispered.

"I'm unstoppable," Easton promised, but my gut twisted at his words. "Let's leave these two to rest. Doctor's orders," he added as he hooked his good arm over my shoulders.

In the cabin's living room a smile broke out on Cash's face when he saw me and he jumped up to wrap me in a hug and swing me around. "Cupcake, I've missed you. How are you feeling today?" he asked as he stared right into my face. "Hungry? We don't have anything too fancy, but I can whip up a bowl of cereal or a sandwich or something." He ran his thumb over my cheek.

I shook my head. "Not now, but thanks." I felt a little better knowing that the twins were alright and that it seemed like maybe Easton was on his way to forgiving Jameson. "What I really could use is a shower," I said just as Oz and Palmer walked through the front door, but they weren't alone.

Behind them was Chad.

"What the fuck." Easton moved to stand in front of me. "What is he doing here?" I couldn't help but peek around his body to see what was going on.

"I'm sorry, man. He came out of nowhere while we were in the middle of Target." Oz coughed nervously. "He threatened—"

"Boys, you should know that you can't hide from me," Chad cut in. "I've always got one eye on you no matter what." He pulled back his suit jacket to reveal the gun on his hip. "Now that I have your attention, why don't you give me back what's mine?"

I felt Cash behind me now as Easton growled a warning. "Brett is mine." His voice was deep. "I suggest you get the fuck out of here now before someone puts a bullet between your eyes. There are five of us, and one of you. You're outnumbered." He reached behind him and gripped my hand tightly.

Chad's eyes narrowed into slits. "Let me let you in on a little secret, Easton." A smile tugged at his lips.

"Chad, don't," Ruby exclaimed as she burst into the room. Her eyes were wide, her hair disheveled and she looked like she hadn't slept in days. "Sweetheart, why don't you come with me? We have a few things we need to talk about."

I looked up at Easton and then at my mother. "Mom, what's going on? Whatever you have to say you can say in front of my boyfriend and my friends." I leaned forward so that my chest was pressed against Easton's back.

"Honestly, I don't think—"

"Mom, after everything, I don't care what you think! My friends almost died because of this man, and I don't want any part of the life you want to build with him. I'm an adult now. I'm staying here where I'm safe."

Ruby closed her eyes as she let out a little sigh. "How can you think you're safe here, Brett?" She spat and I watched as her face twisted in anger. "These boys are killers! Do you have any idea what they're capable of?" Her voice cracked the air like a whip.

My eyes grew wide. "How dare you," I hissed. "That man—"

Chad held up his hand to silence me and without another word slit my mother's throat.

Chapter Thirty

Brett

I t took me a few minutes to realize that the sound that was ringing in my ears was me screaming. Easton had knocked Chad to the ground while Cash grabbed me and wrapped his arms around me to try to keep me from seeing my mother as she bled out on the cabin floor.

"Let me go, Cash, let me go." I struggled in his arms. "That's my mother, she could... I could save her... please!" Wetness covered my cheeks as I sobbed. "Please," I begged, but that only made him tighten his grip.

Cash wouldn't budge. "Sorry, cupcake, no can do." He smoothed my hair down against my head. "She's gone," he murmured softly, but I still continued to squirm against his chest as I ignored the words I knew he said were true.

"You son of a bitch," Easton yelled, and I heard something hit the ground. "I'm going to fucking kill you myself!" he warned, and another scream threatened to escape from my mouth just as J2 rushed into the room.

"Get the girls out of here," Oz demanded as he rushed past Cash. "*Now,* before something happens to them. Take them out of here! I don't care where, as long as they are away from this shit." Keys hit the ground and Cash's grip loosened on me just enough for me to spring free.

I rushed past my mother's lifeless body and Easton who was smashing Chad's body repeatedly against the cabin floor while the rest of the Knights tried to get control of the situation. The front door was still open and I was able to slip out onto the porch into the bright sunshine. I had no idea where I was or where I was going, but I kept moving despite not having on shoes or pants.

"Brett, stop!" Cash called out from behind me, but I kept going into the heavily wooded forest in front of me. "You're going to get hurt running outside like that," he added.

A branch slapped me in the face, and tears hit my eyes, but I didn't care. I stumbled over a rock and nearly went down but somehow managed to keep myself upright.

"Leave me alone, Cash, please," I told him. "I can't..."

This time I couldn't stop myself from falling, and the pain that seared through my knees and palms was more than I could stand. I cried out as I hit the ground, only I didn't bother to get back up. The ground was damp against my skin as I screamed my mother's name, not caring who heard me.

Cash's arms wrapped around me. "Let it out, boo, let it all out," he whispered. "You have every right to be upset," he told me.

"Fuck you!" I slapped at his chest. "This is all your fault! Yours, Easton's, the twins, I hate you! I hate every single one of you!" I tried to shove away from him, but Cash held on to me tightly. "If you hadn't befriended me that day, Ruby might still be... my mother is dead!"

I burst into a fresh set of tears and buried my face in Cash's chest as he stood up with me in his arms. I had no choice but to wrap my legs around his waist and rested my head on his shoulder as he began to walk.

The scent of blood filled my nose when Cash stepped into the cabin, but his hand came down on my head to keep me from looking around. It didn't matter. I knew what had happened here, and I would never be able to forget it. He moved slowly as he walked and then stopped to flip on a light to reveal a spacious bathroom with a large claw-footed tub.

I struggled as Cash started to ease me down into the tub until he pulled me back to look at me. "I know you're angry." His voice was soft when he spoke. "I know you hate me and you have every right. I want you to wash up now. I'll wait outside, but that's as far as I can go."

I let Cash set me down, but when he started to leave, I grabbed his hand as he started to walk away.

"Don't leave me alone."

Cash's brows dipped. "Boo—"

"Please."

A faint smile pulled at his lips. "You got it." He turned around. "Go on, take off your clothes. I promise I won't look," Cash assured me.

I slowly pulled off the shirt, boxers, and panties underneath before I turned on the water as hot as it would go. I grabbed the bottle of soap and dumped it in so that it covered me up before I slowly sank down inside the tub. I hardly even noticed the sting against the cuts on my body.

"You can turn back around now," I said.

Cash did as I told him, but his eyes stayed on my face. Blue eyes that were sad, tired, and told me how sorry he was. He moved a little closer before he knelt down next to me.

"I am so very sorry, Brett. You know I never wanted any of this for you and if I had known—" He dropped his head and sighed.

"You know that I can't stay here, Cash." I watched as his head shot back up. "I can't stay here in Kingston now that my mother is dead and after everything that has happened."

He looked confused. "Where will you go? What about Easton? Or me?" His hands came up to grip the side of the tub.

"I don't care as long as it isn't here."

"Brett, you can't be serious." But the look on my face was anything but. "You're going to destroy him, you know that." Cash sat back on his feet. "You're not going to leave without talking to him, right? You can't just up and leave us."

"I don't want to talk to Easton right now." My heart twisted just a little at the thought of leaving, but I had no choice. "I meant what I said. It's because of all of you that this happened."

"Brett, please." Cash looked close to tears.

"Turn around so I can rinse off," I instructed, and then I quickly washed myself from the soap when I heard the door open.

"What the fuck is this?" Easton growled. "Get out." When I turned around, his eyes were dark and angry. "What are you doing?"

"What does it look like? Cash is my best friend, and he didn't see anything. Can you get me something clean to put on?" I asked just as he dropped the Target bag on the floor before he folded his arms across his chest. I noticed the blood and bruising on his hands. "You killed him, didn't you?" I grabbed a towel to start to dry myself off.

"What's going on, Brett?"

"Answer the question, Easton."

Easton turned away from me before he answered. "Yes, we fucking killed him! I made sure to smash his face like a glass window before we dragged him outside and Jameson put a bullet in his head because he said he should be the one to do it. Is that what you wanted to hear? Huh? Are you fucking happy now?"

His voice caused fear to knot in my stomach.

"He deserved it, babe. He killed your mother, my father, and countless other people. What else were we supposed to do?"

Easton had his back to me as I started to climb from the tub. "I don't know," I whispered before I collapsed onto the floor.

"Jesus Christ." He was by my side in an instant. "You need to rest, Brett, with everything that has happened. Let's get you dressed, get you something to eat, and then—"

I shook my head. "Stop it, Easton." I placed a palm against his chest. "I can't do this."

His brows dipped.

"I'm leaving," I added before I reached for the plastic bag he had dropped when he walked in.

"What do you fucking mean leaving? You're not going anywhere, Dorothy," Easton snarled. "You're safer with me, with Cash, and... why? Why do you think you need to leave me?" He sat back as I began to pull clothes out of the bag. When I didn't answer, he stood up. "You're actually serious."

Palmer had picked out a pair of flared jeans with an oversized blue sweater that were the perfect size. The black underwear and matching bra were cotton, and I'd be lying if I didn't like the fit she had chosen for me. I grabbed the elastic around my wrist and pulled my hair up into a ponytail before I turned to face Easton again.

"If I stay here, I'll only end up hating you even more for what happened," I whispered.

"Don't you love me?"

"This isn't about love anymore."

"Brett." Easton reached for me, but I shook my head. "Please, don't do this. We can figure this out. We need you here. Fuck that, *I* need you. We need one another." His voice was thick with sorrow.

I dropped my gaze. "You were fine before I got here, and you'll be fine when I'm gone," I assured him. "I'm going to have Cash take me back to the house to get my things."

When I finally looked up, the smile Easton wore was cold and cruel, sending chills up my spine. I turned to wrap my hand around the handle only to have the door shut as he slammed me against it.

"Nothing I say or do will change your mind, will it?" His icy smile didn't reach his eyes. "So, that's it? You're going to rip my heart out without giving me a chance to fix things?" Easton's hand found its way to my throat, but he didn't tighten it.

I swallowed as I stared up at him. "You can try to keep me here, but I won't be happy. Is that what you want? For me to be unhappy in a place that ruined my life, or would you rather I find somewhere where I can live and start over again?" Anguish stabbed my insides. "Maybe—"

"Maybe nothing, Brett." Easton released me so that he could take a step back. "I don't want to see your face around here again."

He spun around, and I whipped open the door to run from the bathroom before I actually *did* change my mind.

"Cash!" I called out to my best friend who was sitting in the living room with his head in his hands. "I need to go pick up a few things back at Palmer's house before I leave."

His eyes moved behind me to where I knew Easton stood before he focused on my face. "Whatever you want, cupcake, you know that I'm here for you," he assured me.

Then we walked out of the cabin, and away from the nightmare that had become my life.

The End—For Now
To Be Continued

Acknowledgments

This story has been running around in my head for nearly three years now. It started off a lot sweeter, a lot cleaner, and turned into something much, *much* more. Most of the small town of Kingston is based on where I grew up in right down to the castle that looked like someone dumped it there. When I was in high school we used to joke the town had more cows than people, and there weren't any fast food places. We had way too many pizza joints and four stop lights in the whole town; but the best donut shop in the state. And, yes! Brett and her Knights will be back SOON! She'll get her HEA at some point.

I'm always afraid that I'm going to leave someone out when I write the acknowledgments. Honestly it's right up there with coming up with a blurb, but here we go.

Thank you to—

My own alpha bad ass. My husband who has been my biggest supporter since I started publishing my books. You've done so much more than I ever asked and I know that I couldn't do this without you, baby. *You're the chicken*. Real love is forever. **I love you!**

My best friend, my PERSON! Stephanie, every single time I post something you're usually the first person to like it, share it, or make a comment. We might be separated by over 1500 miles, but you're my ride or die, bitch.

The ladies at Books and Moods who created this gorgeous cover that I was obsessed with the second I saw it. For making beautiful teasers, connecting me with new authors and friends, and for helping me pave a path in this new writing adventure. I appreciate everything you've done.

My dad who, even if he was still alive, I would never let read this book or anything I've written. Not a day goes by that I don't think of you, miss you or wish that you were here with me right now, but I do hope you're proud of me.

Crow on Instagram for making the first reader teasers and making me cry. I'm so happy to know you loved London and Mason as much as I did. I hope you feel the same way about this book, too!

My amazing editor, ellie, for always helping me polish up my work. I knew the moment I saw your Insta posts that we would be a perfect fit.

I want to thank *you* for taking the time to read this. Reviews are super important and if you have the time I would love you to leave one. Good, bad, or whatever you want to say. It helps get indie authors noticed.

About the Author

Sundae Leighton is a romance author who writes sweet stories with a twist. She lives in New England with her husband and cats. She'll tell you she's a coffee snob, enjoys binge watching her favorite shows, loves watching NASCAR, is a bit of a geek at times, an absolute mug hoarder, lover of pumpkin spice, and a complete Jeopardy nerd.

Also available from Sundae: *Picture Perfect* and *Gravity* at shop.sundaeleighton.com or wherever books are sold.

New releases, teasers, sneak peaks, email list, social club: http://www.sundaeleighton.com

Facebook Readers Group: http://www.facebook.com/groups/233608387885905

Facebook: http://www.facebook.com/authorsundaeleighton

Instagram: http://www.instagram.com/sundaeleighton

Twitter: http://www.twitter.com/sundaeleighton

Goodreads: http://www.goodreads.com/authorsundaeleighton